THE LAST DRAGON

WITHDRAWN

THE REVENGE OF
MAGIC
THE LAST DRAGON

JAMES RILEY

ALADDIN
NEW YORK   LONDON   TORONTO   SYDNEY   NEW DELHI

ALADDIN

An imprint of Simon & Schuster Children's Publishing Division

1230 Avenue of the Americas, New York, New York 10020

First Aladdin hardcover edition October 2019

Text copyright © 2019 by James Riley

Jacket illustration copyright © 2019 by Vivienne To

For information about special discounts for bulk purchases, please contact Simon & Schuster Special Sales at 1-866-506-1949 or business@simonandschuster.com.

The Simon & Schuster Speakers Bureau can bring authors to your live event. For more information or to book an event, contact the Simon & Schuster Speakers Bureau at 1-866-248-3049 or visit our website at www.simonspeakers.com.

Jacket designed by Heather Palisi

Interior designed by Mike Rosamilia

The text of this book was set in Adobe Garamond Pro.

Manufactured in the United States of America 0819 FFG

2 4 6 8 10 9 7 5 3 1

Library of Congress Cataloging-in-Publication Data

Names: Riley, James, 1977- author.

Title: The last dragon / by James Riley.

Description: First Aladdin hardcover edition. | New York : Aladdin, 2019. | Sequel to: The revenge of magic. | Summary: With help from his friends, Fort tries to find and bring the last dragon to the Old Ones in exchange for releasing Fort's father, while they continue to seek the books of magic.

Identifiers: LCCN 2018048918 (print) | LCCN 2018053151 (eBook) | ISBN 9781534425743 (eBook) | ISBN 9781534425729 (hardcover)

Subjects: | CYAC: Adventure and adventurers—Fiction. | Magic—Fiction. | Healers—Fiction. | Monsters—Fiction. | Dragons—Fiction. | Books—Fiction.

Classification: LCC PZ7.1.R55 (eBook) | LCC PZ7.1.R55 Las 2019 (print) | DDC [Fic]—dc23

LC record available at https://lccn.loc.gov/2018048918

For my agent, Michael Bourret, for being
my guide in publishing, my teacher in writing,
and my groaner in puns. I'd be lost without him
in my corner, sticking with me through it all,
and hopefully for many years to come.

THE LAST DRAGON

- ONE -

PRESIDENT FORSYTHE FITZGERALD," Fort's father said, pointing at the spots where each word would go above the giant statue of a seated Abraham Lincoln.

This should have been a happy moment, seeing his dad again, but knowing what was coming, all Fort could feel was horror. "We have to get out of here, Dad. *Now!*" he yelled. He tried to grab his father, but his hand swept right through his dad's like he was a ghost.

"I feel like we're going to need a larger statue, though," his father continued, like he hadn't heard a word Fort said. "These ceilings are high enough to fit that head of yours, but you're definitely going to require a bigger seat."

"None of that matters," Fort said, wanting to scream in

1

frustration. "If we stay here, you'll be taken again. I need to get you out of here!"

But his father ignored him, like he was stuck going through the same motions as the day it'd all happened, no matter what Fort did. The other tourists at the Lincoln Memorial didn't seem to hear Fort either, as they continued about their visit, unaware of what was about to come.

"You'll do all of that and more!" his father shouted, and this time, other people *did* look, just like they had six months ago. "There's no time to be lazy, not with all the amazing things you're going to accomplish! And don't forget that I still want a flying car, so I'll need you to invent that, too."

"Dad, *please*," Fort said, tears now rolling down his face. "Come with me? I can't keep going on like this, not knowing if you're alive or if you're . . . you're hurt. Please, just *leave*, you don't have to keep saying everything you already said that day—"

"Um, I'm pretty sure as an adult, I can talk as loudly as I want," his father said. "But stop pushing us off topic, Fort. This is your future we're talking about! You're going to be a great man someday, and I for one can't wait to take pictures in front of your statue as children gaze up at it adoringly!" He waved at two girls who were watching them, giggling. "See? We've already got two volunteers."

"Dad, this is about *your* future," Fort said, trying in vain to grab his father's hand again. "If you stay, I'm going to lose you, and I can't . . . I can't handle that. Not after Mom . . . *please,* Dad, come home with me!" This was all so horrible, knowing what was to come, but even on the day it'd happened, Fort hadn't felt so helpless as he did now. "If you come, you'll . . . you'll see what I've been doing! I've been learning magic! It's wild, I can't even believe it, but I did it for you! I wanted to get revenge on the monster that took you, but then when I had my chance, I couldn't do it. It was almost funny, after all that time wanting to hurt it—"

"It's not *not* funny," one of the two girls said.

"Intelligent youths around here!" his father shouted in response. "Listen to them, Fort. I hear that the children are our future."

"They have to be now," Fort said, hoping his father could hear him at some level. "Because children are the only ones who can use magic. These books of magic turned up, like, thirteen years ago, but only kids can read them and learn the spells. But once some students started using magic, these horrific nightmare creatures found us, and they want to take over the world, just like they did thousands of years ago. They're still

3

looking for us, Dad, and I can't hide from them, not if I want to find you—"

"Low blow, young man," his dad said, then pointed at Lincoln. "Do you think our beloved sixteenth president would have spoken to his father that way? And he's your personal hero!" He leaned closer to the girls conspiratorially. "When my boy here was in diapers, he'd stroll around in a top hat and make us call him Fort Lincoln."

One of the girls snorted, while the other turned away to hide her laughter, but Fort didn't care. At this point, he wasn't sure why he ever had. "Dad, we don't have any more time, it's on its way. It's going to destroy the whole National Mall, and if we don't get out *now*—"

"Oh, we have plenty of time," his father said, taking out his phone. "Besides, I think I have pictures of that in here. Girls, do you want to see?"

"Take me to the Einstein Memorial!" Fort shouted. "Remember? You're just about to mention that. We just need to get out of here—"

"Nonsense!" his father shouted. "Why, we haven't even seen Einstein yet. Did you know there's a statue of Einstein right off the National Mall? And the Gettysburg Address!" He pointed at the speech carved into the wall of the Lincoln Memorial to the left of the president. "Look at this. Two hundred and seventy-two words. Short and to the point."

And then it was too late.

The memorial began to tremble, and Fort knew that nothing was going to change, that his father was going to be taken down into the earth, just like he'd been six months ago, and that all Fort could do was watch.

"I think President Lincoln is waking up," his father whispered to Fort with a grin. "Did you know a second man gave a *two hour* speech before Lincoln at Gettysburg?" He handed Fort a brochure with the Gettysburg Address written out in multiple languages, the same one Fort always kept in his pocket. This version fell right through his ghostlike hand and gently landed on the floor of the memorial like he wasn't even there.

And then the second tremor hit, this time much worse than the first. Several people around the memorial began to shout in surprise, but Fort just turned and walked toward the entrance, not even caring how many tears fell now.

He couldn't see this. Not again. He couldn't watch his father—

But the scene shifted around him, and suddenly he was right

back inside, his father reaching out to steady Fort as the trembling stopped again. "Ladies, maybe you should go find your parents," his dad said to the two girls they'd been talking to before turning to Fort. "Are you okay, kiddo?"

Fort just looked up at him, shaking his head, his mouth hanging open. What was there to say? He couldn't stop this, but he wasn't allowed to leave, either? Why was his mind torturing him like this?

"That's the spirit," his father said. "But maybe we *should* head back to the hotel and grab some dinner. Einstein can wait. After all, time is his relative, I think. Probably a cousin."

His father made his way through the crowd toward the stairs, and Fort just shut his eyes. *Wake up*, he thought to himself. *Wake UP. Don't do this to yourself. You don't have to see it, not again. Not every night!*

When he opened his eyes, though, he was at the stairs with his father, watching as people ran from the Washington Monument in single-file lines. Sierra was causing that, he had learned later. She was using her mind magic to control them all, trying to make sure none of the tourists would be hurt when the creature destroyed the monument. And soon she'd take over Fort's mind too, trying to force him to escape . . . but leaving his father behind.

A third tremor struck, this time far worse than the last two. The stone of the memorial leaped straight up, throwing everyone into the air except Fort, who was still intangible. The stone cracked beneath him in a jagged lightning shape all the way down the steps.

"Out!" Fort's father shouted, pushing the girls toward the exit before trying to grab Fort's hand and run down the stairs with him. Instead, Fort just stood like a helpless bystander, waiting for the horror that was to come.

"Stay alive," Fort whispered after his father. "Please, wherever you are . . . just be okay until I can get to you. I have a plan, and I'm coming for you, so *stay alive*."

He braced himself for the creature to appear from beneath the Washington Monument, hoping he wouldn't have to watch again, over and over like he had every night since he'd first heard Dr. Oppenheimer's secret: The doctor thought Fort's father might still be alive.

But instead of the ground cracking and a giant black scaled hand emerging, a mass of tentacles pushed out of the earth, rising up to reveal crystalline armor, a skull helmet, and the form of the Old One who'd taken over Damian at the Oppenheimer School.

YOU WERE THE CHILD WHO CAUSED US PAIN, it shouted in Fort's mind, sending agony shooting through his skull. He screamed, trying to wake up, to do anything to flee from this monstrosity, but nothing worked. YOU WISH TO SEE YOUR ELDER AGAIN. WE CAN FEEL YOUR DESIRE. BRING US THE LAST DRAGON, AND YOU SHALL HAVE YOUR FATHER BACK—

Out of nowhere, Cyrus's face pushed through the Old One's tentacled helmet, and the sky faded into an ugly green color, the ceiling of the boys' dormitory at the new Oppenheimer School. Cyrus had his hand on Fort's shoulder, shaking him as he stared down worriedly while standing on the bunk below Fort's. "Hey, are you okay?" Cyrus asked. "You were shouting in your sleep again."

His heart still racing, Fort took a deep breath, trying to calm down. This wasn't the first time Cyrus had to wake him up. He'd been having the same dream every night for two weeks now. Though this was the first time the Old One had appeared. That was new.

Not that it could be real. This was just his head finding new ways to torment him, now with promises that his father was still okay. Not that Fort had any idea what a last dragon was,

8

or where that idea had come from. The only dragons he knew of were the skeletons that he'd seen in the old Oppenheimer School's museum room.

"I'm fine," he told Cyrus. "Did I wake you up?"

Cyrus shrugged. "Yes, but that's okay. Because when you did, a vision hit me at the same time. They're being moved. Tomorrow night's going to be our only chance to grab them."

Fort's eyes widened, and he forced a smiled. "*Finally*. Tell the others in the morning, and we'll meet at lunch to go over the plan one more time."

Cyrus nodded, then slipped back down into his bed below, leaving Fort to try to forget the image of the Old One. That had just been a dream. But now he was going to be able to take concrete steps to bring his father home.

I'm coming for you, Dad, he thought. *Just please . . . be okay.*

- TWO -

FORT HAD BEEN IN THE NEW SCHOOL FOR a couple of weeks now, but for some reason he still couldn't find the cafeteria without following the signs. At least that fit with the level of secrecy surrounding the entire school, since he didn't even know where it was located. For all he knew, Fort could be in another country.

After the last school had been destroyed by one of the first students, Damian, while Damian was possessed by the same Old One from Fort's dream, all the students had been transported off the army base first by helicopter, then by plane, and finally driven by bus to the new school, blindfolded until they'd arrived inside the underground hallways.

The soldiers on board claimed that was for their own safety, since if the kids didn't know where the school was, they couldn't reveal it to anyone with supernatural access to their minds. But

Fort just figured the soldiers were used to being secretive, since the only person on the planet with mind magic was presently off with Damian, trying to locate more books of magic.

What Fort did know was that the new school was entirely underground, locked behind three-foot-thick round metal doors. The soldiers claimed those doors would keep them safe even if someone dropped a nuclear bomb within thirty miles. That was comforting, but made Fort wonder what would happen if someone dropped a bomb within twenty miles, or ten. Or, say, right on top of the school.

Not that nuclear bombs were his biggest concern. Given what had happened at the last school, the other students seemed far more dangerous than any missile.

As Fort made his way to the cafeteria, he realized that one reason it was hard to find his way around was that everything was painted an ugly green, something he'd previously only seen in his grandmother's bathroom. But here, all the walls were painted the same nauseating color, making the whole facility feel like it'd been transported from the past to the present. Hopefully that wasn't actually the case, but given that a UK school had a book of time magic, who knew?

It didn't help that there were posters lining the walls from the

1950s and 1960s saying things like "Help fight the red menace!" with cartoon soldiers facing down a hammer and sickle. Over the two weeks Fort had been there, those posters had slowly started being replaced by new ones showing dark, shadowy figures with bony hands reaching straight out at you, saying "Don't trust anything not human!" His favorite, though, was a boy covered in soot who said "Magic is only safe under adult supervision. Don't blow yourself up!"

Good advice all around.

When Fort finally located the cafeteria, he saw that Cyrus had done as asked: Rachel and Jia were both sitting at their regular table in the corner, with Cyrus making a beeline for it from the food line. Fort nodded at them, then quickly jumped into line, knowing he had to eat, even if he was too nervous to keep anything down.

"So get this," Sebastian said, coming up behind Fort in line. "I just talked to Dr. Ambrose, and you won't believe what she's making me do. Me, the top student in her class!"

"Except Jia's the top student," Fort murmured, not looking back. The last thing he wanted to do was listen to Sebastian complain, especially since on a list of his favorite people, Sebastian ranked near the bottom, just above Colonel Charles, the military coheadmaster of the school, and various cartoon villains. And Sebastian only made it *that* high because he'd helped save everyone back at the old school.

"I heard that," Sebastian growled. "Now I'm not going to tell you what Ambrose said about *you*."

Fort frowned. Dr. Ambrose had said something about him? He hadn't seen her since the attack, as classes hadn't started yet at the new school, which meant that days were mostly left up to the students so far. Why would she—

Sebastian banged his tray into Fort's. "Keep moving, New Kid," he said. "Some of us have places to be. And wait until you see where *you're* going." He grinned, which made Fort even more nervous.

He tried to put it out of his mind as he grabbed a burger and some green beans, then jumped out of line. Whatever Sebastian was hinting at could wait. The only thing that mattered now was the plan, and for that, he needed to get back to his friends and hopefully have a moment alone to go over it—

"Fort!" someone shouted as he made his way to their table. Fort sighed and turned to find Trey waving him over. "Come sit with us. Bryce and Chad are being really annoying!"

13

Bryce and Chad both rolled their eyes at this, but for once didn't argue with Trey. Of the three bullies who'd picked on him during his first week at the old school, Trey had been the only one to actually try to be Fort's friend at the new school. The other two had kept torturing Fort for another week or so, but gradually given in to him sitting at their table every so often. Fort barely had any friends as it was, so it was worth a few pranks to have Trey on his side.

But now really wasn't the time. "I promised I'd sit with Cyrus and everyone," he said to Trey. "How about I see you guys at dinner?"

Chad snorted at this, and Bryce grinned. "Looks like your pet bandage doesn't want to sit with you, Trey," Bryce said, using the Destruction kids nickname for Healing students. "How pathetic is that, to get shot down by the new kid?"

Trey's eyes narrowed, and he waved Fort off. "Whatever. I'm busy at dinner. See you never."

Fort winced, but it couldn't be helped. Everything was happening *tonight*, which meant he needed to go over the plan with Jia and Rachel. It all hinged on them knowing their parts, and he couldn't let anything get in the way of that.

"Sorry," he whispered at Trey, who didn't acknowledge that

he'd heard. Fort sighed and walked over to the table where Rachel was glaring at the three boys.

"Want me to burn their behinds?" she asked as Fort sat down. "I'm always up for tormenting the Chads."

"*Rachel,*" Jia said. "You're going to use magic outside the classrooms? You know we're not supposed to!"

"*Jia,*" Rachel said, mimicking her voice. "You know I have a moral duty to set jerks' behinds on fire."

"Oh, I'm not saying you shouldn't," Jia said, her eyes lighting up with excitement. "I'm saying I want to help!"

"I'm okay, but thanks," Fort told her. "Did Cyrus tell you what he found out last night?"

Rachel and Jia both nodded. "Let's not forget that these things make everything cloudier than I'd like," Cyrus said. "But I'm *pretty* sure that I saw what we need."

Fort clenched his fists beneath the table, trying not to let his impatience over the last few weeks make him more anxious than he already was. "'Pretty sure' has to be enough, then," he said, gritting his teeth. "We'll just be extra careful. But that means it's even more important to go over the plan one more time, so that everyone knows what they're doing."

Rachel groaned, and even Jia looked irritated. "There's such a thing as overplanning," Rachel said. "Besides, you know everything's going to go wrong as soon as we start, so why not just let us improvise?"

"This is *too important*," Fort said, leaning in closer. "If we don't get them now, before they're locked away again, Cyrus says we won't have another chance."

"We'd have a ton of chances if one of you Healing people would learn that ghost spell again," Rachel pointed out.

Jia shook her head. "Fort had all of his magic wiped by the Old One, so it'll take him months to learn Ethereal Spirit again. And *I* never should have to begin with. Dr. Ambrose banned it for a reason."

"Because it was *awesome*?" Rachel asked. "And what about your imaginary friend, Fort? Is she going to be here for all of this?"

Fort gave Rachel an annoyed look. "First, she's *not* imaginary. Second, I haven't had a chance to talk to her yet today, but she told me she'd be ready when the time came."

"You can trust her," Jia confirmed. "But we need to know for sure she'll be here at the exact right moment. If she's late or doesn't show, then we're all going to get kicked out of school, if not something worse."

Cyrus held up a hand to interrupt. "Ah, I think we're going to have to cut this short. Something's about to happen."

Fort stared at him. "Something like . . . another attack? Or more like someone's about to spill their cereal?"

"And here, students, we have the cafeteria!" shouted a voice from the twin yellow doors leading out to the halls. "This, of course, is where you'll be eating all your meals."

They all turned to find Colonel Charles leading a bunch of kids through the doors, walking backward like he was some kind of tour guide. Strangely, Fort didn't recognize any of the students he was talking to. Was the school bringing in more students?

"And to our older students," Colonel Charles continued, turning around to address those already in the cafeteria. "I want to introduce you to our *new* class here at the Oppenheimer School. Please mentor them whenever you can, so they can follow in your footsteps."

Fort threw a glance at Rachel, raising an eyebrow. New students?

She shrugged, not seeming to know what was going on either.

And then Fort caught Sebastian's eye, and the other boy grinned evilly.

"Enjoy your lunch, kids," Colonel Charles said. "I'll be back when you're through to show you where your classes will be starting tomorrow." He nodded as the students dispersed, then walked over to Fort's table, where everyone straightened up at his approach.

"Colonel!" Rachel said, and saluted him, then stuck her hand in the air.

Colonel Charles smiled slightly and high-fived her. "I'm actually here for Forsythe, Rachel." He turned to Fort. "Can I speak to you for a moment alone? There will be some . . . changes in your situation."

Fort's eyes widened, and he glanced at the others, who seemed just as worried.

"Changes?" Fort asked, his mouth suddenly dry. After the attack at the old school, he'd assumed he'd be expelled for breaking so many rules, but Colonel Charles had assured him at the time that he was going to be kept on, as they needed more healers. But now, with so many new students, maybe something had changed.

"You'll see," Colonel Charles said. "Let's take a walk over to the dormitory. You'll need to gather all your things."

- THREE -

COLONEL CHARLES LED FORT TO THE door as the Chads all clapped ironically. Jia and Rachel both looked worried, while Cyrus gave him a pitying look, which was never a good sign from someone who could see the future.

Once they stepped outside the cafeteria, Fort assumed the colonel would stop and share whatever was happening, but the man kept moving, walking just ahead of Fort in silence, back to the dormitory. When they reached it, he waved Fort inside. "Grab everything you've got here, please."

Fort didn't move. "Are you . . . expelling me?" If it was happening, then Fort would have to do . . . something. He wasn't sure what, but there was no way he could leave now, not when he was so close. If he got sent home, he'd be giving up his chance to rescue his father forever.

"Expelling? Of course not," Colonel Charles said, and Fort let out a huge sigh of relief. "But you'll be moving out of the dormitory here. So do as I say, please."

That didn't make any sense, but Fort went to gather his things, which didn't amount to much. He'd packed a bag when he'd left his aunt's apartment almost a month ago now, but the bag had never reached the school, so all he really had were his uniforms and boots. That, and the last thing his father had given him, a brochure of the Gettysburg Address translated into multiple languages. Fortunately, he kept the brochure with him in his pocket at all times anyway.

The only other things that were sort of his were some old mystery novels he and Cyrus had found lying around in unused rooms here at the new school. He took one he hadn't finished and left the rest for Cyrus. For some reason, Cyrus loved the books, probably because he refused to use his magic to see how they ended.

With Fort's hands full of clothes and boots, Colonel Charles turned and walked back out of the dormitory without another word. Fort took a long look at his home of the past two weeks, beginning to worry again. Where was he going? And why was he being separated from his best friend?

"Don't make me wait on you, Fitzgerald," Colonel Charles said from outside the door, and Fort hurried to catch up.

The colonel led them through the ugly green halls, down corridors Fort had never been in, which just made him more lost than ever. Thick green pipes ran along the top of each wall, with black wires snaking in and out of them. Here and there, a construction worker adjusted wiring inside the walls, bright blue sparks flying.

"This bunker was built for Congress, in the event of a catastrophe," Colonel Charles said, walking Fort past one of the workers. "That was back in the late nineteen-fifties, if you couldn't tell by the decor."

"What are they doing?" Fort asked as someone pushed a cart with two huge metal barrels down the hall past them.

"Renovations," Colonel Charles said. "All of the electronics in here were out of date, and we needed communications to the outside world that wouldn't go out the first time a Destruction student learned how to cast an electromagnetic pulse." He snorted, and Fort figured that was supposed to be a joke.

Somehow, he couldn't make himself laugh. "So the school isn't ready? I thought classes were going to start tomorrow."

"Oh, it's ready enough," Colonel Charles said as they passed a horribly carpeted room that looked like it had enough desks and chairs to fit almost five hundred people, all facing a raised podium in front. Maybe that was where Congress would have met? "This was our backup school from the beginning. But ever since the attack, and thanks to your discovery about Healing magic hurting the Old One, we decided to increase attendance. And that required upgrading more of the facility than we'd originally planned on."

They passed by another large room, this one with glass walls so Fort could see soldiers inside sitting at computers that at least looked more modern than the rest of the place. He also noticed several televisions around the ceiling of the room, televisions that showed—

Fort's breath caught in his throat, throwing him into a coughing fit as he struggled to believe what he'd just seen.

Colonel Charles paused and followed Fort's gaze to where the television showed pictures of Damian, the boy who'd been taken over by the Old One, and Sierra, the girl who'd linked to Fort's mind accidentally during the attack that had taken his father.

And the text above each picture labeled them as terrorists.

"We're saying they're part of the Gathering Storm," Colonel

Charles said, turning back to Fort now. "It's a bit easier to say that than reveal that the girl wiped our memories and escaped after waking up from a coma and destroying the first Oppenheimer School. And we *do* want people afraid of them, so the public will be on the lookout. It makes sense all around."

Fort stared at the screens for a moment, then realized what he'd heard. "Wiped our . . . memories?" he asked.

Colonel Charles stared at him for a moment, then pulled out a small tablet. "That brings us to the first thing I needed to speak to you about." He typed something on the screen that Fort couldn't see. "Did you know we had cameras up all over the base, back at the old school?"

"Sure," Fort said, not liking where this was going.

"Now, during the attack, most of them were destroyed," the colonel said, then paused his typing and gave Fort a long look. "Most, but not all."

A deep chill went sailing down Fort's spine. When Sierra and Damian had left, Sierra had wiped herself out of Colonel Charles's memory entirely, so that he wouldn't hunt them down while she and Damian tried to find the other books of magic. Clearly something had changed, since Colonel Charles knew exactly who she was now. Sierra had left Dr. Opps with *his* memory of everything, so maybe the doctor had betrayed them, or—

Colonel Charles turned the tablet around, and Fort's eyes widened as he saw himself on the screen, waving his arms around while talking to Damian and Sierra. The three of them looked like they were arguing for a moment, then Damian and Sierra passed Fort and ran offscreen. There was no sound, but from Fort's perspective, what had happened was pretty obvious.

His mouth suddenly as dry as a desert, Fort blinked, not sure what he could possibly say here. There he was on camera, letting two wanted magicians go free. At the time, he'd wanted Damian to stay, to get judged for what he'd done—even if Damian had been possessed by the Old One when he'd done it—but Sierra had convinced Fort that she and Damian would never be treated fairly.

And now Colonel Charles had Fort on video letting them walk. "Uh . . . ," he said, trying to decide if he should run, and if the colonel could catch him if he did.

But then Colonel Charles put his hand on his shoulder, and it was too late. "So first of all, I just want to tell you," the colonel said, "that I'm proud of you."

That was it, he was getting kicked out, and . . . wait, *what*?

"You're . . . proud of me?" Fort said, his voice breaking.

"From what I see here, you tried to stop them," Colonel Charles said. He squeezed Fort's shoulder, then removed his hand, and Fort almost collapsed, not able to believe his luck. "Considering you had no magic at that point, and both of them could control your mind, that speaks highly of your bravery."

"It . . . does?" Fort said, still struggling to catch up.

"Not many would have done it," the colonel continued. "In fact, it looks like you're the only one who tried. Probably because they'd already paralyzed the others, so they must have assumed you were no threat. Still, I want you to know that I saw what you did, even if like the rest of us, you got your mind wiped so don't remember doing it. I saw it, and I admire that you tried."

"I . . . I *don't* remember it, no," Fort said, just happy that he wasn't about to be thrown in jail or something.

"And don't you worry," Colonel Charles continued. "We've got agents in the field tracking Sierra and Damian down as we speak. Each agent is fully protected against mind magic, so it shouldn't be long before we have them back in custody."

"Oh, that's . . . that's great," Fort said. "Where, um, are they looking?"

"Oh, here and there," the colonel said. "And don't worry about not remembering, either: One of these two wiped my mind completely of both of them. I had to be caught up to date by my staff, once we determined Sierra and Damian had gone missing during the attack. Do you know how embarrassing that is?"

Fort just shook his head silently, not trusting himself to say anything.

The colonel gave him a sympathetic look, then his eyebrows furrowed. "By the way, Forsythe, I'm told that you were once . . . connected to Sierra, from when she used her mind magic on you, back at the National Mall. I'm even told you could see her memories while she was in a coma. You don't still feel any sort of connection to her *now*, do you?"

Fort looked Colonel Charles right in the eye, knowing there was only one right answer to this question. "No, I don't. Whatever that was, it's completely gone now."

The colonel nodded. "As I suspected. It must have been something unconscious while she was in the coma. Now follow me, I'll take you to your new room." And with that, he set off down the hall.

Next to Fort, a brown-haired girl wearing a black leather

jacket and ripped pants appeared in the hallway, glowing yellow. "*Completely* gone?" Sierra said, raising an eyebrow at Fort.

"Maybe not, like, a hundred percent," Fort said, and grinned at her.

- FOUR -

IERRA'S MENTALLY PROJECTED IMAGE followed Fort down the hall after Colonel Charles, and for some reason Fort felt much better having her along.

Where are you two right now? he asked her in his mind.

"Oh, we're still trying to get a flight to the UK," she said, stopping to stare into various rooms. "Wow, this place is old, huh? Glad *we* got nice rooms in NSA headquarters."

He grinned. *How's the savior of the world?*

She rolled her eyes at him. "Give Damian a break. He feels really bad about what happened. And now he's doing everything he can to make sure we can fight them, if they ever come back."

Assuming he's not the one to let them in again. How do you put up with his attitude all the time?

She laughed. "You'd be surprised. Last night, I actually almost got him to talk about where he came from before Dr. Opps brought him to the school. That would have been a major victory." She clenched her jaw, giving Fort her most serious look. "But no," she said, mimicking Damian's voice. "I couldn't possibly burden you with my secrets. The enemy could pull them from your mind, and then we'd all be lost."

Fort groaned out loud, forgetting where he was. Colonel Charles turned to give him a questioning look, and Fort coughed to cover it. "Sorry, something caught in my throat at lunch," he said, turning red as Sierra moved behind Colonel Charles to make faces at the man.

"We're here, anyway," the colonel said, and knocked on a random door in a long line of them in a hallway Fort wasn't sure he could find again with a map. "Gabriel? Can we come in?"

"Gabriel?" Sierra said, raising her eyebrows. "Who's that?"

Fort shrugged as the door opened, revealing a boy at least a foot taller than Fort, with long dark hair that fell over his face. He was built like a football player, and could probably give the soldiers guarding the school a fight if it came to that. His eyes had dark rings beneath them, as if he hadn't slept in a while. He saluted when he saw Colonel Charles, and the colonel saluted back. "Yes, sir?" Gabriel said to the colonel.

"*Whoa,*" Sierra said, moving within inches of Gabriel's face to give him a closer look. "Look at the size of him!"

"Gabriel Torrence, I'd like to introduce your new roommate," Colonel Charles said, turning to gesture to Fort. "This is Forsythe Fitzgerald. He's been at the school before, but only for about a week, so he'll be joining you first-years in class."

"He'll be what?" Sierra said, grinning widely.

"I'll be *what*?" Fort said, much less enthused than Sierra.

Colonel Charles gave him a patronizing smile. "From what you've told me, you had all the magic erased from your mind during the fight against that creature, back at the old school. So now you're starting over from scratch. We wouldn't want the more experienced students being held back, waiting for you to catch up." He turned back to Gabriel. "Forsythe will be showing you around and tutoring you in Healing. I've arranged for special access to the magic book for you both, in the hopes that you can eventually catch up to the second-years and potentially join their class."

"Tutoring?" Sierra said, raising an eyebrow. "Doesn't he know you're terrible at magic?"

Right? Fort thought in shock. *What is going on? I don't have time to tutor someone. And I can't be his roommate! What if he finds out about the* plan?

Gabriel turned toward Fort, who unconsciously took a step back. His new roommate was *big*. "Nice to meet you, kid," Gabriel said, smiling slightly, before turning back to Colonel Charles. "Respectfully, sir, I don't think I need a tutor *or* a roommate. He might be better off helping someone else."

"I don't think you understand, Gabriel," Colonel Charles said. "I wasn't asking. Consider this an order."

Gabriel blinked, then nodded. "Yes, sir. Then I'll do my best to learn from him." With that, he gave Fort a look that almost seemed apologetic.

"That's all the school can ask," Colonel Charles said, then nodded. "Dismissed. Forsythe, stay out here with me for a moment."

Gabriel nodded and closed the door as Colonel Charles led Fort a few feet down the hallway. "Gabriel is a special project of mine," Colonel Charles said, putting a hand on Fort's shoulder. "He has . . . a lot of potential, and I'd like to see what might come of it. For that, I think you're uniquely qualified to help, Forsythe."

Fort just stared at the colonel in confusion. "You want me to tutor him? Why? Was he born on Discovery Day?"

31

For a second Colonel Charles looked like he was going to say something, but he seemed to change his mind.

"No, his birthday is in January," the colonel said. "However, that shouldn't limit him any more than it does you." Behind the colonel, Sierra began making faces at him again. "I'd view this as a personal favor if you'll take him under your wing, Forsythe. Show him around, eat meals with him, become his friend. But most of all, get him up to speed as quickly as you can on magic. Consider Gabriel your *top* priority at the school, even over your own studies. Do I make myself clear?"

What? Who *was* this kid? "Not especially, sir," Fort said, more confused than ever.

"Then consider it an order," Colonel Charles said, growing irritated. "And if I find out you're not following my instructions, then we'll reassess your usefulness in remaining at the school. Does *that* help clarify things?"

Fort nodded, glaring back at the colonel.

"Good," Colonel Charles said. "Now go bond with your new roommate. Classes won't begin until tomorrow, so you'll have plenty of time today to get to know each other."

With that, the colonel turned and walked back down the

hall they'd come from, with Fort just watching him go, not even sure what to say to any of this.

"Well," Sierra said, wincing. "This isn't going to make stealing the book of Summoning any easier, *that's* for sure!"

- FIVE -

FORT SLOWLY OPENED THE DOOR TO his new room, silently taking it all in as Gabriel didn't bother looking up from his book. Two beds were pushed up against one wall with a nightstand in between, and a dresser sat against the opposite wall with room enough for all their clothes. The walls were bare and painted the same ugly green as everything else.

Another door opposite the one Fort stood in led to what looked like a bathroom, which was the first good news he'd seen all day. Having to use the bathroom way down the hall in the middle of the night was never fun, especially if the soldier guards caught you out there. That automatically made this room better than the dormitory.

Except here he wouldn't be sleeping above his best friend anymore. He wouldn't have Cyrus around to talk to whenever he wanted, to go over the plan, or just to chat. Instead, his new roommate was a huge, intense boy that he knew nothing about but seemed to be important enough to get his own room and be given a permanent tutor.

Fort closed the door behind him, then dropped his uniforms on the dresser and opened the drawers to find an empty one. Gabriel had taken the ones on the left, so Fort stuffed his spare clothes into the top drawer on the right, though he left the Gettysburg Address brochure in his pocket. Then he moved over to the free bed and sat down, not saying anything in spite of the dozens of questions going through his head.

Sierra passed right through the closed door like a ghost, and Fort had to remind himself that she wasn't actually here but was just projecting her image into his mind, so of course she'd follow him in. She looked between Gabriel and Fort, slowly shaking her head. "It already smells like boy in here. How do you people do that?"

How would you know what it smells like? he asked her silently.

"'Cause *you* can smell it, smart guy," she said, tapping her nose. "Now watch out, I think the big one's moving."

Fort turned to find Gabriel putting down his book and sitting up. "Listen," he said, giving Fort a look that could have been either apologetic or angry, it was hard to tell which. "It wasn't my idea to come here, and there's nothing I'd rather do less than learn magic, okay? So don't worry about whatever Colonel Charles ordered you to do. He thinks he's big-time here because he's in charge, but he's just a little man who let a small amount of power go to his head. You let me deal with him, and just do your thing. Sound good?"

Fort bit his lip, not sure how to respond to that. "That'd be great, except Colonel Charles said I'd be expelled if I didn't do what he said. I haven't known him that long, but I do know he's not big on being disobeyed."

Gabriel snorted. "Like I said, leave it to me. You seem like a good kid, and I'm sorry you're getting mixed up in all of this. If the colonel gives you any trouble, just blame it on me. It's not like you could carry me to class."

"See?" Sierra said. "Everything's going to be fine! He doesn't even want your help, so you're free to go talk to Jia and . . . the others whose names I can never remember." She took several baby steps toward the door, like she was trying to encourage him to go.

"Fair enough," Fort said, and followed Sierra to the exit. "I'll be around if you have any questions or anything."

"Thanks," Gabriel said, barely listening as he picked his book back up and lay down on the bed.

Fort nodded and opened the door.

A soldier stared back at him. "Sorry, kid," the guard said. "No one's leaving until dinner. Colonel Charles's orders."

"Are you serious?" Gabriel shouted, leaping up from the bed. For such a big guy, he moved surprisingly fast. Fort quickly got out of his way as Gabriel confronted the soldier. "You can't keep us here. *Let us out.* Do I have to go over your head?"

The soldier shook his head but looked much more nervous than he had when just talking to Fort. "Sorry, uh, sir, but I have to follow the orders I was given. No one can exit this room until dinner."

"Sir"? Fort thought at Sierra, who looked confused too.

Gabriel growled at the soldier, then seemed to deflate. "I get it. You're just doing your job," he said, and tossed off a salute to the soldier, then fell heavily back to the bed as the soldier closed the door again. "Sorry, kid. I guess the colonel *is* going to be a huge pain in the behind about this."

Who is *this guy?* Fort asked Sierra.

"Let me check. Hold on." She closed her eyes, and her hands glowed brighter for a moment. But the light quickly disappeared, and she frowned. "Whoa. He's wearing one of my amulets, Fort. The ones I made for Dr. Opps back at the NSA, to protect the wearer against mind magic. Why would they give *him* that?"

Fort snuck a look at Gabriel and saw that she was right. He'd mistaken it for just a chain around Gabriel's neck at first, but now he could make out the shape of a silver ball beneath the boy's shirt. Why would a first year student have protection against his mind being read? That didn't make any sense. None of the other students had an amulet; only the teachers and high-ranking military had them, since there weren't enough to go around.

"Oh shoot, I have to go," Sierra said, looking annoyed. "Damian thinks he's got a way onto a plane. You wouldn't believe how many people's brains we've had to magic already and still can't even get a ticket. The TSA does *not* mess around."

Wait, you're still going to be around tonight, right? Fort asked, knowing she could feel his worry but not able to hold it back. *We can't pull this off without you.*

"Oh, I know," Sierra said, wiggling her eyebrows at him. "Don't worry. I won't stand you up like that girl Denise did when you were six, when you two were going to put on that little dance show for your parents."

Fort's eyes widened, and he felt his entire face light on fire. *You said you'd stop looking at my memories!*

"Oh, I say a *lot* of things," Sierra said, grinning evilly, then disappeared.

Fort smiled in spite of himself as he sat down on his bed. Gabriel had gone back to reading, so at least he had some quiet to think, and his mind soon turned back to the book of magic they were stealing tonight. Nothing was going right so far. He didn't have time to be sitting in his room, trapped by the guard, not when he should be going over the plan with Jia, Rachel, and Cyrus again. At least he'd be allowed out at dinner and could meet up with them then, but that was cutting it close.

Because tonight was their only night to steal the book of Summoning. And it all came down to Dr. Opps.

It was the doctor's own fault, too. *He* was the one who wondered if Fort's father might still be alive, given that the unthinking monster that had stolen his dad was controlled by an Old One. And why would the Old One kidnap someone unless it intended to keep that someone alive?

Of course, other reasons tried to pop into Fort's head, just as they always did, but he forced himself to ignore them. He had to believe his father was okay out there. Even his subconscious seemed to think it, if his dreams were any indication.

Assuming they were just dreams.

Unfortunately, there was only one way to go after his father, and that was by opening a portal to the monsters' dimension using Summoning magic. And only one person on earth knew how to do it.

Sierra had run it by Damian, of course, but he'd immediately refused, saying that the Old Ones were waiting for him to use his Summoning magic again, so they could use it to return to this dimension. It annoyed Fort to no end that the boy was probably right, so he couldn't exactly argue.

Plan B had been asking Sierra if she'd copy the spell he needed from Damian's head, just like she'd done by accident with some of Jia's spells, back when she'd been in a coma at the old school. But even the suggestion had offended her.

"I am *not* going to just steal a spell from somebody's mind!" she'd yelled at him, and the intensity of her repulsion that traveled through their telepathic connection overpowered him to the point he'd never asked again.

But that meant he had no other choice, if he wanted to rescue his father. He'd need the book of Summoning, one of two books of magic that Dr. Opps had kept secret and hidden beneath the old Oppenheimer School. Cyrus had reported that the books had been brought to their new school at some point in the last ten days but were being kept under close watch by Colonel Charles.

But tonight they'd be on the move again, probably to be taken to some special room and locked up. It was hard to say exactly, as Cyrus had trouble with his future visions around the books themselves; they always seemed to create a blind spot for him. But if that happened, Fort might lose access to Summoning magic forever, meaning his father would stay lost.

Fortunately, they'd had plenty of time to come up with a plan to steal the books while waiting for them to emerge again. But Fort needed each of his friends to do their part if the plan was going to work. And that meant making sure everybody was in the right place at the right time.

What he *didn't* need was Gabriel, a total stranger, finding out what they intended to do. Who knew what he'd do? The worst thing was, telling Colonel Charles about it wasn't even the most terrible thing that could happen. For all Fort knew, Gabriel would take the book of Summoning himself and accidentally bring the Old Ones back.

41

Fort glanced over at the boy, who was still reading, and wondered who he could be to get such treatment here. Someone like Sebastian, the son of a congresswoman who controlled the school's budget? Someone like Damian, who they'd identified early as having a real gift for magic? Or something entirely new?

The third option scared Fort the most, because the last thing he needed right now was unknowns. But if they could get through tonight, then the mystery of Gabriel wouldn't really matter. As soon as Fort had his hands on the book of Summoning, he was going to use the magic to rescue his father then and there. There was no way he was going to take the chance that someone would catch him first, so he couldn't wait.

He knew that if he made it back safely with his dad, the school would immediately expel him, and that was fine. All he wanted was his father back. He'd miss his friends, yes, but there was no comparison. And so all of this with Gabriel would disappear, as long as he could get to the book as planned.

Still, maybe it wouldn't hurt to befriend the other boy, just in case?

"Good book?" Fort asked.

"The colonel ordered you to be friends with me, didn't he,"

Gabriel said, not looking up. "Let's not give him the satisfaction."

. . . Right. Okay. Fair enough.

Fort lay back on the bed, covering his face with his hands. He'd be able to see his real friends at dinner and not have to worry about this new roommate situation for one meal, at least.

- SIX -

MEET GABRIEL," FORT SAID, SIGHING deeply as he gestured to the taller boy next to him. Two soldiers waited just behind them for Fort and Gabriel to sit down together, something that wasn't voluntary, according to their orders. "Gabriel, this is Jia, Rachel, and Cyrus. Gabriel's my new roommate, and he's going to be sitting with us for . . . well, until we're told otherwise."

Jia's eyebrows shot up in surprise, and Rachel looked suspicious, but Cyrus stood up solemnly and offered his hand. "Nice to finally meet you, Gabriel," he said, more serious than Fort had ever known him to be. "I've seen a lot of you in the future."

Gabriel frowned as the soldiers finally gave them some room. "You mean, you'll *be* seeing a lot of me in the future?"

"Not exactly," Fort told him as they both set their trays

down. "I'll explain later." He turned to Jia and Rachel, who were both giving him questioning looks with varying levels of annoyance. "Colonel Charles assigned me to Gabriel, since he's new. Not only are we roommates, but we're going to be hanging out pretty much all the time, including at meals." He let his long stare illustrate exactly what he thought about *that*. "And I'm going to be tutoring him too. You know, just like how all new students are given tutors?"

"None of this was my idea," Gabriel said, starting in on his meal. "Including those soldiers making me sit with you all, so I'm sorry about that. Just pretend I'm not here."

Rachel gave Fort a pointed look that said everything he was already thinking, but Jia tried to change the subject. "If you remember, Fort, *you* got some tutoring when you first came to the Oppenheimer School," she said. "Not that you needed it, since you had your . . . friend."

"Let's not bring *her* up again," Fort said, hoping Jia picked up on the fact that Sierra as a topic was *way* off limits. "I got enough of her at the other school."

"Did you?" Sierra said, sitting down in an empty spot at the table. At Fort's surprised look, she gave him one back. "What? It's a long ride to the airport, and I'm not even sure we'll get on this flight, so I told Damian to wake me when we're there. I want to make sure I know everything that's happening too."

"Anyway, I know we all had plans for tonight," Fort said. "But I wouldn't want to abandon my new roommate, so let's maybe talk about those later."

"Later?" Cyrus said. "But tonight's the only—"

"The only night we won't be tired from classes," Jia quickly interrupted.

"No, that's not what I was going to say." Cyrus looked confused. "Are we really not going through with the plan? Because I still see us—"

"Having fun anyway?" Fort said. "I'm sure we will! Let's all talk to Gabriel now, so he doesn't feel left out."

Gabriel, though, hadn't looked up from his food since he'd sat down. "Eh," he said, shrugging slightly. "I say go through with this plan of yours. Like I said, don't worry about me. Sounds like you're breaking rules, and I'm all for it."

"Oh, we are," Cyrus said. "Almost all of them."

Jia snorted water out of her nose, and Rachel quickly jumped in. "He's kidding," she said, handing Jia her napkin. "He thinks it's funny to make things up like that, don't you, Cyrus?"

"Do I?" Cyrus asked, looking even more confused now. "I'm not sure I know what's going on here."

"I do," Gabriel said, looking up from his burger. "You all had something planned for tonight, but you don't know me, so you can't talk about it in front of me. Like I said, don't worry about me. I'm not going to snitch to anyone."

"We're not doing anything that's *actually* wrong," Jia said. "Besides, some rules were meant to be broken."

Rachel sighed. "Don't listen to her. She's looking for her next thrill after trying to take down an Old One."

"Um, *succeeding* in taking one down, thank you," Jia said.

"It was just going to be one last night hanging out before classes start," Fort said, not sure how much worse this could get.

"Just the four of us," Rachel said quickly. "It's like we're a club or something. No new members until school officially starts."

Sierra dropped her head into her hands. "You guys are *so* bad at this, Fort. Do you want me to just wipe his memory of this whole meal?"

Maybe? he thought at her, clueless about how to bring this back under control. And more importantly, they really did need to go over the plan, just in case this was their last chance before Dr. Opps brought the book of Summoning out of hiding. *Can you just make him hear a fake conversation for a minute or two?*

Sierra frowned. "I was kidding. You really want me to do this? I'm not entirely —"

I don't want you to, I need *you to! We have to have that book if we're going to get my dad back. Nothing else matters, okay?*

". . . Okay, Fort," Sierra said, and he could feel the worry coming off of her, but he couldn't let that bother him now. "But he's still wearing that amulet, so you're going to need to remove it first."

Ugh, right, the amulet. Fort winced, then turned to Gabriel. "Hey, what's that chain thing you're wearing? Can I see it?"

Sierra groaned loudly as Gabriel slowly turned to stare at Fort. "Excuse me?" he asked.

"It just looks like one of the protective ones that Colonel Charles wears," Fort said, which was true, since the colonel always wore his, probably ever since he heard that Sierra wiped his memory. "I've always wanted to see one."

Gabriel snorted. "That's what he said. I kinda doubt it does anything. Take it if you want it." He yanked it over his head and tossed it to Fort, who missed it, letting it hit the table loudly. He quickly grabbed it as the guards turned to stare, and he nodded at Sierra.

"I *really* don't feel good about this," she said. "It's the thing with Cyrus all over again, and I still don't like that we did that."

You're going to be doing it to Dr. Opps later!

"Yeah, but *he* deserves it," she said. "This kid hasn't pushed anyone into experimenting with magic to the point they get possessed by ancient evils. Well, that I know of, I guess."

He gave her a long look, and she rolled her eyes. "Fine!" Her image wavered for a moment as she cast the spell, only to solidify a moment later. "Happy? Now all he's hearing is a fascinating monologue from you about your most embarrassing memories. I made sure to give him the greatest hits."

"Great," Fort whispered to himself, then turned to Gabriel, needing to test things. "Gabriel? Hey, Gabriel? Can you hear me?"

But the other boy just continued eating, completely oblivious.

"Okay, Sierra's fixed things so we can talk for a moment," Fort told the others. "Cyrus, what time is Dr. Opps bringing the books out?"

"Just after curfew," Cyrus said, looking at Gabriel with some confusion.

"What does he think we're talking about?" Rachel asked, waving a hand in front of Gabriel's face. The other boy immediately looked up and stared at her curiously.

"He can still see you," Fort hissed at her.

"Don't worry, I've got this," Sierra said, looking even more annoyed. "I had Rachel tell him that she wanted to share embarrassing things too."

Fort sighed. *Glad* you're *having fun at least.*

"Oh, always."

"Everyone just pretend like you're eating, okay?" Fort told them. "Sierra's got him listening to . . . our life stories. Just act casual. Cyrus, where's the best spot to grab the books?"

"There will only be one hall along his path that will be empty at the time and doesn't have cameras installed yet," Cyrus said. "It's two floors up, just before an elevator. After that, he and the guards go down to a basement level and things get really fuzzy, so I think that's our only shot at this."

That was what Fort had been afraid of. "Okay, so the hallway it is. Everyone's clear on their jobs, right?"

Jia nodded. "I cast Paralyze on Dr. Opps and the guards with him, so that we can remove their protective mind amulets."

"Then I grab the books and replace them with the fakes,"

Fort said. "Sierra will convince them the books I give them are the real books of magic, as well as make them forget we were ever there."

"That spell on the books won't last for more than a couple of days, so you better hope they don't check in on them after that," Sierra pointed out.

It won't matter, Fort thought at her. *I only need the book of Summoning long enough to open a portal and find my dad. After that, they can throw me in jail for all I care. All that matters is that he comes back safely.*

"That's not *all* that matters," Sierra said, but Rachel was talking over her.

"Cyrus, did you find somewhere for my part of all of this?" she asked.

He nodded. "There's an unused kitchen on that floor with some strong ventilation. If you do it in there, it'll carry away any smoke."

Rachel nodded, leaning forward. "Okay then. So for my part, as soon as Fort brings me the books, I burn them both with fireballs until they're *ash*. Everyone still agrees that this needs to be done, right? That they're just too dangerous for anyone to use their magic ever again?"

First Jia, then Cyrus nodded. Rachel turned to Fort, who nodded as well.

"Agreed," he lied. "They need to be destroyed."

"Oh right," Sierra said, dropping her head into her hands and groaning. "I'd almost forgotten about the part of the plan where you betray all your friends. Great. This is going to go so, *so* well."

- SEVEN -

TELL ME AGAIN WHY WE'RE LYING TO everyone?" Sierra asked, lying on Fort's bed with a sleep mask on and a travel pillow around her neck. In the next bed, Gabriel read by the light of a lamp clipped to the headboard. Somehow Gabriel had been able to bring a whole box of books to the school, as well as the light, compared to Fort's just enough uniforms to fill a drawer and a beat-up old copy of the mystery novel he'd found.

Because I can't let Jia or Rachel come with me, assuming they wouldn't just try to stop me in the first place, he thought at Sierra from the opposite end of his bed, staring up at the ceiling. It was still a few hours until Cyrus's appointed time, and Fort could barely sit still. It'd been almost seven months since his father was taken, and every minute that passed just made it worse. What had his father been going through this whole time? Had he been tortured for information? Had they just thrown him in some prison and forgotten about him?

"Why not?" Sierra asked, peeking out from under her sleep mask only to make a disgusted face. "Ugh, someone in the airport is eating something really stinky. Who does that? At least they're not waiting to inflict it on us on the plane."

Are you sure you're going to get on the flight?

"Damian thinks so," she said, then started rubbing her temples. "But between entertaining you and making sure everyone in the airport sees me and him as an old British couple, I'm getting a headache."

That's right, your face is all over TV, Fort thought. *I forgot you'd need to disguise yourself.*

"You'd think Damian could help, but no, he says he senses someone's after us, so he has to be prepared for an attack." She rolled her eyes and replaced her mask. "He *senses*. Like that's a thing. It's like he doesn't even have the courtesy to make up some spell I don't know. At least lie to me convincingly, if you're going to do it."

Fort grinned. *Anyway, how's disguising yourself any different from what I asked you to do to Gabriel? You were awfully judgey about that.*

She sat up and pointed at him. "Because Damian and I don't have a choice, and you *do*. Because Gabriel wasn't going to turn you in. And because it's just a thing I don't feel great doing, okay?"

Sorry, Fort thought, and pushed along some apologetic feelings. *But how do you know he won't turn us in? Did you read his mind when you were in there?*

"No, I make it a habit to only read yours," Sierra said. "Gabriel isn't exactly thrilled with authority, so he doesn't seem like a snitch."

Fort nodded, glad he'd been able to change the subject from having to lie to his friends. After all, he didn't—

"Hey, I *heard* that," Sierra said, pulling the mask off again. "We're not done here. Why couldn't you bring them along? Them stopping you, *that* I understand, and yes, they probably would have. But you're going to need all the help you can get, and taking them with you would be smart."

They totally would try to stop me, Fort thought. *Jia still blames me for stealing her spells and using them to wake you up. Rachel almost murdered me when she thought I might be a danger to the school. What do you think they'd do if they found out I was taking an even bigger risk than last time? There's no way they'd let me do this.*

Sierra narrowed her eyes. "Why are you avoiding my question? You can't fool a telepath, Fort. Why don't you want them along?"

He growled to himself, then sat up and glared at her. *Because Cyrus told me if I brought anyone else with me, I'd lose one of them forever. Okay?*

She sat back in surprise. "Whoa, okay, yes, that'd do it. When did this happen? You never told me he checked your future."

Because it wasn't a great sign! Fort shouted back in his mind. *You think knowing that if I don't go alone, one of my friends could die, or get left behind . . . you think that makes me excited to do this? I have to get my father back. But I also know how dangerous it's going to be. I just can't let myself think about that.*

She looked at him sadly. "I get it. Still, you could have told me. I've seen your memories of potty training. There's nothing you can't tell me, Fort."

Nothing except— he thought, then immediately cut himself off, his eyes widening.

"Wait, what was that?" she said, jumping up off the bed. "What are you hiding? Something about going alone, and what Cyrus told you would happen."

Fort winced. This was exactly the reason he hadn't men-

tioned any of this to her. *He said . . . he said that if I went alone, I could bring him back, but that it'd be dangerous. That I might get hurt. That was it. That's why I didn't want to tell you.*

Okay, it wasn't the full truth, but it was close and all he could afford to let her know.

Even that much was probably over the line. "Are you kidding?" she screamed. "He told you that you might get hurt? But you're not going to do the safe thing and bring the others, because no, Fort Fitzgerald can't let anyone help him, not even to keep him safe!"

Because it would mean putting them in danger! he shouted back. *How is that better? At least this way I'm the only one taking the chance!*

"But what if—"

There isn't a what if, not according to Cyrus! There are only two options: I lose a friend, or I might get a few scratches. That's no choice at all.

She looked away. "And that's why I had to use my magic on him, to make him think he saw you destroying the books instead of using them, because you couldn't have him telling the others. I still hate that we did that."

I know, me too, Fort thought, and he did, honestly. Cyrus

was his best friend, but he knew that the boy couldn't keep a secret to save his life, and if it got out that Fort was going, this would all fall apart.

She sighed and turned back toward Fort. "Fine. I don't agree with this, but at least I get now why you're hiding it from them." She looked down at his hands, which had clenched into fists. "But you're about to claw through your sheets, you're so anxious. Why don't I magic you to sleep or something? I promise I'll wake you up at the right time, and then you won't be sitting here for hours about to explode."

Still angry, Fort started to say what a terrible idea that was, but even in his annoyance he knew she was right. He *should* really be at his freshest when he got to the dimension where his father was being held. And if nothing else, he wouldn't be sitting here waiting for another few hours. *Okay,* he said. *And thanks. Just make sure . . .*

"I know, I know, the plan," she said, rolling her eyes but smiling gently at him. "I'll be where I promised I'd be. Just trust me, okay?" Her hands glowed brighter, and she gave him a worried look. "I'll see you in a few hours. Don't have nightmares."

A wave of sleepiness hit him then, and it was all he could

do to lay his head on his pillow before he drifted off, as Sierra faded out from the other side of the bed.

The dream, as it always did, started within seconds.

A giant black scaly hand pushed up through the stairs of the Lincoln Memorial, closing around Fort's father and the woman he'd been carrying to safety. Fort's heart stopped as he watched his father disappear behind those fingers.

The old woman came tumbling out from between the creature's fingers, crashing to the grass next to Fort. His father tried climbing through just behind her, but he was going to be too late. He was *always* too late.

"Dad!" Fort screamed as the creature roared, then started pulling back below the ground.

"Fort!" his father shouted. The creature's hand curled around him, rupturing the remains of the memorial as it descended back into the ground. "FORT—"

The creature's massive hand disappeared within the earth, and his father went silent.

"NO!" Fort shrieked, but part of him knew that he couldn't do anything, even if he wasn't a ghost here, because the dream would play out just like real life had, and Sierra would be commanding him to run any second now.

But her voice never appeared in his head. Without waiting to find out why, Fort dove into the hole after his father.

Down and down into darkness he fell, unable to see or hear anything but the creature's scales ripping against the dirt and stone. His father stayed silent as the creature descended. Though Fort was falling, somehow he stayed right with the monster's fist moving at the same speed.

A green glow lit the tunnel from below, shining off of the creature's scales as it dug back down, the earth collapsing in a strangely organized way behind them, almost as if by magic. The glow intensified, and now Fort could see the portal, just like the one he'd seen below the old Oppenheimer School when the same creature (or a very similar one) had almost pulled him through.

If only he'd known then that his father might still be alive, he would have gladly gone with it.

The creature passed through the portal, and Fort followed, holding his breath with anticipation. He knew that this was just his imagination, he *knew* it. But what if he was wrong? What if he was going to see what had happened to his father? Maybe he could see where his dad had been taken, and—

The creature stopped, slamming into solid stone, then lowering its hand toward the ground as Fort floated down next to it. Its fingers opened, releasing Fort's father, who groaned as he rolled onto the stone below. The creature stepped away into the darkness, and suddenly it felt like Fort was entirely alone with his dad.

When the monster was gone, his father slowly got to his feet, the glow of the portal the only light that Fort could see him by.

"Hello?" his father said, and Fort's heart almost broke to hear his dad so alone and scared.

"I'm here, Dad!" he shouted, but he knew his father couldn't hear him.

"Hello!" his father yelled again. "Is anyone—"

He abruptly went silent as two red-eyed monsters appeared in the shadows just in front of him. Another pair appeared next to the first, then another, and another, until Fort's dad was surrounded by the creatures.

"Hello?" his father said, his voice shaking with fear.

And that's when the monsters all leaped forward, straight at his father.

"NO!" Fort shouted, but some unknown force pulled him back up the way he'd come, up and out of the ground, and back into shadows at the now-destroyed National Mall.

And the Old One was waiting for him, filling the sky with its horror.

WE CAN GIVE YOUR ELDER BACK TO YOU, it said. GIVE US WHAT WE ASK, AND YOU SHALL HAVE HIM ONCE MORE. GIVE US THE LOCATION OF THE LAST DRAGON. HE IS HIDDEN TO US, BUT YOU CAN FIND—

"Time to wake up!" someone said, and Fort bolted upright, right through Sierra, who'd been leaning down over him. He almost screamed out loud in surprise but managed to hold himself back, which was good since Gabriel snored quietly next to him, his reading light still on, his book tented over his chest.

"Whoa, are you okay?" Sierra asked him. "You look *terrified*. What were you dreaming about?"

I'm fine, he said, pushing the nightmare out of his mind as quickly as he could. The last thing he needed was her seeing what he'd dreamed, real or not. *Is it time?*

She gave him a concerned look, but nodded. "Damian got us tickets, but our flight doesn't leave for another hour, so I'm good to go. You all ready to lie to your friends, steal a book of magic, and go find your dad?"

You have no idea, he told her, and leaped off the bed.

- EIGHT -

HEY, THIS IS PRETTY COOL, Rachel said in Fort's head. AND I'M GLAD YOU WEREN'T MAKING UP YOUR IMAGINARY FRIEND. THAT WOULD HAVE BEEN PRETTY SAD. LIKE YOU SAYING YOU HAD A GIRLFRIEND IN CANADA.

SPEAKING OF GIRLFRIENDS, DOES ANYONE WANT TO KNOW ABOUT THE GIRL FORT USED TO DANCE WITH IN FRONT OF HIS GRANDPARENTS? Sierra asked, and Fort immediately felt Rachel's burst of excitement.

No! he thought as loudly as he could. Next to him, Jia coughed to hide a laugh, but he could feel her own joy at the idea in his mind. *Everyone needs to be serious. This is important! And Sierra can't keep track of everyone's minds if we're all talking at once.*

ACTUALLY, I TOTALLY CAN, Sierra broadcast in their

minds. THIS SORT OF THING IS EASY, ASSUMING I DON'T HAVE TO WIPE ANY OF YOUR MEMORIES OR TAKE OVER YOUR BODY. THAT'S WHEN THINGS GET MUCH MORE COMPLICATED. I COULD CONNECT THE WHOLE SCHOOL LIKE THIS IF I HAD TO. SO BACK TO THE DANCING—

We're coming up on the hallway, so no time for that now, Fort thought quickly, stopping around the corner from where Cyrus had said they'd be able to ambush Dr. Opps and the two guards carrying the books of Mind and Summoning magic. Wires hung from the ceiling where cameras were still being installed, so Cyrus had been right: This was the perfect spot.

Fort felt Jia's joy turn into anticipation as they reached their destination, and he remembered what Rachel had said about Jia looking for thrills. Jia flattened herself back against the wall and squeezed her hands together to keep them from shaking. "Are you ready?" she whispered to Fort. "Because *I'm* ready. I'm *so* good to go. We're going to nail this. Isn't it exciting? We're making the world a safer place, and all it took was breaking a few rules!"

"That's right," he whispered back, not thrilled to be deceiving her. "Once they're gone, only Damian will have the power to bring the Old Ones back, and we already know we can handle *him*. The last thing we need is for the military to decide they need mind control or to summon something and teach some new student. They're too dangerous."

Jia sighed. "I know, though it'd still be fun to play around with them for a little bit. Not long, but just, like, one or two spells, you know?"

I THINK THEY'RE ALMOST THERE, Cyrus said in their heads. MY VISION GETS ALL WONKY AROUND THE BOOKS, SO IT'S HARD TO TELL FOR SURE.

The reminder of Cyrus's "wonky" vision around the books wasn't great at this moment, but footsteps sounded from down the hallway, so Fort couldn't worry about that now. *Cyrus is right, I hear them,* he thought to the others. *Everyone ready, and know what you're going to do?*

I'M GOING TO PARALYZE THE THREE OF THEM FIRST, Jia said, grinning widely at him. THEN I'LL TAKE THE MIND AMULETS OFF OF DR. OPPS AND THE SOLDIERS, WHILE YOU GRAB THE BOOKS, REPLACE THEM WITH YOUR FAKE ONES, AND MAKE YOUR WAY TO RACHEL.

Fort looked down at the two roleplaying books that Rachel had donated, even if she hadn't been happy about it. Unfortunately, they were the only thing even close to the size of an actual book of magic, and Sierra had said that would help with the spell to disguise them.

YOU STILL OWE ME FOR THOSE, NEW KID! Rachel yelled in his mind, and Fort winced, forgetting she could still hear him. THOSE ARE CLASSICS.

Sorry! he thought. *So, like Jia said, I take the books to you, Rachel, two halls down on the right from here, in an unused kitchen.*

A KITCHEN THAT SMELLS LIKE FEET FOR SOME REASON.

Fort immediately smelled exactly what she meant through Rachel's nose. Everyone on the mental "call" groaned in disgust.

Thanks for that, Fort thought as the footsteps came closer. *I should be there, like, thirty seconds after Jia hits them with the paralyze spell.*

RIGHT, Rachel thought. AND THEN WHILE I'M BURNING THE BOOKS, WHICH IS THE LAST TIME I HOPE TO EVER SAY THAT, SIERRA IS GOING TO ERASE THEIR MEMORIES OF SEEING US AND ENCHANT THEM INTO THINKING MY INCREDIBLY PRECIOUS ROLEPLAYING BOOKS ARE THE BOOKS OF MAGIC.

IS "ENCHANT" THE RIGHT WORD? Sierra asked. CAN'T

WE CALL IT SOMETHING COOLER, MAYBE MORE SPY-ISH? LIKE I'M MAGICALLY COVERT ACTIONING THEM INTO THINKING THEY'RE RECEIVING THE DROP WHICH WE'VE INTELLED INTO . . . HEY, YOU KNOW I CAN HEAR ALL OF YOUR JUDGMENT, RIGHT?

Shh, they're just around the corner! Fort thought to the others, and he saw Jia tense up, her hands starting to glow a cold blue. *Everyone ready?*

READY, Jia said, shuddering with excitement.

READY, Rachel said.

READY, BUT IT'S NOT TOO LATE TO RETHINK THIS, Sierra said, and Fort let her feel his annoyance. OKAY, OKAY, FINE, YES, READY.

UM, FORT? Cyrus said in their heads. WE MIGHT HAVE A—

"Now!" Jia shouted, and leaped around the corner. Whatever Cyrus had been about to say would have to wait as Fort ran out behind her, ready for anything.

Dr. Opps's eyes widened in shock as Jia hit him with her Paralyze spell, freezing his body in place. Before the two guards could make a move, she hit them as well, and they stopped dead in their tracks.

Only, none of them were carrying books.

Um, Cyrus? Fort thought, panic beginning to take over his mind. *Where are the books of magic?!*

THAT'S WHAT I WAS GOING TO SAY, Cyrus said, guilt coming in waves from his mind. SOMETHING CHANGED SINCE I LAST LOOKED, BUT I COULDN'T GET A SOLID VIEWING OF THE FUTURE BECAUSE THE BOOKS WERE TOO CLOSE TO EVERYTHING. I THINK . . . I THINK SOMEONE SURPRISED THEM AND TOOK THE BOOKS ALREADY.

You think?! Fort shouted in his head, unable to stop his frustration from boiling over

STICK WITH THE PLAN, Rachel said. GET THEIR AMULETS OFF SO SIERRA CAN WIPE THEIR MEMORIES. CYRUS, YOU KEEP TRYING TO FIND THE BOOKS!

ON IT! Sierra said, while they could all sense Cyrus nodding.

Fort grabbed the amulet from around Dr. Opps's neck as Jia handled the guards. He caught Dr. Opps's eyes and winced, giving the doctor an apologetic shrug. "Sorry," he whispered. "We didn't have a choice."

Dr. Opps just glared at him, and Fort was happy that the paralysis spell kept the doctor from speaking.

OKAY, I'M IN THEIR HEADS, Sierra said, and Jia canceled

her spells. All three men instantly relaxed, but didn't otherwise move.

I FOUND THEM! Cyrus said. I FOUND THE BOOKS. THEY'RE . . . UM, UH-OH.

Don't say "uh-oh," Fort told him. *Just tell us where they are.*

YES, RIGHT. WELL, LIKE I SAID, I COULD BE WRONG ABOUT THIS, BUT AS FAR AS I CAN TELL . . . COLONEL CHARLES HAS THEM IN HIS PRIVATE OFFICE.

- NINE -

FORT WANTED TO DROP TO HIS KNEES and punch the floor, he was so frustrated. How could such a simple plan go so wrong? It was all down to Cyrus's magic not working on the books. He *knew* they should have been more careful because of that. They should have confirmed that Dr. Opps had them, and—

FORT, IT'S TOO LATE TO SECOND-GUESS, AND THIS ISN'T CYRUS'S FAULT, Rachel said in his mind. WE CAN STILL GET THE BOOKS!

He nodded, hoping she was right. *Cyrus, is Colonel Charles alone at least?* Fort said in his mind, trying to keep his panic from passing to the others.

HE IS, AND THERE AREN'T ANY CAMERAS IN THERE, Cyrus said. SO IF YOU CAN GET IN THERE AND SUR-

PRISE HIM, YOU CAN STILL GET AWAY WITHOUT ANY-
ONE KNOWING.

Right, okay. This was all terrible news, but they could work with it. Fort knew where the colonel's office was, though only because it was close to the cafeteria, and there was always a bunch of guards nearby, not to mention cameras in the hallways, even if the cameras weren't in the office itself. That meant they couldn't just walk out with the books, if they even made it in.

Does anyone *have any ideas?* Fort shouted, but the others were starting to feel hopeless too.

A hand settled on Fort's shoulder, and he turned to find a fully awake Dr. Opps staring at him. "I think I might know what to do," the doctor said, and Fort's heart stopped dead in his chest.

"Dr. Opps, you're . . . I mean . . ." Fort couldn't make his brain work correctly, with words deciding to float out of his reach all of a sudden. But just as he was sure he was going to be thrown in jail for the rest of his life, the doctor smiled and slowly poked his finger into Fort's ear.

"Hey!" Fort shouted, and the doctor laughed.

"You should see your face," Dr. Opps said. "Do you really not know who this is?"

Fort's eyes widened. "Sierra?"

"C'mon," Sierra said in Dr. Opps's voice, then gave Fort a firm push down the hallway.

"Um, what do I do with the guards?" Jia asked, still standing next to the two soldiers.

"They're fine!" Sierra said, looking back over Dr. Opps's shoulder. "Just shove them down some hall and run. You've got, like, two minutes until reality clicks back in for them."

Jia's eyes widened, and she began pushing the guards toward the next hall as Fort and Sierra/Dr. Opps reached the end of theirs. Fort paused, waiting for the doctor to lead, but Sierra just stared at him. "Do you think *I* know where to go?" she said. "I've never been here, not outside your mind."

"Oh, *right*," Fort said, looking both ways at the intersection, having no better idea where they were than Sierra did. Fortunately, a sign pointed to the elevator, so he grabbed the doctor's hand and pulled him in that direction. "I think we go this way."

"You're not really inspiring a lot of confidence, Forsythe," Sierra said, mimicking Dr. Opps's tone. She giggled, which sounded even odder coming out of the doctor's mouth. "Forsythe. I can't even say it without laughing."

"It was my grandfather's name," Fort whispered as a guard turned the corner. The soldier gave them an odd look and it took Fort a second to realize he was still pulling someone who looked like the headmaster of the school down the hall by the man's hand. He immediately dropped it, and Sierra laughed again.

The guard passed them with a few more looks, but didn't say anything, and Fort pushed the elevator down button so hard he nearly broke it. "Can you please take this seriously?" he hissed at Sierra as the doors finally opened, and they moved inside.

"I'm in the body of a grown man, and all I want to do is make him pick his nose," Sierra told him, slowly raising a hand toward her face. "So, no, I'm not sure I can." Seeing Fort's expression, she put up her hands in surrender. "Okay, okay! I get it. I'll play nice. Lead on, Forsythe." She covered her mouth to stifle a giggle, but Fort just shook his head as the elevator descended.

Two floors down and four guards later, Fort turned a corner toward what he was sure had to be the way to Colonel Charles's office . . . and almost collided with the colonel himself, carrying a duffel bag over his shoulder. Colonel Charles looked from Fort to Dr. Opps in surprise, then narrowed his eyes. "Forsythe, why are you out after curfew?" he asked.

Cyrus, Fort hissed in his head. *He's not in his office yet!*

DON'T WORRY, Cyrus told him, entirely not helping. I THINK HE'S HEADING THERE NOW.

"Ah, I was just bringing him to see you," Sierra said, using her Dr. Opps tone again. "We've, um, got something to speak to you about, ah . . . Charles?"

Fort bit his lip hard. *You don't know his first name?!*

NO, DO YOU? I'M NOT EVEN SURE HE HAS ONE!

Charles was clearly not the right answer, as the colonel clenched his jaw tightly. "I know you don't agree with the committee granting me control over the school, Oppenheimer, but I'd appreciate it if you respected my rank."

"Right, I apologize, Colonel," Sierra said, then did a little bow. Fort rolled his eyes.

Colonel Charles just stared for a moment before speaking. "Now, what is so urgent?" he asked finally. "If this is about . . . the matter we just went over, then I have nothing more to say."

Sierra's mouth opened, but no words came out, and Fort's eyes widened as he realized she had no idea what to say. "It's not that," he said, then noticed the cameras above. "But it's sensitive, and it has to be discussed in *secret*."

"Yeah," Sierra said. "We should go to your office so we have some privacy. Can't have anyone overhearing, Colonel."

Colonel Charles nodded. "I was heading that way now, to secure the . . . items. It's just down the hall."

"Oh, that's great news," Fort said, relieved that the books were in the duffel bag. At Colonel Charles's odd look, though, he quickly added, "I mean, about your office. Being close. To talk in. For privacy."

Sierra slapped him on the back of the head, and he closed his mouth.

"And this can't wait?" Colonel Charles asked, hefting the bag with the books.

"It's *very* urgent," Sierra said. "It involves Sierra, the little genius who wiped your mind. Fort thinks he knows where she is."

What? Fort said. *You want me to tell him where you are?*

OF COURSE NOT! she said in his head. WE'RE GOING TO LIE. TELL HIM DAMIAN AND I WERE SPOTTED IN CANADA OR SOMETHING.

"Of course," Colonel Charles said. "This way, then."

He walked them back to his office and led them inside. It wasn't big, but at least it looked like it'd had its technology updated. The decor matched the rest of the facility, though, with two puke-green chairs facing a desk in a small, cramped area. Could this be the best office the facility had for the coheadmaster of the school?

"Sit, please," the colonel said, waving Fort and Sierra into the two chairs. "Now, tell me what you've got for me."

"She's in Canada," Fort said, right as Sierra said, "We've tracked her to California."

They turned to each other, Fort blushing, Sierra glaring. *I thought you said "Canada"!*

I SAID MAYBE CANADA! I'M STILL IMPROVISING!

Colonel Charles looked between them, frowning, then abruptly opened a drawer and pulled something out in his closed hand. "Oppenheimer, I notice you're missing your protective amulet," he said, quickly standing and walking around to stand behind them. "And between that and the fact you called Fitzgerald here 'Fort,' I'm going to assume I'm speaking to . . . Sierra?"

- TEN -

SIERRA LEAPED TO HER FEET, BUT Colonel Charles was faster. He slammed something down over her head, and Sierra shrieked, collapsing to her knees.

"Ah, I wasn't sure that would work," the colonel said, grabbing a pair of handcuffs from his desk and placing them on Sierra's wrists behind her back. "I'll have to give Oppenheimer credit for that, if he ever regains control."

Sierra thrashed around on the floor in pain, and Fort finally made out what Colonel Charles had put around her neck: a protective mind amulet. With Sierra's mind inside Dr. Opps's, there was no telling what kind of damage the amulet was doing to her.

"What are you *doing*?" Fort shouted, jumping to his feet too. "Stop it! She's in pain!"

Colonel Charles stepped between Fort and Sierra and pushed Fort back to his seat. "Ah, now that's disappointing. Here I was hoping you were under her control as well. But considering she's barely able to think right now, I think we can safely guess you're here all on your own." He gave Fort a curious look. "What exactly did you want with me? To take over my mind, and control the entire school? Wipe my memories again? What was the plan, Forsythe?"

Fort just stared at him, then launched forward, trying to pull the amulet off. Unfortunately, the colonel was faster, grabbing Fort by the wrist before he could reach Sierra. Colonel Charles twisted his arm painfully, pushing Fort's head and chest down against the desk, pinning him there.

"She'll be fine," Colonel Charles told him. "Unless, that is, you pull a stunt like that again. Now, can we talk like civilized adults, or do I need to keep this up?" He wrenched Fort's wrist again.

Fort gritted his teeth to keep from crying out. "Okay," he hissed. "But *please*, let her go."

"What . . . what are . . . ," Sierra tried to say, slowly pushing to her knees, only to drop back to the floor. "I'm . . . you're . . . splitting me in . . . *half*!"

"Really?" Colonel Charles said, looking back at her. "Honestly, that's news to me. Oppenheimer never claimed it'd be painful. Just thought it might be a last-ditch way to drive one of those monsters out if it took over a student again." He leaned down to give Sierra a closer look. "But instead, I'm guessing it's interfering with your spell, while not allowing you to leave his mind. That's actually perfect."

"Take it *off*," Fort said, practically begging now. "Please! We weren't going to do anything, we just wanted the Summoning book."

"And why would she need that?" Colonel Charles asked. "She has Damian, and he can summon whatever he wants, clearly."

"It was for *me*," Fort said. "Dr. Opps thinks my father might still be alive, and I had to use the magic to get him back!"

This made Colonel Charles stand back up in surprise. "Oppenheimer thinks that?" He seemed dumbfounded for a moment, then leaped forward and grabbed Fort by the uniform, his eyes wide. "What proof does he have? *Why has he never told me this?*"

"I don't know," Fort said miserably. "He just thought it was possible."

"My *son* was taken by the same creatures!" the colonel said, releasing Fort and turning around. "Why would he never tell me this? It can't be true, not this long after . . . can it?"

Sierra whimpered on the ground, and Fort's stomach hurt just hearing her. "Please, I'll do whatever you want, just let her go!"

"Ah, no, we won't be doing that," Colonel Charles said, barely giving Fort a look. "Now that we have her, I intend to keep her. I don't know how we'll get her out of Oppenheimer's mind, but even if we can't remove her, she'll still be an asset."

Sierra slowly looked up at him, her face—Dr. Opps's face—contorted in pain and fear. "You . . . you *can't* . . . keep me . . . locked up!"

"Locked up?" Colonel Charles said, still distracted. "Of course not. You'll be *working* for us. Oppenheimer wasted you while we had you. Think of the good I could do around the world with your magic. I've been testing both the Mind and Summoning books for the last week or so, but Oppenheimer declared that they had to be put back in storage for safety. I agreed at first, then realized this was ridiculous. His passivity has been holding us back, keeping us in danger, when we should be *using* the magic we have! So I took them back."

"I . . . will never . . . be your . . . *prisoner*!" Sierra shouted, and Dr. Opps's body seemed to bulge strangely, like it was too full or something. Fort's eyes widened, but Colonel Charles didn't notice.

"Call it what you want," he said. "But you *will*—"

And then his mouth dropped open as his own amulet floated up and off of his chest, then over to Sierra's hands behind her. As it did, the handcuffs around her wrists ripped in half, freeing her.

"How did you do that?" Colonel Charles demanded, stepping back to pull a glowing red orb out of his pocket.

But Sierra just stared at him with hatred in her eyes as she slowly rose from the floor, floating in the air now just like the amulet had. "You have no *idea* the power I have," she hissed, her voice low and dangerous. She clenched her fist and crushed the amulet in her bare hand. The one around her neck cracked, then tumbled to the floor.

The walls around them began to creak, and Fort backed into the center of the room, scared for Sierra, but also now terrified of whatever magic she was using. Where had it come from? How could she be doing this?

The chair behind Sierra exploded into pieces as a strange

wind picked up, swirling around Colonel Charles. The colonel held the glowing orb between them, his eyes now wide with fear. "You . . . you don't have this kind of power! This can't be happening. The amulet protected me. *Stay back!*"

But Sierra just sneered at him as Dr. Opps's body fell to the floor, leaving Sierra's glowing yellow form still floating in midair. Unlike the other times Fort had seen her in his mind, he could actually *feel* her presence now, just like he'd felt the Old One in the mess hall at the previous school. Magic emanated from her like heat from the sun as she slowly reached for Colonel Charles.

"You were going to keep me locked up here?" she said, squeezing her hand again, and the red glowing ball in his hand shot away, cracking against the far wall. And then Colonel Charles rose into the air, hanging by his shirt collar.

"Please, *let me go!*" he croaked. "I wasn't going to hurt you. I just . . . just wanted to . . . protect . . ."

Fort started to stand—he couldn't let her just choke the man. But as he got up, Sierra's magic seemed to surge in power, like her anger was feeding the magical energy, making her almost too bright to look at.

Fort dove back to the floor, hoping to escape the power that he could now feel throughout the room, like the air before a lightning strike. He crawled under the desk as the room creaked again, and something fell from the ceiling. Someone screamed, but he couldn't tell who, and then . . .

And then the light faded back to normal, the eerie wind died down, and there was only silence.

Fort slowly pulled himself out from under the desk, terrified at what he might find. Sierra stood on the ground again in front of him, glowing normally now, with Colonel Charles lying on the floor, breathing steadily, but otherwise not moving. At least he was still alive!

"I will take your memories of this moment," she said, raising a hand, and Colonel Charles's head glowed yellow. His mouth opened and closed without any sound coming out. "And I will take your memories of the books of Mind and Summoning magic." His head glowed again. "But I will leave you with the memory of *me* holding your mind in my hands. And any time you even *think* of coming after me or my friends, you'll remember this moment, how I could have wiped your mind completely. And you'll know *fear*."

Colonel Charles nodded over and over, breathing faster now. "I . . . promise . . . please—"

She lowered her hand, and the colonel's head slammed back to the floor, not moving. Sierra's glowing self also returned to the floor, and she fell exhaustedly against Fort, only to stumble right through him. He reached out for her, but just like in his dream, there was nothing he could do to help.

"Are . . . are you okay?" he asked, unable to hold back his fear.

"I . . . *no*," she said, looking up at him with a scared expression that he knew matched his own. "What did I just do?!"

And then she collapsed to the floor and disappeared.

- ELEVEN -

IERRA? FORT SHOUTED, LOOKING around the room uselessly. *Sierra! Can you hear me? Are you okay? Talk to me!*

YES, she said in his head, but didn't reappear. I'M . . . I'M OKAY, I THINK. JUST SO *EXHAUSTED* ALL OF A SUDDEN. AND DAMIAN IS YELLING AT ME. I GUESS . . . THAT LIGHT IN THE OFFICE, IT . . . IT HAPPENED *HERE*, TOO. EVERYONE SAW. SECURITY'S LOOKING FOR US, AND DAMIAN SAW . . . A BUNCH OF AGENTS. AGENTS WITH AMULETS.

A chill went down Fort's spine, but at least her voice was back to normal. This was the Sierra he knew. The power to tear apart the room seemed to be gone—for now. Where *that* had come from, he had no idea, but that mystery could wait until they were safe. *You need to get out of there!* he thought. *Can you run?*

WE'RE HIDING, she said. SO TIRED. CAN BARELY MOVE. BUT I CAN . . . I CAN GET YOU OUT OF THERE. BACK TO . . . RACHEL.

Next to him, Dr. Opps's body slowly picked itself up from the floor, only to stumble, falling against the wall. Fort quickly went to help, giving the doctor his shoulder.

"Sierra?" Fort whispered, not sure who was in there.

"Obviously," she said, standing up straight and pushing him away. "Grab the duffel bag with the books. I'll carry it, for the security cameras. And don't try to help, it'll look suspicious."

"You shouldn't be here," Fort said, his worry for her overpowering any thought of the plan now. "Go back to Damian, and make sure no one finds you—"

"Shush," she said. "I'm not leaving . . . until I've done my part." She swayed for a moment, only to catch herself. "But maybe let's go quick."

Through their connection, Fort could feel that all her fear at what had just happened had been replaced, if temporarily, by determination. He knew that arguing would just prolong things. Silently he led her out of the office, glancing outside quickly to see what the halls looked like after all the commotion inside.

As Fort figured, there were guards everywhere. The first sol-

diers to see them quickly ran to help Sierra, but she shook her head. "Colonel Charles needs you more than I do," she said as Dr. Opps. "That amazingly smart mind-reader girl got to him. She was in this boy's head too, but he doesn't remember anything, so I'm taking him back to his room."

"Shouldn't we sound the alarm?" one soldier asked. "Lock down the facility and alert Agent Cole?"

"It's too late," Sierra told him. "The girl's already gone. She's just way too clever to be caught. I have no idea what to do about her, really. What *is* there to do when—"

Fort elbowed her to wrap it up.

"But I'm rambling. Now *go*, the colonel needs you!" Sierra shouted, waving the soldier back toward Colonel Charles's office. "Go, go, go!"

Still, getting from the office to the elevator felt like a marathon. Every few feet, Sierra would have to stop and lean against the wall for support, and even the guards who she sent back to help Colonel Charles would stop and look back, not quite sure if she was okay.

By the time they reached the elevator, Fort was ready to just take the duffel bag and run, no matter what kind of trouble they got in. DON'T YOU DARE, Sierra said in his head, glaring

at him through Dr. Opps's eyes. WE STILL HAVE . . . TO FIN-
ISH THIS. RACHEL THINKS SHE'S . . . GOING TO BURN
THE BOOKS . . . REMEMBER? AND I HAVE TO . . . CON-
VINCE HER SHE DID.

She was making sure she did her part to fulfill Fort's lie to
his friends, after almost getting caught by Colonel Charles, and
whatever that surge of magical power had been.

So much for keeping his friends out of danger. And Sierra
had already suffered so much—

OH, STOP IT, she said, but Fort saw a blush rising on Dr.
Opps's cheeks.

Once they made it back up two floors, where the cameras
hadn't been installed yet, Fort grabbed the bag from Sierra and
gave her his shoulder again, which she thankfully accepted this
time. They slowly made their way to the kitchen where Rachel
was waiting, Fort's guilt rising with every step.

After what felt like hours, Fort pushed the kitchen door
open to find a darkened room lit only by two exit signs, their
red light giving stainless steel counters around the room an
eerie glow.

"Rachel?" he said as he helped Sierra to the floor, leaning her
back against the wall. "Are you here?"

The lights turned on, momentarily blinding Fort. When he could see again, he found Rachel standing in front of them, her eyes on Dr. Opps, but her face expressionless. "That's Sierra?" she asked.

Sierra weakly raised a hand to salute. "Mission accomplished."

"You got the books, then?" Rachel said, turning to Fort. "Colonel Charles had them?"

Fort nodded. "We were right to do this. He was going to use them to teach more students."

Rachel gave him a long look. "Yeah, and we all agreed we couldn't let anyone else use the books. Right, Fort?"

UH-OH, Sierra said in his head.

"That's right," Fort said, slowly handing over the duffel bag to Rachel. "We burn them so no one can use them ever again." What was happening here? Why was Rachel so suspicious?

She pulled the bag open and grabbed both books, letting the duffel fall to the floor, then opened them one by one. She glanced over the first few pages of both, then set them down on the floor. "They definitely *look* like the real thing," she said, and stared at Fort again.

"They better be real," he said, and forced a laugh. "Otherwise we just put Sierra through a lot of pain for nothing."

YOU SOUND SO GUILTY, Sierra said.

"Then let's get this over with," Rachel said, and pushed Fort away from the books. "Take a few steps back. We don't really know what will happen if we try to destroy these things. Let's hope it doesn't release evil ghosts that we end up having to hunt down for the rest of our lives."

"Let's hope," Fort agreed, backing away to the wall to where Sierra sat. He glanced down at her in concern. *Are you okay? You can still make sure she doesn't burn the books, right?*

She nodded, then closed her eyes. I THINK . . . I HAVE TO LEAVE DR. OPPS THOUGH. PUT HIS BODY OUTSIDE . . . FOR WHEN HE WAKES UP.

And without another word, Dr. Opps slumped over.

Rachel separated the books, kneeling down next to the Mind magic book first. "I'm going to do it," she said, looking up at Fort as if for confirmation. When he didn't say anything, her hands began to glow red, and she launched a small fireball directly at the book.

It hit the cover . . . and immediately went out.

"Okay," Rachel said, furrowing her brow. "This might be

harder than I thought. I didn't even singe the thing."

Fort frowned. *Sierra, did you do that? We want her to* think *she burned them, remember? You don't have to lay it on so thick.*

But Sierra didn't answer.

"I'm going to try it a different way," Rachel said, the power already glowing again. Another fireball formed, but this time, instead of releasing it, she kept it floating between her palms and slowly brought it down to the Mind book until they touched. "Maybe it just needs a little more time to get started."

You can let her think it's burning now, Sierra, Fort thought, hoping she was listening. *Sierra? Are you still here? You've got this, right?*

"There it goes!" Rachel said, and Fort turned back to watch the cover of the telepathy book slowly light up under the force of her fireball. He breathed a sigh of relief. Sierra had come through, creating the illusion just as they had planned.

Something beeped, and Fort looked down to find a phone at Dr. Opps's side glowing. He glanced at it and saw some kind of news alert. Curious, he picked it up, and his eyes widened.

JFK AIRPORT IN NEW YORK CITY SITE OF NEW ATTACK. GATHERING STORM MEMBERS REPORTEDLY INVOLVED. THAUMATURGIC DEFENSE AGENTS ON SITE.

"No," he whispered, then looked up. *Sierra? SIERRA? Are you okay? Did they find you? What's going on? Talk to me!*

But there was no reply as smoke began to fill the room. "Let me get the vent going," Rachel said, moving to turn on the fan above the stove. Fort turned back to her, his eyes wide.

She'd *really* burned the Mind magic book! This wasn't an illusion. Sierra was gone, and he was about to lose the Summoning book forever if he didn't say something, if he didn't stop Rachel *right now*.

Strange yellow light seeped out of the pages of the telepathy book as the pages burned, rising with the smoke into the vents above the stove. "Yikes," Rachel said, almost emotionlessly. "I hope this stuff isn't going to play with my *mind* at all." She turned to the Summoning book and knelt down next to it. "Guess it's time to burn the second one now?"

Fort thought about calling for Sierra again but stopped himself. She was in real danger, and he couldn't distract her any further. Definitely not for something so pathetic as covering for his lie. "Rachel," Fort said, "wait."

"For what?" Rachel asked, her tone sounding far too innocent to be real. "Is there something you wanted to say to me?"

Fort opened his mouth, ready to apologize, tell her everything . . . but even now, he couldn't bring himself to do it. *If she finds out, you'll be pulling her into this, her and Jia and Cyrus too. And if they come, one of them won't be making it back.*

"I just think maybe we should hold off on that one for now," he said, knowing how ridiculous he sounded. "Maybe . . . maybe we'll need it. You know, later."

Rachel took a deep breath in, closing her eyes, then let it out and stood up. She picked up the book and slowly walked over to Fort. For a moment, she looked at him with an unreadable expression.

Then she threw the book right at his face.

The book of Summoning slammed into his nose, and the pain and shock sent Fort tumbling backward to the floor, the book landing heavily on his chest. As the shock wore off, the pain intensified, making Fort groan.

"What was that for?" he started to yell, only to look up and find an enraged Rachel glaring down at him.

"Sierra didn't shut down our mental 'call' while you were in with Colonel Charles, you *jerk*," she said, her hands glowing red as she pointed them at Fort. "We *all* heard everything you told him! You lied to us! You never wanted to destroy the books. Why would you do that? Why would you betray all your friends?!"

Fort winced and tried to sit up, but she shook her head, shoving him back to the floor with her foot. "No, you don't say a *word*," she whispered as a fireball appeared in her hand. She slowly aimed it at the book on Fort's chest. "I should have known. You lied to me from the start, back at the old school. Why should now be any different?"

Fort spread his hands in surrender, his eyes on the fireball. "Please . . . *please* don't. My father is still alive, Rachel. I know he is."

"So?" she said. "You could have *told* us. We'd probably have all helped you! I would have, you *know* I would have." The fireball grew brighter.

"I know," Fort whispered, shaking his head. "That's why I couldn't let you know. Cyrus—"

The fireball shot out from her hand, and Fort shouted in surprise. There wasn't enough time to dodge, to get out of its way . . . but the fireball flew right over his head and exploded against the tile floor a few feet away. "I hope you find your dad, New Kid," she said. "But don't ever speak to me again."

She walked past him, and he wondered if there was any way to make this right, to explain . . . but before he could think of the words, he heard her drag Dr. Opps out the door and close it behind her.

And then there was silence as she left Fort with the book of Summoning, completely alone.

- TWELVE -

FOR A MOMENT, FORT JUST LAY IN THE middle of the kitchen as the smoke from the book of Mind magic dissipated. Apparently it really had been destroyed, then. Whatever was happening to Sierra, she must have been pulled away before she could make the illusion.

Sierra? he thought. *I'm sorry. I hope you're okay?*

Again, there was no response, and Fort slowly sat up, grabbing the book of Summoning before it fell to the floor. He checked to see if Dr. Opps's phone was still there and had any updates, but there was no sign of it, so Rachel must have taken it with her.

Rachel, whom he'd completely betrayed. Not to mention that Jia and Cyrus had heard the same things Rachel had. He'd effectively lost every friend he'd made at the Oppenheimer School, all in one night.

Even after all of that, though, Rachel had left him the book. For someone who'd attacked Fort when she'd just *overheard* Dr. Opps saying he was a danger to the school, leaving him the book was a sign of how much she trusted him.

Or *had* trusted him.

He groaned again, then turned to the book lying in the middle of a dusty kitchen floor, the book he'd given up everything he'd cared about just for this moment.

The Magic of Summoning, and Creating Gateways to Other Realities.

Even with everything he'd been through, Fort couldn't help a chill going down his spine at having the book in his hands after all this time. In a matter of moments, he'd be off to the monsters' dimension, and if everything went well, he might be back with his dad within hours. And maybe his friends would see that it'd all been worth it when he returned with his dad, safe and sound?

Probably not, but stranger things had happened.

But hadn't he been *right* not to tell them? Rachel had admitted she would have come, and then he'd have been putting her in danger. And look what had happened with Sierra, when Colonel Charles had caught her in his trap. That was even in friendly territory, not some dimension of horror! He couldn't imagine the terrible things that might have happened to his friends in the creatures' homeworld if they'd come along.

No. He'd do this on his *own*, and keep his friends as safe as possible, whether they hated him for it or not.

"I'm coming, Dad," he whispered. His hands trembling, Fort slowly opened the book, mentally readying himself for the monsters' home domain. He took a deep breath, then read over the first page.

One for the body, bones and skin,
One for the spirit, its spectral kin,
One for the mind, thoughts and dreams,
One for the world, from dirt to streams,
One for all space, wide and vast,
One for all time, future and past.
Seven from six, the rest unearthed.
One saves all, if proved their worth.

Oh, right. The opening page was the same in all the books of magic. Fort had seen those words back when he'd first arrived at the original Oppenheimer School. Dr. Opps had taken him to be tested on which form of magic he had more natural talent with, Destruction or Healing. At the time, he'd had no idea what the poem meant, but now the words took on a different meaning.

"One for the body, bones and skin" had to be talking about Healing magic. The mind line was telepathy, and time probably referred to Clairvoyance, the magic that Cyrus had studied. So had a bunch of other students, but Cyrus was the only one to not go insane doing so. Fort shivered at the very thought of what that school must be like now.

The other lines, though, he wasn't quite sure about. Destruction had a spell to control the ground, which had dirt and streams in it, so maybe that was the one about the world? Which left only spirit and space. Summoning *had* to be space, which sort of made sense . . . Summoning opened portals to other dimensions, which was like crossing through space. Not that Fort understood how in any way.

So what was the line about spirit referring to?

He was getting distracted. The poem didn't matter, not while his father was waiting.

His heart beating faster with anticipation, Fort turned the page, ready to absorb the Summoning magic spell to create a portal to another world. He took a deep breath, then read the words for the first spell:

Teleport Within the Same Plane.

A horrifying sinking feeling turned Fort's stomach over, and he shook his head, quickly turning to the next page, which was blank.

No. No! The next page was also blank, and the following one, and the rest of the book. Fear closed around his heart, and he quickly turned back to the first page and read over the first spell.

When an object must pass between nonadjacent spaces, yet still within the same reality/probability time line, a teleportation circle can be opened, connecting those two spaces.

NO! Teleportation, *not* dimensional travel?! Within the same reality, it said.

"*No, no, no, no, no, no,*" Fort whispered, shaking his head, staring at the words on the page before him. Something began bubbling up inside him, and he wasn't sure if he was going to laugh or cry or just set the book on fire. "No. No! NO!"

Suddenly he couldn't even think past his rage, and he threw the book as hard as he could straight at the nearby kitchen cabinets. The crash as it hit was so loud that someone might have heard it, but Fort didn't care. He slammed his fists down on the floor until pain shot through his hands, then bent over and curled up over his knees, holding his head down as he screamed into the floor.

The first spell wasn't the one he needed, and to get to the next one . . . he'd need to master the Teleport spell. After everything he'd done, he couldn't even get to his father. Mastering teleportation would take days, maybe even a week, time he didn't have, time his *father* didn't have!

He could feel it all slipping away from him, and his anger faded, pushed out of the way by a deep, devastating despair, one that sank all the way to his core.

He'd lied to and betrayed his friends. Sierra might have just gotten caught by TDA agents because of him. And all Fort had gotten out of it was a teleportation spell, leaving his father still beyond reach.

Teleportation magic? he could hear his father saying. *Why, you could go anywhere, see anything with that spell! That's maybe the most amazing magic I've ever heard of!*

Except it wasn't, because it couldn't do the one thing Fort *needed* it to do.

"Stop it," he whispered to himself, digging his nails into his palms. This wasn't helping, this wallowing. Yes, things were awful and terrible, but he still had the book, and more spells

would come after he mastered Teleport. And he knew the right spell was in there somewhere, because Damian had used it to bring the monsters here in the first place.

It would mean at least a week of practice. But maybe the portal spell would be the second one. Or worst case, the third. He'd already waited two weeks just to get the book. He could survive three more.

More weeks while his father suffered who knew what—

Stop! he shouted in his mind. *Focus. That doesn't help. You need to master this spell as quickly as you can, not worry about what's out of your control for now.*

He quickly stood up and grabbed the book from where it lay on one of the counters, opening it back to the teleportation spell again. This time, he read the description, just in case there was anything he'd missed.

When an object must pass between nonadjacent spaces, yet still within the same reality/probability time line, a teleportation circle can be opened, connecting those two spaces.

Though true magicians know that space is a false equivalency, and everything lies within our own reach, to convince the cosmos of this, one must first bring to mind one's destination location and merge it to your starting point.

Even through his roller coaster of feelings, Fort's eyes started to glaze over at the text, completely unable to concentrate enough to figure out what it was trying to say. The Healing book's language had been nice and simple; why couldn't whoever had written the Summoning one spell things out in plain English? Or whatever magical language this actually was?

Please note, it continued. *Distance can only be traversed when the mind accepts that reality is naught but a figment of our imagination, and what we see as separated can never truly be.*

"Ugh, get to the point!" Fort hissed, scanning down to the bottom of the page:

A portal shall open, bridging the distance like a termite eats through wood, and remain *open until such time that the magician desires it to no longer exist. Please do not leave your various teleportation circles open, as it may create hazards to indigenous life.*

All right, see, *that* he needed to know! If he made a teleportation circle, it'd stay open until he canceled it. Fair enough. Now all he needed were the spell words . . .

Something began to glow at the bottom of the page, and when he looked closer, two words filled his mind, followed by a flood of energy he hadn't felt in weeks.

Gen urre'plat. The words to the teleportation spell.

Weirdly, the magic didn't feel the same as when he'd learned Healing spells. That energy had felt cold, whereas the Summoning magic almost made him itchy, like he wanted to jump out of his skin.

That didn't matter, though. He'd take some itchiness if it'd help him master the spell faster. As it was, he'd still have to cast it a few thousand times to master it. And then, *finally*, he might get to a spell to open a portal and save his father.

There was no time to waste, either way.

"Gen urre'plat," he said, bringing to mind the first place he could think of and opening a teleportation circle there on the wall of the kitchen.

That same itchy energy filled his hands, making them glow a strange green color, which matched the circle of energy that appeared on the wall, a tiny circle no bigger than his hand. He concentrated on increasing the circle's size, and it widened to about the size of his torso, letting a frigid wind into the room, making Fort's teeth chatter.

He stepped closer, then slowly stuck his head through the hole and found himself staring out of the very top of the Empire State Building in New York.

For just a moment, all of the anger and worry were put aside, and Fort actually found himself staring in wonder at the lights of the city spread out below him, as the high winds a thousand feet in the air buffeted his face.

His father was right. This spell was pretty amazing.

And soon, he'd show his dad in person.

- THIRTEEN -

ORT PULLED HIS HEAD BACK THROUGH the teleportation circle, but instead of closing the circle right away, he just stared through it for another moment, letting the wonder of it all wash over him.

Okay, so he couldn't open a portal yet, or go rescue his father. But teleporting would probably still prove pretty useful in the monsters' dimension, so the time he spent mastering it wouldn't be a complete waste.

And, well, if he had to go visit some of the biggest landmarks around the world in the process, who could blame him?

Something creaked out in the hallway, and Fort immediately froze, not sure if someone was coming, or if the facility was just settling. Looking around, he realized what it would look like if a guard came in: He was standing in the middle of a smoky-smelling kitchen, holding a book of magic he'd stolen from the headmaster. That might not go over so well.

Fort quickly hid behind one of the counters, just in case someone barged in to expel him, but the hallways went silent now, and no one emerged. Taking a deep breath to calm his nerves, he stood back up and shut off the fans, hoping they'd done enough of a job to pass a quick inspection, and then turned off the lights. He went to leave the kitchen to find a safer spot to practice teleportation, only to stop. *Was* there a safer spot anywhere at the Oppenheimer School?

He couldn't open teleportation circles in his room, not with his intense new roommate around at all times. And there were cameras basically everywhere else. At least the kitchen was out of the way, and there shouldn't be a reason for anyone to come to the unfinished areas of the facility at this time of night. Besides, Cyrus had said it would be safe for them to destroy the books there, so hopefully that applied for a few more hours.

Fort flipped the lights back on, still worried about staying, but what choice did he have? Not to mention he now had a bigger problem. He'd been so focused on just getting the book and then immediately portaling off to find his father that he hadn't considered where he could hide the book of Summoning if he needed to.

The kitchen definitely wasn't secure enough. If nothing else, Rachel knew about it, and as angry as she was right now, he didn't want to tempt fate by letting her get another crack at burning it. And his room wasn't any safer, not with one bureau and a nightstand. Gabriel would find it for sure.

The problem was the book's size: It was just too big to hide easily. The only place it might fit would be under his bed, and that just seemed like the most obvious spot in the world. And considering they hadn't switched the two books of magic with their fakes, it wouldn't be long before Colonel Charles or Dr. Opps came around looking for them.

If only there was a way to hide the book *outside* the school, someplace where he could still get to it. But that wouldn't . . . wait a second. Fort slapped his forehead, amazed at his own ignorance.

Of course he could hide it outside the school. He could hide the book anywhere on earth, now that he had the teleportation spell!

He quickly flipped the book open, and read the spell again, letting the magic fill him. All he had to do was cast the spell, relearn it quickly, then deposit the book on the other side of the circle. Then he could open a new circle whenever he wanted and retrieve it.

So where in the world should he leave one of the most dangerous books in existence?

What he needed was something secure, like a bank vault. Only it had to be a vault that people didn't go into very often, a vault that would remain undisturbed, yet still guarded. Something like . . . Fort Knox?

That could work! Fort prepared the teleportation spell in his mind, picturing the vaults full of gold at Fort Knox in his head. He whispered the words, gestured to the nearby kitchen wall again, then waited for the circle to open.

Nothing happened.

Fort frowned, not sure what he'd done wrong. The spell had worked fine the last time. Was Fort Knox magically protected somehow? No, that couldn't be possible. The only one who knew anything about Summoning was hopefully hiding from federal agents in an airport with Sierra right now, and there was no way Damian would have cared about protecting the United States' gold.

So why wouldn't it work?

He started to open the book to relearn the spell, only to realize the words were still in his head. That made sense . . . he hadn't been able to use the magic, so it hadn't faded from his mind.

But what was the problem?

He pictured the Empire State Building again and recast the spell. This time, the green circle opened without any problem, and the cold New York wind quickly sent a shiver down his spine. Fort winced at the chill and immediately closed the circle.

So the magic still worked, but something about Fort Knox was stopping him.

Fort quickly relearned the spell and tried a new destination, one he knew well: the room he'd lived in at his aunt's house. Again, the portal opened easily, and he found himself staring at a rowing machine, the one his aunt had moved to storage back when she'd taken in Fort.

But beyond bringing back the exercise equipment, she hadn't changed anything else. The blanket on the bed was still the one from his old bedroom, and she'd kept all of his pictures up around the room.

As he stared at the bedroom, part of Fort wanted to step through the teleportation circle, find his aunt, and tell her that everything was going to be okay, that he'd be bringing her brother-in-law back soon. But instead, he canceled the spell and sighed deeply.

Either she'd see her brother-in-law soon, or she was better off not knowing. And he still had a teleportation issue to work out.

Reading the spell again, Fort considered the problem. Clearly the magic was still functioning okay. The only time a circle hadn't opened was when he tried to jump into Fort Knox. But why would that one in particular not work?

Or was he thinking about this the wrong way? Maybe it wasn't something about Fort Knox that didn't work, but something about the other two places that *did*. What did the Empire State Building and his aunt's apartment have in common? He'd never actually been to the Empire State Building, even though he'd seen pictures of it, so it couldn't be that he needed to have visited a place first. But he'd also seen photos of Fort Knox, and—

Wait. Had he?

Fort frowned, trying to remember. Was there ever a time he'd actually *seen* pictures of Fort Knox? Thinking back, he realized instead of photos he'd just been imagining random piles of gold inside a huge vault, and that didn't seem likely to be what it actually looked like. And now that he was searching his memory, he couldn't remember what the outer building looked like, what color it was, or even where it was located.

Could that be the answer? He could only open a teleportation circle to somewhere that he'd seen, either in a photograph or in person?

There was only one way to find out.

Fort whispered the words and pictured in his mind what he imagined Jia's hometown in China looked like.

Nothing happened.

Next he tried to open a portal to Dr. Opps's office at the school.

Nothing.

The Oval Office.

Noth . . . wait, *no*, that one worked!

Fort's eyes widened as he watched the president of the United States reading over some papers at a huge brown desk. He immediately canceled the spell, closing the teleportation circle as his heart threatened to explode out of his chest. That had been close! If the president hadn't been reading at that exact moment, Fort might have been seen. And that would have been the end of everything.

And why had he even tried the Oval Office? Of *course* he'd seen pictures of it. He'd seen it thousands of times, probably! For some reason, he'd lost track of what he was doing and just started focusing on places he'd never visited. He needed to be a *lot* more careful in the future. Teleportation was just too powerful to mess around with.

But at least he'd figured out the problem: He could only open a teleportation circle to somewhere he'd seen photos of or had visited in person. Not that solving the issue helped narrow down where to stash the book to keep it safe.

What did that leave? Where was somewhere that no one else would go, but that Fort had seen before? Was there a place that only *he* had ever been? He couldn't imagine anything, unless it was like a locker in one of his old schools? But even a locker would have been given to other kids by now.

Maybe he needed a different approach. Not someplace only he'd been, but maybe a place that only he could *reach*, with the teleportation spell. Not many people would be hanging out just below the spire on the Empire State Building. Or maybe like someplace inaccessible, someplace . . .

Someplace underground.

The solution came to him in a flash, and he immediately knew he had to try it, just to see. No one would be able to get there, so the book should be safe. Assuming there was any *there* left to stash it.

Fort bit his lip, then pictured the place in his mind. He unleashed the magic, and a circle large enough to fit the book opened in the kitchen wall. He slowly pushed his head into the darkness on the other side of the circle, and was happy to see that not only was there plenty of room to stash the book, but it looked like no one had been there since the attack.

He quickly relearned the spell, since if he didn't, he'd lose the book forever once he closed the circle. For luck, he pulled out the Gettysburg Address brochure and stuck it between two pages. He wasn't sure why, but it felt like his father would be watching over the book if the brochure was in there. Then, with a final pat good-bye, he slowly pushed the book through the glowing green circle into the darkness.

He gave one last look at the tunnel beneath the old Oppenheimer School, the one created by a giant scaly black monster when it had attacked Fort, trying to drag him down into its own dimension two weeks ago.

"I'll be back, Dad," Fort whispered, patting the book again. "Soon."

And with that, he closed the circle, leaving the book behind in the darkness.

- FOURTEEN -

FORT SLIPPED INTO HIS ROOM, CLOSING the door as slowly as he could so he wouldn't wake Gabriel. Without the light from the hall, he had to carefully pick his way around the other boy's bed to his own, but he wasn't going to chance switching on a lamp. It'd taken him what felt like hours to get back from the kitchen, avoiding the guards and cameras as best he could. Now, he just wanted to hide in bed for a few days and process everything that had happened.

He successfully made it to his bed without stubbing a toe or whacking his shin, which was maybe his biggest victory of the night. Now he could just lie there in silence for a minute and think about what had—

"How'd the plan go?"

Fort bolted straight up, panic exploding in his brain before he realized it was just Gabriel. "You're awake?" he whispered, trying to calm back down.

"I'm talking to you, aren't I?" Gabriel said as Fort's eyes adjusted enough to see his roommate sitting up in bed now. "I think it's safe to assume I'm awake, yes. So? How was it?"

"We were just hanging out, like I said at dinner," Fort told him. "That's it. Nothing exciting."

"You don't have to tell me what's going on, Forsythe," Gabriel said, lying back down. "But don't lie to me either. There's no need. Just say you don't want to talk about it."

Fort felt warmth slowly run up his face. "Okay, sorry. Yeah, I don't want to talk about it."

"Fair enough," Gabriel said, staring up at the ceiling. "So did you get caught?"

Fort groaned. "You *just* said that if I didn't want to tell you—"

"I didn't say I'd stop asking," Gabriel told him. "Were you stealing one of these amulets?" He tapped his chain that was now sitting on the nightstand. "Do they have ones that do cool things, unlike this one? If there are some that turn back time, I'm going to go steal one myself."

"We weren't stealing amulets," Fort said, his embarrassment now setting his face on fire.

"So what were you stealing?"

"Nothing! No stealing. Can we just go to bed?"

"I *did* go to bed," Gabriel pointed out. "You're the one who snuck out after curfew. Don't worry about that, though. I'll tell them you were here the whole night if they ask."

For a moment, that actually seemed nice of him. And then Fort remembered how many soldiers had seen him and Sierra in the hallways. Well, Sierra in Dr. Opps's body, at least. "You, uh, shouldn't do that," he said. "Just . . . it's fine. They won't ask. Nothing happened."

"Sounds like it," Gabriel said.

"Gabriel?" Fort said after a moment of silence.

"Yeah, kid?"

"You can call me Fort. Forsythe was my grandfather's name. Just . . . just call me Fort."

"Sure, kid. Fort."

Fort lay back, dreading any further questions, but when none came, he slowly started to relax and go back over everything they'd done that evening.

Rachel wasn't going to forgive him any time soon, if ever.

Neither would Jia. Cyrus might, but that was more because he was just that easygoing, not because Fort deserved forgiveness.

And was Sierra okay? He'd tried calling her name several times on the way back to his room but eventually had given up, worrying that she was trying to hide or something and couldn't be distracted. Mostly he wished he had some way of getting news about the outside world down here in the school. There was the room with the computers and the TVs, where he'd first seen Sierra and Damian labeled as terrorists, but that had been filled with soldiers and wasn't really a place he could just wander in and crank up the volume to hear what was happening.

Of course, he could have used a teleportation circle to find out what was going on. Maybe even go to the airport and try to rescue her and Damian?

Of course, Damian could teleport himself, except that the Old Ones would be watching for it. And even if Fort got away with it, he had no idea where they were. Or which airport they were at. Or what it looked like. Or if *he'd* get caught by the same agents.

Okay, maybe it made sense to just wait for Sierra to get back to him. If he found out later that Colonel Charles had captured her, he could find a way to rescue her at that point. At least

he knew that they wouldn't hurt her, considering how much Colonel Charles wanted the power of Mind magic.

Or *had* wanted it, before Sierra's powers had gone crazy in his office. What had *that* been? How did her Mind magic work on physical objects? Even if there were spells like that, where had they come from? Had she . . .

Ugh, none of these thoughts were helping. He was just going to make himself more anxious, if he kept up with questions he couldn't answer. Besides, he had enough to worry about, with mastering teleportation.

Everything he'd heard about mastering spells at the last school told him he'd need about a week. He'd done it faster at the time, but that had been because Sierra had cheated and stolen spells from other students' minds for him without realizing she was doing it.

So he'd need to get through another week or so of school, with Colonel Charles and Dr. Opps both now on high alert from what they probably thought of as Sierra's attack. Not to mention that he was seen by the guards and the security cameras with Dr. Opps after Colonel Charles had been knocked out, so they'd for sure be questioning him soon.

He'd just have to tell Colonel Charles that Sierra had taken

from him. He leaped off his bed in surprise, and the bed disappeared behind him, as did Gabriel and the rest of the bedroom. Instead of the school's ugly green walls, Fort now found himself surrounded by crystal tubes with bolts of lightning passing through them at random, illuminating the area as they passed.

The tubes were built in and around a carefully carved stone cave, pushing in and out of the stone, flowing off in all different directions. Without meaning to, Fort slowly floated along one row of tubes, leading toward what looked like a sort of gate made out of lightning.

As he drew closer, Fort realized that whatever had ahold of him wasn't going to stop, and he threw up his arms to protect himself from the lightning . . . only for a hand from behind him to reach out, palm facing the lightning. The electrical energy seemed to part in midstream, turning back on itself, and opening a path through the gate.

Fort tried to turn around to see who it was behind him, but he couldn't move, frozen in place by whatever force was moving him along. Was this another dream? Or was it more like what he'd seen when Sierra was asleep, her memories coming to life around him?

Any thought of what was happening was thrown from his

mind when Fort saw what was up ahead. A huge pit opened wide before him, circled every ten to twenty feet down with buildings made from crystal, with gold and silver roofs. Lightning shone off of everything as it crackled through the tubes that now led into the city, and his mouth dropped open at the sheer beauty of it all.

Here and there he could see movement, something that looked vaguely like people, but he couldn't see what they were from this distance, especially with just the lightning to see by. There were no other lights in the city, though something seemed to glow in the center of the pit, rising up from the middle of the circles of buildings. It almost looked like a statue made of diamond, but all Fort could see was the very top, and he couldn't tell what it was supposed to be.

And then a roar shook the cavern, and somehow the city in the pit morphed into a darkened abyss, just as large, but less deep. Even in this strange place, he recognized that roar, he *knew* that roar by heart. He'd heard it first on the National Mall, and then again below the Oppenheimer School, as well as in far too many nightmares.

One of the monsters roared again in the darkness below him, and huge red eyes opened, staring up at him. Fort heard the sound of claws digging into rock just seconds before the red eyes came straight for him, flying far too fast to avoid.

Fort screamed in terror, knowing there was nothing he could do. The last time he'd faced one of these creatures, he had his magic, his advanced Healing spells that caused pain, but now he was completely defenseless, with no magic except for one teleportation spell. And if he cast that, he'd lose the book of Summoning forever. But if he didn't, and this thing ate him—

Massive jaws opened wide and swallowed him whole, the creature's teeth slamming shut behind him. Only now, they weren't teeth, but instead had morphed into stone stalactites, closing off the entrance to a tunnel Fort now found himself in.

Some light shone in from behind those stone teeth, illuminating the sides of the tunnel, if only barely. A hot wind came from the other end of the tunnel, and Fort felt himself drawn in that direction, floating again against his will.

He could hear something happening down at the other end of the tunnel. There were voices, one that sounded human, and the other . . .

He shuddered just hearing it. It sounded like . . . it *felt* like the voice of an Old One.

He flew faster now, completely out of control of his body,

but for some reason, he wasn't surprised by that. Nothing surprised him here, in fact, even if plenty of it terrified him. That was enough to prove this was all a dream, even if it didn't matter, because somehow it was also real. It was happening . . . or *had* happened already, to someone if not him.

The voices grew louder as he moved, and a strange reflected light began to illuminate the tunnel from that end. Fort emerged into a room that extended far beyond his sight, easily larger than a football stadium, with a rock ceiling so tall that he could barely make it out above him.

And the whole room was filled with gold.

Nuggets of gold, like something you could mine from the ground, were piled everywhere. The mounds of gold were enormous, many threatening to topple over at any moment as nuggets tumbled down from the heights every few seconds.

"Please!" he heard a voice say, and Fort's heart stopped as he instantly recognized his father. "I don't know what you want, but—"

"YOU HAVE NO POWER, HUMAN," the other voice said, reverberating in Fort's chest from its force. This voice was different from the Old One with the tentacles, though, which erupted in his mind. Whatever this creature was, it was speaking out loud, though that didn't make it any less horrible. "HOW DID YOU LOSE YOUR MAGIC?"

Fort began to float up alongside the nearest pile of gold, rising to the level of the voices. For now the mounds still blocked his view, but in moments he'd be high enough to see.

"Magic?" his father said. "What . . . what are you talking about?"

The horrific voice began to laugh, and Fort tried to cover his ears but couldn't. It was inescapable, that laughter, and it soon began to echo in his mind, changing into something more familiar, into words—

IF YOU WISH TO HAVE YOUR KIN RETURNED, YOU WILL TELL US WHERE TO FIND THE LAST DRAGON.

As the tentacled Old One roared in his mind, Fort shouted in pain, only to bolt up in bed, the scream dying in his throat. He was back in his room, and it *had* all been a dream. But he'd seen his father! Had that really happened? Was it a memory somehow?

Was the Old One showing him where his father was so Fort would do as it asked, revealing where this last dragon was, whatever *that* meant? Maybe it wanted the dragon skeletons in the school?

Gabriel leaned into the room from the bathroom, a toothbrush sticking out of his mouth. "Whoa, you okay?" he said. "You were screaming for a second there."

"Just a . . . a nightmare," Fort said, trying to keep his hands from shaking. "Is . . . it morning already?"

Gabriel gave him a sympathetic look. "Yeah, it is," he said. "And I get it. I've been having weird dreams too. This place brings 'em out, I think." He reached over and grabbed one of Fort's uniforms from the bureau, then tossed it at him. "Come on, get dressed. They'll hassle me all day if I show up to breakfast without you."

His roommate popped back into the bathroom, and Fort sighed, picking up his uniform. He felt like he'd gotten no sleep at all, which wasn't surprising given what he'd been dreaming about.

Maybe breakfast *would* help, though. If nothing else, today couldn't go any worse than yesterday had.

He quickly got dressed, then opened the door to find a man and a woman in dark suits waiting for him. "Fitzgerald?" one asked.

"Um," Fort said, completely panicking.

"Right, this is him," the other said, grabbing Fort's arm. "Come with us. Agent Cole would like a word."

- FIFTEEN -

AGENT COLE TURNED OUT TO BE waiting in Colonel Charles's office. Unlike Fort's escorts, she wasn't wearing a suit but instead had a green jacket with the letters TDA printed on the back. She turned around and smiled warmly as Fort entered, extending her hand.

"Forsythe?" she said, and he nodded, trying to play it as cool as he could, considering he was about to have a heart attack. "That's not a name you hear very often. Is it a family name?"

"My grandfather's," Fort said.

"That would do it. Sit, please," she said, and gestured for Fort to sit in the same seat he had been using the night before. "My name is Christina Cole, and I'm head agent at the TDA in charge of locating our infamous two missing students. Usually, Colonel Charles or Dr. Oppenheimer would be speaking to you now, but unfortunately, both are recovering from the attack last night."

Fort nodded, trying not to stare at the pieces of the other chair that still lay on the floor. "You want to know if I remember anything," he said, since Sierra had told the guards that he'd been mind-controlled and had his memory erased. "Is that it?"

Agent Cole sat down in Colonel Charles's chair and leaned back, her finger steepled in front of her. "Part of it, yes. I'd also like to know what Sierra wanted with you and Dr. Oppenheimer."

Fort took a deep breath, trying to keep his hands from shaking. "All I remember is going back to my room after dinner last night and reading a book, then waking up in the hallway outside with Dr. Opps walking me back to bed. He told me we'd both been taken over by that girl you mentioned . . . Sierra, that's her name?"

"Yes, that's it," Agent Cole said, nodding at him.

"Right. Beyond that, I have no idea what happened." He looked around like he'd never been in the office before. "Looks bad, though. How did the chair break?"

Agent Cole smiled gently, then leaned forward. "Forsythe . . . do you go by that, or something else?"

"Fort," he said.

"Fort, I can appreciate that you've gotten used to dealing with regular administration here at the school," she said, looking him straight in the eye. "They're good at what they do, but there's a reason that I've been put in charge of bringing our two fugitive students back into the fold. I'm very good at seeing through falsehoods, whether magical or otherwise. So why don't we start again?"

His eyes widened, and he gripped the arms of the chair tightly. "I don't know what you mean . . . I told you, I can't remember anything."

"Two books of magic went missing last night," Agent Cole said, standing up to come around toward him. She stopped a few feet from Fort and sat back against the desk. "Now, no one went in or out of the building, so there would have only been one person who could have removed them. Unfortunately for you, he was busy running from my agents last night. So why don't you tell me where the books are?"

Fort tried to speak, only to swallow the wrong way and launch into a coughing fit. "I *told* you," he stammered. "I don't know anything about that."

"I've got agents searching your room as we speak," she said, watching him closely. "And this will go much easier on you if you admit what happened before we find anything."

"You're searching my room?!" Fort said, incredibly thankful that he'd thought to hide the book elsewhere now. "I'm telling you, I didn't take any books."

"So what, you're going to say Gabriel stole them?" She shook her head, smiling again. "I think we both know better than that."

"No, I'm not saying that Gabriel did anything. I'm . . . I'm trying to say that no one . . . that I don't know who took the books! I didn't even know they were gone!" He could feel sweat running down his neck now and fought the urge to wipe it off.

She sighed and leaned in closer. "From what I can tell, you're not a bad kid, Fort. You shouldn't even be here at this school. But the colonel decided to bring you in, to see if that would wake Sierra up, and here we are. Now, the connection you shared with Sierra wasn't your fault. But getting her help to steal the books . . . that's not something we can forgive, not unless you tell me what happened so I can fix this. "

"I'm telling you, she was in my head! I don't know why, or what happened!"

Agent Cole looked down for a moment, then stood up and

went back to sit behind the desk. "Do you know what's going on in London right now?" she asked.

The alert on Dr. Opps's phone came to mind, but Fort shook his head. "No. They don't let us watch the news or anything."

"Sierra and Damian somehow made it on an international flight, but we were waiting for the plane when it landed. They evaded capture but haven't left the airport yet. I have four squads of agents going terminal by terminal at Heathrow, all wearing these." She pulled on the amulet chain she had around her neck. "No one's being let in or out until we find Sierra and Damian." Her phone buzzed, and she picked it up. "Ah, they've swept terminals four and five, and are moving on to three." She looked at Fort. "Like I said, this will all go easier on you if you cooperate. We're going to find her and the boy. But if you help us . . ."

Fort gripped the chair even tighter and shook his head. "Last I saw or heard from Sierra, she and Damian were leaving the old school," he said quietly. "Other than that, I have no idea what you're talking about, with any of this."

She studied him for a moment, then shrugged. "Fair enough! Listen, I hope you're telling the truth, I really do. I don't see that as a possibility, but until I find those books, I can't prove anything." She paused. "Well, that's not entirely true. I'm told some of these memory wipes turn out to be just temporary, so I'm sure Dr. Oppenheimer and Colonel Charles will be glad to volunteer anything they remember. And you, of course, should do the same."

Fort barely remembered to nod, busy wondering what would happen if either of the two headmasters could recall what had happened the night before.

"Don't worry about your room, by the way," she said, opening one of Colonel Charles's drawers. "We'll put everything back where we found it. Got to run a tight ship here at the Oppenheimer School, you know!"

"Thanks," Fort said, still distracted.

"Oh, and since you say you've just had your mind taken over by a fugitive," Agent Cole said, pulling out another amulet from the desk. "I'm going to need you to wear this at all times. I'll alert all the guards to make sure you've got it on, just in case she tries again." She held it out to Fort, and he slowly took it.

Sierra? he shouted as loudly as he could in his mind as he sat back down with the amulet. *I don't know if you can hear me, but the TDA is looking for you and Damian with a bunch of agents.*

They're going terminal by terminal, and have already checked four and five! You need to run, get out of there before—

FORT? Sierra said in his mind. I CAN HEAR YOU. YOU'RE SURE SHE SAID FOUR AND FIVE?

"Put it on *now*," Agent Cole said, and Fort began to put the amulet over his head, stopping to let it get caught in his hair.

Yes! Where are you?

TERMINAL FIVE! IF THEY'RE GONE, THEN WE CAN GET OUT OF HERE. YOU'RE A LIFESAVER!

Agent Cole stood up and grabbed the amulet from Fort's hands.

YOU HAVE NO IDEA WHAT WE'VE BEEN THROUGH. I NEED TO TELL YOU—

The agent placed the necklace over his head, and as soon as the amulet dropped against his chest, Sierra's voice disappeared.

"That's better," Agent Cole said, her smile returning. "Now run off to breakfast while we finish with your room. The moment we find anything, you'll be sure to know!"

Fort nodded and stood up, anxious to slip into the bathroom or someplace private to get the amulet off and see what Sierra had to tell him.

"Oh, by the way?" Agent Cole said as Fort put his hand

on the door. "That amulet is a bit . . . special. I guess Dr. Oppenheimer had Sierra rig a few to knock someone out if they tried to take it off. So make sure you don't lose it! Wouldn't want to find you unconscious in the bathroom or something, now, would we?"

Fort just stared at her for a moment, shook his head, then walked out without another word.

- SIXTEEN -

AFTER EVERYTHING WITH AGENT Cole, all Fort wanted to do was see a friendly face. But the chill coming from his friends' table in the cafeteria made Fort shiver as he entered. Rachel gave him an evil, dead-eyed stare as he walked in, and Jia caught his eye, then immediately looked away. Cyrus at least looked concerned, though considering everything that had gone wrong, that could be about a lot of things.

"Hey," Gabriel said, waving at Fort from a different table, where he'd already taken some cereal. "Did you know that there are a couple of suits in our room going through our stuff? What's that about?"

"You don't want to know, trust me," Fort said.

Gabriel raised an eyebrow, then seemed to notice the looks

from Fort's table of friends. "*Yikes*. I can see why you don't want to talk about things. What'd you do to them all?"

Fort sighed deeply and moved to get in line for food, ignoring the question. He grabbed a tray and slammed it down on the counter, not even sure who he was most angry at: Gabriel for asking more questions, Agent Cole for catching him, or himself for betraying his friends in the first place.

Himself. Definitely himself. With Agent Cole a close second.

After choosing something that he hoped was oatmeal, Fort slumped into a seat next to Gabriel, where he could still see his friends. Only Cyrus seemed to be looking, and he waved at Fort like he wanted to say something, but Rachel grabbed his hand and pulled it back down to the table.

Great.

"Listen," Gabriel said. "I get that you don't want to tell me what happened, and I accept that. But here's what you *don't* realize: I'll stop asking about it if you tell me. That's called a win-win."

Fort dropped his head into his hands, groaning softly. "You know what? *Fine*. Here's what happened: I did something . . . not so great. I lied to them about it so that they wouldn't be in dan—in trouble too. And now they're a little upset about it all. Understandably."

Gabriel nodded, then dug into his own cereal. "And which part involves our room getting searched?"

Fort didn't look up. "That's somewhere in there too."

"Are they going to find anything?"

"*No,*" Fort said, probably too angrily. "Because there isn't anything to find, okay?"

"Smart," Gabriel said. "But back to the death looks from behind me, it sounds like, if I'm hearing your incredibly vague description right, you were trying to protect your friends. Considering what's going on in our room, you had good reason to. What's the problem, then?"

Fort frowned. "The problem is that I didn't tell them the truth. I *lied* to them."

Gabriel took another bite. "Would they have gotten pulled away by agents too, if you'd told them the truth?"

"I don't know. It doesn't matter. I wasn't going to take that chance."

"Then I still don't see the problem," Gabriel said, flying through his cereal. "You were trying to protect people you cared about, so don't sit there and tell me you did anything wrong. You watched out for your friends, and they're only mad because they wanted to watch out for you, too. But you did the right thing here. You kept them safe, even if it meant them getting mad at you. That takes guts."

Fort frowned. "I guess. But—"

"There's no buts here, kid," Gabriel said. "Listen, Fort. You remind me of my little brother. He's kind of a goofball and always getting into trouble. But I watch over him, because that's what big brothers do." Gabriel smiled, just a bit. "And wow, did he hate it. But I never let that stop me. Because I knew that if I ever looked away for just a minute and he got hurt . . ." He trailed off, looking into the distance for a moment before turning back to his cereal. "Friends are no different. It's us versus the world, kid, and the world isn't pulling any punches. You protect those you care about no matter what."

Fort just stared at his roommate, his annoyance at Gabriel slipping away. "I really remind you of your brother?" he asked, a little surprised by that.

"Yeah, not so much in the face or anything," Gabriel said, not looking up. "But he's a good kid, and from what I'm hearing, you are too. Don't beat yourself up for trying to help people, Fort, no matter how you have to do it. It's not always pretty, but it's still the right thing to do."

"Um, thanks," Fort said, and really meant it. For some reason, he actually did feel better, though he had to admit it was a bit new to him, having this semistranger say Fort reminded him of his brother. Maybe that was because Fort was an only child and didn't really understand what having a brother or sister was like? Still, right here and now, with everyone else he knew angry at him, it didn't feel that bad to have Gabriel in his corner.

Gabriel nodded, then rose to get back in line for seconds, while Fort got to work on his own breakfast, suddenly famished now that he felt a bit less guilty. Out of the corner of his eye, he saw Jia and Rachel leave, neither looking at him as they went. Cyrus hung around, like he was waiting for Fort, but a soldier came in and waved him out of the room.

It took Fort until just then to realize he didn't recognize any of the remaining students in the cafeteria, which meant that all the old Oppenheimer School students must have left already.

And here was Fort, stuck with the new kids.

After Gabriel plowed through a second bowl of a cereal, two more soldiers entered the room, each holding a list of names.

"The following students should accompany me to the Destruction classroom," one said, and read off a list of names Fort had never heard before. There seemed to be more girls than boys overall left in the cafeteria, and ten girls and five boys followed the first soldier out. That left about a dozen girls and ten boys, but instead of reading names, the second soldier just shrugged and told the remaining students to come with him.

Gabriel was also in the second group, which Fort figured would be the case, since Colonel Charles said Fort would be tutoring his roommate. After their talk just now, though, that seemed less of a pain than it had when he'd first heard about it.

As they exited, one of the agents who'd escorted Fort to Agent Cole stopped him for a moment. "Cole wanted me to tell you that your room is clean," she said. "And that she knows the books are around somewhere, so she won't stop looking until she finds them. In case you *hear* anything."

- SEVENTEEN -

THE SOLDIER LED THEM THROUGH the halls, pointing out markers here and there to help them find their way toward what would be their Healing classroom. Each of the hallways was labeled with a number and letter, which Fort had noticed during his weeks here but hadn't really taken into account every time he got lost. But now that they were getting farther away from the area he knew, he welcomed finding out that the base was built in a sort of grid, so at least he could find his way around better in the future. Hopefully.

Finally, the soldier stopped at a large theaterlike room with American flags surrounding the walls. Here and there a seat or two remained bolted to the floor, but it looked like most of those had been removed, and the room was now filled with familiar-looking steel tables.

Up onstage, right next to a podium, Dr. Ambrose sat at a desk covered in papers. She didn't look up as the students filed in, each of the kids making their way through the tables to gather in front of her desk. When they had all arrived, and Dr. Ambrose still didn't say anything, a few of the students began to talk quietly to each other.

Dr. Ambrose's head immediately shot up. "Who said you could speak?"

The crowd went silent.

She narrowed her eyes. "So no one's going to answer me? And here I had hope for you new kids. Assistant!" She clapped her hands.

Someone sighed heavily from offstage, and then Sebastian strode out from behind a curtain, looking no happier to be here than Fort was to see him. "Yes, Dr. Ambrose?" he said.

"Your students are here," she told him, nodding at the assembled kids below the stage. "Get to it. I have things to do."

Sebastian nodded, still looking annoyed, then stepped forward to address them. "Good morning. I'm Sebastian Thomas, but you can and *will* call me 'sir.' I'll be teaching you, since as has been explained to you, none of you were born on Discovery Day, and therefore you need extra help."

Fort glanced around in surprise. None of these new students were born on Discovery Day? The Oppenheimer School hadn't taken that type of student before, so maybe he'd actually proven something, back at the old school.

Or maybe there just weren't that many available kids born on May 9.

"Dr. Ambrose will be around for part of each class," Sebastian continued, "but otherwise she'll be occupied . . . "—he trailed off, like the next bit was painful for him—"with a *special* project, one that my class is helping her with. But instead of being there, probing the limits of Healing magic, I'm here, teaching you how to take out splinters." He glared at them. "Which means you're all going to work *extra* hard to learn your magic, or I'm going to be annoyed. And you don't want to see me annoyed."

One of the kids snorted at this, and Sebastian slowly turned his head. "You think I'm joking?" he said, his hands glowing with a blue energy.

The boy shook his head, suddenly nervous. All the students around him backed away, leaving the boy alone in the crowd. Sebastian jumped down from the stage and patted the boy's shoulder, the glow flowing from his hand into the boy. "I hope you liked having your tonsils out, because now you'll be going through that a second time."

"Wait, what?" the boy said, then put his hands up to his throat. "What did you *do*?"

"You will *listen* when I speak, or you'll be spending a quiet few days in the infirmary as the rest of your class leaves you behind," Sebastian said to the others. "Am I clear about that?"

The students nodded, all except for Fort, who rolled his eyes.

Sebastian, of course, locked onto Fort immediately. "Ah, our former sole New Kid," he said, moving toward Fort through the crowd as the other kids parted like the Red Sea. Sebastian's hands began to glow blue again, and he reached them both out toward Fort's shoulders. "So happy to be teaching you, Fort!"

Fort put his hands up defensively, but Sebastian was too quick, clamping his hands down on Fort's shoulder before he could dodge. But instead of making him ill, the energy in Sebastian's hands gave Fort a small burst of energy. "You looked like you were about to fall asleep on your feet," Sebastian said, releasing his shoulders. "That better?"

"Yes, actually," Fort said, not sure what he was being set up for.

"Good," Sebastian said. "Because I need your help with

something. Everyone else, grab a spot at a table and wait for my next instructions."

As the other kids began to maneuver through the tables to find one near their friends, Fort just stared at Sebastian, not liking where this was going. "What's this about?"

"I know you're supposed to be tutoring someone," Sebastian said. "Which kid is it again?"

Fort nodded at Gabriel, who'd waited nearby instead of taking a seat at one of the tables.

Sebastian nodded. "Yeah, okay. That's not going to happen. I need you for something more important."

As much as Fort hadn't wanted to tutor Gabriel, the last thing he was going to do was admit that to Sebastian. "Well, you should take that up with Colonel Charles, since he was the one who ordered me to tutor Gabriel."

"Don't give me that," Sebastian whispered, stepping closer. "You think I don't remember how many rules you and Cyrus broke at the last school? You don't care about orders. And this is important."

"*What's* important?" Fort asked, getting more annoyed the longer this lasted.

Sebastian nodded up at Dr. Ambrose, who was gathering her

things just out of earshot. "Ambrose is working with my class to see if they can come up with spells without using the book of Healing, just like you did back when you fought that Damian kid. If they succeed, we'll never have to bother with mastering spells again, and we'll be free of that stupid book."

Ah, so *that's* why Sebastian needed him. He wanted to know how Fort had come up with the pain spells. "No way," he said. "I'm not telling you how I did it. I don't even *remember* what I did, so I couldn't even if I wanted to, which I definitely don't." That was mostly the truth, since he really couldn't remember the exact words to the spells he'd come up with. But he did remember *how* he'd learned them. All it'd taken was figuring out what each spell word had meant, and then mixing and matching.

Sebastian's eyes narrowed. "'No way'? You do what I say here, New Kid."

"Tell that to Colonel Charles, Teach," Fort said, and turned around, only to stop as a cold hand pressed into his shoulder.

"Like I told the others," Sebastian said, "you call me '*sir*.'"

And then he pulled his hand off of Fort's shoulder, letting his magical flu hit Fort so hard it almost knocked him off his feet.

- EIGHTEEN -

GABRIEL GRABBED FORT AND PROPPED him up as the room chose that moment to start spinning. "Whoa, are you okay, kid?" his roommate asked, looking worried.

"I'm fine," Fort said, his teeth beginning to chatter as it felt like the temperature in the room dropped twenty degrees. "Must have . . . eaten something bad."

Gabriel narrowed his eyes. "I'm going to get help. You look like you're about to pass out." He put Fort's arm over his shoulder and slowly led him to the theater stage, helping him sit down.

"Fitzgerald, are you kidding me?" Dr. Ambrose said, looking up as she packed her papers. "Did you already give yourself a disease? Class barely started!"

"It was that one," Gabriel said, pointing at Sebastian, who waved back at them with a smile. "*He* did it."

"Oh," Dr. Ambrose said, then shrugged. "Sounds like it's part of the lesson, then. Carry on."

"You can't just leave him like this!" Gabriel said. "Is there something I can do to help him?"

"Have you mastered Heal Minor Wounds yet?" Dr. Ambrose asked.

"I've got literally no idea what you're talking about."

"Then no, you're useless for now," she said. "You won't learn Cure Disease until your second spell. Sounds like you need an older student."

"Jia," Fort croaked, his mouth weirdly dry as all the moisture in his body sweated out his skin. "She'll help. She . . . did last time."

"Forget that," Gabriel said, and helped Fort lie back on the stage, then turned away. As Fort stared in wonder at how the ceiling was breathing in and out, he heard shouting a little ways away. Dr. Ambrose said something, then someone yelped in pain, and Fort began to wonder if this was all the ceiling's fault.

And then Sebastian appeared above him, looking even more annoyed than before, if that was possible. "You're *so* lucky he's got special treatment," he whispered to Fort as he laid a glowing hand on his forehead, then pulled it away, disgusted. "Ugh, you're so sweaty!"

Instantly his fever disappeared, and Fort sat up with a clear head, though Sebastian was right, he *was* covered in sweat. He found Gabriel standing behind Sebastian with a firm grip on Sebastian's arm, in what looked like an uncomfortable position behind his back. "You fixed him?" Gabriel asked.

"Do you know who my *mother* is?" Sebastian said, looking over his shoulder. "She runs this place, and— OW!"

"I do know her, actually," Gabriel said, so quietly that Fort almost couldn't hear. "I *also* know she wasn't going to let you come back here, not after the attack at the last school. That when she finally gave in, she told you that if there's even the slightest hint of trouble, she's going to yank you back home quicker than you can say 'please stop hurting me.' So I'm guessing this is the last I'll be hearing about this. Am I right?"

Sebastian rolled his eyes. "You're still lucky that you're— OW FINE OKAY, you're right!"

Gabriel released Sebastian's arm, then patted him on the shoulder. "Glad we understand each other," he said to the other boy.

"Who *are* you?" Fort asked, staring at Gabriel in astonishment

as Sebastian began yelling at the rest of the class for staring. "How did you know that about Sebastian and his mom?"

"Don't worry about it," Gabriel said. "Now what are you supposed to be teaching me?"

"No, I'm *going* to worry about it," Fort told him. "Why *am* I tutoring you? Why did Colonel Charles put me in a room with you? I'm only at this school because someone tried something like this before, and it didn't lead anywhere good."

Gabriel stared at him blankly for a moment. "I assume it's a trick for learning healing magic, right?" he said, completely ignoring Fort. "From what I hear, it takes about a week to master each one, so if you can help me get done here faster so I can find a way out of all of this, that'd be great."

Fort glared at him. "I *just* told you something personal at breakfast. You're really going to hold out on me?"

Gabriel shrugged. "Guess I'm better at keeping secrets."

Fort almost laughed. Was he serious? The whole stealing-a-book-of-magic thing had distracted him at first, but now that he'd be here for at least another week, the mystery of Gabriel was suddenly becoming a lot more important.

If Colonel Charles wanted Gabriel to become another savior like Damian, learning each kind of magic, that was going to

be a problem, considering the book of Mind magic was now ashes.

But no, Gabriel wasn't born on Discovery Day. That meant he wouldn't be as talented at magic as those kids were. So what set him apart? Sure, he'd just intimidated Sebastian, which was amazing, but knowing how to pin an arm behind someone's back didn't really suggest magical savior.

Whatever was happening, clearly Gabriel wouldn't be sharing. Fine, let him be secretive. That'd just give Fort more time to master teleportation, move on to the next Summoning spell, hopefully open a portal, and finally rescue his father.

"Okay," he said to Gabriel. "I'll teach you some of the tricks that I was taught, quicker ways to learn healing magic. But I don't like not knowing what's going on."

"Like anyone does," Gabriel said with a snort. "Let's get moving. What's the first trick?"

As Sebastian began lecturing the other students on proper use of the book of Healing, rubbing his shoulder, Fort found a pack of needles up on Dr. Ambrose's desk. He grabbed two and brought Gabriel over to the book, which was sitting on the podium, open to the first spell, Heal Minor Wounds.

Like Jia had shown him back at the old school, Fort walked

Gabriel just shrugged at her. "If we can't get access to the book now, it doesn't make sense to wait around here. Let's just come back when it's not being used."

Without waiting to see if Fort agreed, Gabriel turned and walked out of the room.

"Ugh, you kids," Dr. Ambrose told him, and for once she seemed annoyed at someone other than Fort. "Be careful around that one, Fitzgerald. There's a lot you don't know about him." She gave Fort a quick look. "Remember how you were when you first got to the school? He's even worse. And look what damage *you* caused."

- NINETEEN -

MATH AND SCIENCE FOLLOWED HEAL-
ing one after the other, not leaving Fort much
time to think about what Dr. Ambrose had said,
let alone anything else. The guards around the school seemed
to be watching him more closely now, stopping him to make
sure he was still wearing Agent Cole's amulet.

All in all, he wasn't sure things could get much worse. But
considering lunch was next, Fort stayed optimistic that running
into his friends again would prove him wrong.

This time, Jia, Rachel, and Cyrus were leaving as he and
Gabriel entered, now on a completely different schedule
than he was. Jia avoided his look again, but Rachel glared
at him the whole time, bumping his shoulder hard as she
passed him. Behind them, Cyrus looked like he was about
to explode, he wanted to talk to Fort so badly. Fort told

Gabriel to go on ahead. "I'll be right behind you," he said.

"Don't let him guilt you," Gabriel said, loud enough for Cyrus to hear. "You did the right thing."

"Don't worry, I won't!" Cyrus said, waving at Gabriel. As the other boy left, Cyrus gave Fort a worried look. "There's a lot I need to tell you, and I don't have much time. Can you come with me for a minute?"

Fort winced, staring at two guards watching him from the cafeteria entrance. "If I go too far, the guards will bust me for not having lunch with Gabriel. Colonel Charles wants us together twenty-four seven for some reason."

Cyrus made a face. "This is *really* important, and it might be the last time I see you."

Fort's eyes widened. "The last time? What . . . *why?*"

Cyrus nodded. "Dr. Opps wants me out of here. He said something about how Colonel Charles is dangerous, and we needed to figure some things out."

Colonel Charles *was* dangerous, and no one knew that better than Dr. Opps, who'd first been imprisoned by the colonel at the last school, and just yesterday had the books of Summoning and Mind magic taken from him. Not to mention that Dr. Opps wanted Sierra and Damian finding the other books of magic. "What do you mean, out of here? Where are you going?"

"Back to the school in Wales. A lot's going to happen there, and they'll need me. But that's not what I have to tell you. The bad things that are coming are going to happen because of *you*."

Fort stopped dead in the hallway at this, but Cyrus yanked him into an empty side room, this one with the presidential seal on a podium and a bunch of seats facing it. Maybe this was where the president would address the nation if the government had to be evacuated underground for protective reasons?

"I don't know how, but I didn't see your *real* plan," Cyrus said, looking apologetic. "If I knew you were going to take the Summoning book to find your father, I would have told you what was coming. But for some reason, I saw you destroy the books, so I messed up."

"You *did* tell me," Fort said, blushing badly. "But I didn't want you to give it away to Rachel or Jia, so I asked Sierra to make you remember things differently. I'm . . . I'm so sorry, Cyrus."

His friend seemed taken aback for a moment, then shrugged. "Well, that explains a few things," he said, leaning in. "So you know what happens if they go with you?"

Fort nodded, unable to forget their previous conversation. "You told me that if *anyone* comes, I'll lose one of my friends forever." He cringed. "You had a long list of what might happen. Jia would get taken over by an Old One. Rachel would shut down the portal from the other side to save everyone. It was awful."

"That's not all," Cyrus said quietly. "If you bring them both along and you, Jia, Rachel, and your father all make it back safely . . . that's when everything falls apart."

"What?" Fort said. "You never told me that. I can make it back okay with everyone?"

"No, not everyone," Cyrus said. "That's not what I said. And if you do, the future looks *awful*, Fort. The worst-case scenario." He shuddered. "I don't even want to tell you some of the things I've seen. They're terrifying. The Old Ones make it back, and that's not even the scariest part."

Fort went cold at the image of the Old Ones returning, but at least it confirmed what he had thought. "Okay. Then it's back to my original plan, then. I just go alone."

"What? No, you can't!" Cyrus yelled. A guard looked into the room at the sound of his voice, staring at them both, then slowly continued on. "I must not have told you," Cyrus continued, his voice lower now. "If you go by yourself, you might rescue your father, but *you* won't make it back!"

Fort looked away. "I know. You told me that, too."

Cyrus's eyes widened. "Are you joking? You're still going to do it, even if you know you might get trapped there forever? Or *worse*?" He grabbed Fort's uniform and pulled him closer, more upset than Fort had ever seen him. "You can't do that, Fort! Why are you—"

"If I take anyone, I lose one of *them* instead," he said sadly. "Either that, or I cause some horrible future. It's not even a choice, Cyrus. It's my fault that my dad is there in the first place. If I had been closer, I could have helped him escape, and none of this would have happened. I'm doing this, and by myself. That way no one else suffers because of me."

"So what *then*?" Cyrus asked. "How do you know we won't all go after you, too? Things could end up even worse, Fort! There's only one way to keep everyone safe here."

"I agree," Fort said, moving toward the door. "By me going alone."

Cyrus just shook his head, looking a bit sick. "No. You'd have to . . . to leave your father there."

Cyrus's words hit him like a punch in the stomach, and Fort

backed away, his mouth hanging open. "Not going to happen," he said finally. "See you around, Cyrus."

"Fort, wait!" Cyrus said as Fort turned around and made his way to the door. "I'm not finished! Rachel said I should come up with some story to make you take off that 'stupid amulet,' as she put it, or else she won't be able to—"

But Fort shut the door behind him, cutting off whatever Cyrus had been trying to say. The last thing he cared about was Rachel's feelings about his amulet. It wasn't just her, either. He felt dead inside, after Cyrus telling him to leave his father behind. Everything felt more numb, less important.

The only way to save everyone was to leave his father trapped in the hands of the Old Ones, or something worse? *No.* No matter what it took, there was *no way* Fort would allow that to happen.

And if all it took was trading himself for his father, then that's just what Fort would do.

- TWENTY -

GABRIEL TOOK ONE LOOK AT FORT'S face and didn't say a word to him for all of lunch, which Fort was thankful for. He almost immediately regretted closing the door on Cyrus as soon as he entered the cafeteria, especially if this really was the last time they were going to see each other for a while, but it wasn't like his list of regrets wasn't already full of him being a jerk to his friends. Just another item to add to it.

As lunch ended, something happened to take his mind off of Cyrus, though. Two soldiers came by with lists of students for their next classes. "We'll be splitting you up for weapons training, so when you hear your name, stand and follow me," one said.

Weapons training? Fort looked at Gabriel, who just shrugged. What did *that* mean? Wasn't the whole point of the school for students to add magic into various items for soldiers to use? What were they going to need weapons for?

The first group called was for archery training, which sounded fun, but neither Gabriel nor Fort made the list. Gabriel was named for shield training, which didn't sound much like a weapon, but even more shockingly, Fort wasn't with him. For the first time, he and his roommate would be able to do something alone, and Fort was a bit surprised to find he wasn't looking forward to it.

Finally, Fort's name was called for a third class, which the soldier said was "Bow training."

That seemed confusing. Weren't bows used in archery?

But as they entered a medium-sized room with old, dusty gym mats covering the floor and mirrors on the wall, things got even stranger, as there were no bows, arrows, *or* targets.

"Everyone grab a broomstick," said a soldier in camouflage, who introduced himself as Sergeant Tower. In spite of his name, he wasn't that tall. In fact, he looked pretty average in almost every way, if extra muscular.

The only thing that made Sergeant Tower stand out was that he actually *smiled* at the students when they all entered, and it genuinely seemed authentic, like he was happy to see them. For the Oppenheimer School, that was definitely *not* average.

Several broomless sticks lined the wall with the door, enough for every student. Not that he was shocked, but again Fort didn't see any of his friends, or even Sebastian this time. A few of the other students in the class were completely new faces, so were probably first-timers in Destruction. The rest he recognized from Healing class earlier.

Fort grabbed a stick, not entirely sure what the point was, but glad that at least without the head of the broom, they wouldn't be sent out to clean the facility. Who knew with this new, strange Oppenheimer School.

Sergeant Tower organized them into two rows, with enough space in between each student so that they wouldn't accidentally whack one another with their stick. Once he was satisfied, he moved to stand in front of them.

"It's been decided by those much higher in the chain of command than me that you kids should know how to defend yourselves," Tower said, smiling again. "While I'm all in favor of that, I'm not sure how using a weapon will do what magic can't. But maybe you'll all prove me wrong. Let's find out together, shall we? I'll be training you once a day in the use of what we call a 'bo staff.'" He twirled one of the broomsticks around in his hand. "A bo is a great place to start, as it's a well-rounded weapon for both offense *and* defense."

Fort looked down at the wooden stick in his hand. A bo staff? That at least explained his confusion with archery, but *this* was the weapon they were going to be trained on? At least he wouldn't have to deal with the Destruction students shooting each other with it, but it did seem sort of . . . lame.

"Now, I know what you're thinking," Sergeant Tower said, pacing in front of them, his own broomstick held easily at his side. "This isn't the fanciest of weapons, for sure. What good is it going to do against a heavily armed intruder?"

"I'm not sure what it'd do against my *grandma*," one of the kids Fort didn't recognize said, and a few of the boys around him laughed.

Sergeant Tower beamed. "Great, we have a volunteer! Come on up here, Jaworski. You're going to help me illustrate how a staff like this can be your best friend."

The boy named Jaworski suddenly looked a lot less sure of himself, but he moved to the front to stand before Sergeant Tower, who raised his staff diagonally in front of him, planting his feet. Jaworski matched their teacher's stance, and Sergeant

Tower nodded supportively. "You're a quick study, Jaworski, great job! Everyone take a look at how he's got his feet shoulder width apart, better to keep a firm stance. And holding the staff like that, he's ready in case I go high *or* low. Nice one!"

"So are we done, then?" Jaworski said, flashing what was probably supposed to be a smug look to his friends.

"Ah, not quite yet," Sergeant Tower said, then moved faster than Fort could even see. His staff struck out like a snake, spinning Jaworski's staff into the air with one end before sweeping the boy's feet out from under him with the other.

As the boy slammed into the floor, Tower spun his staff straight at Jaworski's face, freezing it just inches from the boy's nose, all in one smooth movement. "Lesson one," the sergeant said. "Never take your eyes off your opponent!"

Jaworski stared up at the staff in terror, his mouth opening and closing like a fish out of water. Tower grinned, then reached down and yanked the boy to his feet, hard enough to send him flying for a moment. "Still, a good first attempt! Now, after you're fully trained, each of you will be given your *own* staff, and it won't be wood. Yours will be formed of segmented steel, which will obviously be heavier, but—"

"Steel?!" one of Jaworski's friends said. "Isn't that dangerous?"

"Only for your opponents, when I'm done teaching you," Tower told him. "And I'm glad to see we've got another volunteer for the next lesson too! Thanks, Johnson."

Johnson groaned. "You're welcome."

"Now, as I was saying," Tower said, twirling his staff around absently. "We'll start with wooden staffs to get the techniques down, then switch to your school-provided segmented-steel staffs. Not only will the weight add force to your attacks and defense, but each segment will hold its own magic spell, I'm told. You'll be adding those spells to your staff as you go, so none of them will be unfamiliar."

Fort's eyes widened. They were making their own magical staffs? Okay, *that* was kind of awesome. Suddenly this whole weapons practice thing made a lot more sense. Not only did it give them something to defend themselves with, but it also gave them an easy way to train on making magical items for the military, too.

"We're going to start with simple defense strategies," Sergeant Tower said as he knocked Johnson's staff out of his hands, leaving the boy standing there awkwardly. "Disarming will be the most important thing I can teach you here, as that will give you time to escape a more powerful opponent, especially if they have a firearm. Keep in mind you're only learning this to keep yourself safe, *not* to hurt anyone. Any attacks I teach you will only be used as a last resort. Does everyone understand?"

No one said a word.

Sergeant Tower laughed. "That's okay, you're not volunteering if you answer my questions." He launched his staff out and swept Johnson's feet out from under him just like he'd done to Jaworski. "Now let me repeat myself: Does everyone understand?"

"Yes, Sergeant Tower," they all said, almost in unison.

"Good!" Tower said, grinning. "We're all going to get along great, then. Now everyone find a partner, and let's start disarming."

- TWENTY-ONE -

AN HOUR LATER, FORT'S WHOLE body ached from head to toe. Training with the wooden staffs had not only been harder than it looked, but the girl he'd partnered up with, Jocelyn, had slammed him in the shins multiple times, trying to sweep his legs. Each new hit was a lesson in pain, and Jocelyn hadn't seemed very sorry, considering she laughed every time.

Now at least he had some free time before dinner, which he was probably meant to use tutoring Gabriel. But following Colonel Charles's orders was the last thing on his mind right now. What he needed to do was master teleportation so he could move on to the next Summoning spell as quickly as possible. That *had* to be a spell to open a portal . . . if it wasn't, he didn't know if he'd be able to last a second week, the way things were going. Certainly Agent Cole might have locked him up by then, the way all her agents in suits seemed to be everywhere now.

Since they hadn't had weapons training together, Fort avoided going back to his room, where he figured Gabriel would be. Not that he disliked the boy . . . in fact, Gabriel was growing on him. But he didn't want to come up with an excuse to cover where he was going and why he'd be gone for a couple of hours.

Still, with all the guards and agents watching him, not to mention cameras everywhere, finding a place to practice was almost impossible. That left him only one option.

Fort pushed the door open to the boys' restroom and made a face. Someone clearly had issues with the cafeteria food, based on the smell. But the bathroom looked empty, at least, and all the stall doors stood open. And that was all he needed, enough privacy to retrieve the book of Summoning, then open a teleportation circle to somewhere he could practice in peace.

Fort stepped into a stall and quickly closed the door, locking it behind him. He cast a teleportation circle on the nearby stall wall back to the cavern below the old school, and a glowing green circle opened on the metal, revealing the book of Summoning.

Fort quickly grabbed it and closed the circle, letting loose a sigh of relief. He knew intellectually that no one would have been able to find it there, but he was still incredibly thankful to see it hadn't been disturbed. He opened the book to the first spell and took in the spell words again so he could at least leave the smell in here behind.

As his body filled with magic once more, the bathroom door opened, and two boys wandered in, talking loudly. Fort froze, the book of Summoning still in his hand, and a spell at his lips. But if he cast it, the light of the teleportation circle might be bright enough for them to see.

"I'm just saying, it's weird that they're not having us learn more magic," a boy that sounded like Bryce said. "If we're only going to make more fireball bows, this is going to get boring fast."

"It's just the first day," said a voice that Fort recognized as Chad's. "Calm down. And besides, they're awesome. Shooting a fireball instead of an arrow from a bow? That's just cool."

They chose stalls on either side of Fort's, and he cursed silently. Ugh. Was he going to have to wait for them to finish their business now?

"Did you hear what Trey was working on?" Bryce said from

Fort's right. "He and a couple of others are trying to put the earthquake spell into some kind of hammer or something. I guess that's *one* way to tunnel underground."

Fort stared in disgust at the wall. Who talked while going to the bathroom? What was *wrong* with these two?

"I don't know, man," Chad said. "Trey said they couldn't get it to work right. Like it was way overpowered still. It just seems like he's not into things anymore. He told me yesterday after seeing that Foresight idiot that he was thinking of switching to Healing."

Bryce snorted. "Healing's for losers. Did you hear what they've got *them* doing? They're not even making bandages anymore. Ambrose told 'em they're going to just make shields with protection spells now, and fill up those staffs with Healing spells. How boring would that get?"

"I don't know," Chad said. "I saw that Jia girl working on something else. Rachel was in there too. No weapons, just talking to Ambrose in some other language."

"Teacher's pets," Bryce said, and flushed his toilet. "So what do you think is wrong with Trey?"

"I think New Kid got to him when he beat that tentacle monster," Chad said, flushing now too. Wow, had they synchronized themselves? Both stalls opened, but the conversation never paused. "I don't know, man. Maybe he's not cut out for Destruction anyway. He never really had his heart in it."

"Aw, bro, that'd be downright depressing to lose him," Bryce said as water started running. At least they were washing their hands. *That* was something. "Trey's a good listener, and sometimes you just want to let loose with your day-to-day problems, you know?"

"I hear that," Chad said. "He and I went to the cafeteria yesterday after dinner and just laid it all out on the line about my mom and that new guy she's seeing. I won't lie, bro. Tears were shed and hugs were had."

"He'll come around, bro," Bryce said. "Give him time. But if he does want to go into Healing, no matter how pathetic it is, we'll totes be his guys and support him. You with me?"

It sounded like they slapped hands for, like, five minutes. "For life, my bro," Chad said.

As the door closed, Fort let out a huge sigh of relief, though he was careful not to breathe in again. Not willing to wait for anyone else to happen in, he opened another teleportation circle to the first place he could think of, the kitchen he'd been in the night before, and after a quick look to make sure it was still empty, he dove through the circle, closing it behind him.

The kitchen was dark and looked just like it had last night, so hopefully no one had been in it since. Just to be safe, he opened the book again and read over the spell words, just to have a new teleportation circle ready. He'd thought he'd be safe in the bathroom, and that hadn't ended well. So who knew about the kitchen—

"Did you get the microwave installed yet?" shouted a voice from outside the door.

"No, Billy's bringing it in now," said another voice from a lot closer.

Fort sighed. Right, not here, either. He readied the spell words, only to pause midcast as a workman appeared in the doorway, holding a microwave.

"Hey, you're not supposed to be down here," the man said, giving Fort a suspicious look. "You're not one of the students, are you?"

"No, no way," Fort said, shoving the book behind his back. "I just got lost in all the hallways."

The man nodded, looking relieved, but still not happy. "Well, no families are allowed down here either. I don't care how high up your mom or dad is, okay? Now get back to the government quarters before I turn you in."

Fort nodded. He had no idea what the man was talking about, but he wasn't going to question his good luck. Instead, he walked quickly out past the workman, careful to keep the book out of sight as much as he could. Out in the hallway, he paused at the sight of people working everywhere, most of whom seemed to be looking at him suspiciously. Fort waved at them, then picked a direction and hurried away, just trying to get out of sight.

"Hey, kid!" the workman from the kitchen called, and Fort froze, his heart racing. He slowly looked back over his shoulder, sure he was busted, but found the workman pointing in the other direction. "You're going the wrong way. Government quarters are back there."

"Oh, right, sorry, I got turned around," Fort said, and turned to walk in the other direction.

"Don't worry about it," the workman said. "I get lost here, like, every other day."

The others let him pass without saying anything after that, and Fort made his way down the hall, then made a quick turn as soon as he could, just to get out of sight. He wasn't sure what the government quarters were, or why there were families here, but he knew he'd get caught if he ended up there.

What he needed was another empty room, one that *didn't* have anyone working in it. Even another bathroom might be worth the risk, if it'd give him enough time to cast another teleportation circle and get out of here.

He continued down the hall, passing rooms with people working on the wiring in some, installing beds in others, and for a moment Fort wondered how big the facility actually was.

Unfortunately, it was way too large to find his way around, and the farther he went, the more lost he became, until finally he turned a corner and found himself at a dead end. A giant round metal door hung open at the end of the hall by just a foot or two, enough to see that the door had to be at least three feet thick, as he still couldn't see inside whatever lay beyond it.

Fort sighed and started to turn around, only to hear footsteps back the way he'd come. Moving quickly, he ran to the huge door, not even sure he could move it, considering how heavy it must have been. But as he pulled, the door opened easily without even a squeak. He yanked it open just enough to slip inside, and then pulled it back shut again from the other side, unfortunately cutting off all the light to the room too.

At least if it was this dark, it had to be empty, so that was something. Fort felt around on the wall near the door and located what felt like a lever. Hoping it was for the lights, he pulled it, and the room lit up, instantly revealing something familiar, if still unnerving.

The room was huge, just like it'd been in the last school. But this time there were no wooden crates containing weird artifacts or inhuman remains. This version didn't even have glass displays on the wall.

Instead, large metal boxes were pushed against the far side of the room, both of them opened. Inside the boxes were the skeletons of two dragons, a large catlike creature, and four magicians, the source of the books of magic that had been found on Discovery Day.

- TWENTY-TWO -

ALONE WITH THE DRAGONS, FORT wasn't able to resist getting a closer look. To keep it safe, he hid the Summoning book behind some packing material in the corner, then slowly approached the skeletons. He knew he should just teleport out of here, go somewhere he could practice in peace, but being alone with the bones of actual dragons was just too amazing to pass up.

This was only the second time he'd ever seen the dragon skeletons outside one of Dr. Opps's memories, let alone seen the bodies of the magicians who'd been masters of each type of magic.

And this time, they weren't behind glass.

He tentatively reached a hand toward the largest dragon skull, feeling guilty about touching it. Even without the glass, the display still felt like a museum, and a lifetime of being told not to touch things was hard to break.

176

But this wasn't just history; it was *magic*. And when else would he have the chance to touch a dragon?

His fingers brushed the dragon's teeth, and he quickly yanked them away, just in case the monster came alive and tried to bite off his hand. But when nothing happened, he reached his hand out again, and this time touched the creature's jawbone. A feeling just like magic flowed through him, and—

"Hey," said a voice from behind him, and Fort's heart stopped completely as he whirled around in terror to find Gabriel, of all people, standing in the doorway. "I don't think you're supposed to touch those, you know," his roommate said, grinning.

"You almost gave me a heart attack!" Fort hissed, trying to calm himself down. "What are you doing here?"

Gabriel pushed his way in, then closed the enormous door behind him. "Isn't the more important question, what are *you* doing here?"

"No? I know why *I'm* here."

Gabriel snorted. "That kid with the silver hair told me I'd find you here. He said you needed a friend." Gabriel stepped closer, a thoughtful look on his face. "You know, if it was *me* who all the guards were after for taking something

I shouldn't have, I might pay more attention if I was being followed. I was at the end of the hall when you came in here."

Ugh. Cyrus was too good to be real. Even after Fort slammed a door on him, Cyrus still sent someone to check to see if he was okay.

But why Gabriel? Unless he was the only one Cyrus could find who'd still even want to talk to Fort.

"I don't know what Cyrus meant," Fort said, incredibly glad he'd hidden the Summoning book. "I'm just here to see the dragons."

Gabriel nodded. "They walked us through here on the tour," he said. "I never wanted to come, but even I was pretty blown away by this. I'm surprised they left it open."

"They've been doing a lot of work on this floor," Fort said, giving him a little space as Gabriel neared the dragons. "Probably just a mistake. I didn't realize they gave all the new students a tour of everything. Last time I saw something like this, I had to . . . well, rules were broken."

"Oh, there weren't any other students," Gabriel said, staring at the dragon. He reached out a hand and touched it in the same spot Fort had. "Just me and my mom."

"You got a private look around?" Fort said, wondering again who Gabriel was. "Why?"

"Why were *you* out past curfew last night?" he asked, giving Fort a sidelong glance.

"Okay, fair."

Gabriel turned back to the dragon and went silent for a moment. The other boy seemed lost in thought, so Fort took a chance and glanced over at where he'd hidden the Summoning book. From where they stood, it was still out of sight, but if Gabriel moved toward the large cat skeleton, he'd probably be able to see it.

"Do you think there are any left?" Gabriel said out of nowhere.

"What, dragons? Don't you think we'd have heard about it if there were?"

"Unless they only woke up when magic did," Gabriel said, running his hand down the dragon's neck bones. "They could be out there now, anywhere. It's kind of crazy to think about, huh?"

"If something this size started flying around, I'm going to guess it'd make the news."

Gabriel snorted. "Use your imagination, kid. Who says they

have to look like dragons? Birds are descended from dinosaurs. Maybe dragons hid when magic disappeared. Maybe they look completely different now."

"Like what, Komodo dragons?" Fort began to get antsy, anxious that he didn't have the book on him. Why had he put it down? Now he wouldn't be able to grab it without Gabriel noticing. "We should probably get out of here. If you go first, it'll look less suspicious—"

"Maybe those Old One things started as dragons," Gabriel said, ignoring him. "Or maybe these magicians did. Dragons turned into all kinds of things in old stories, and for all we know now, those could be true."

"I'm pretty sure dragons are just dragons," Fort said, pointing at the skeletons in front of him. "Why would they hide what they looked like?"

"To keep hidden, maybe," Gabriel said. "If you were the last dragon, would you want to stand out?"

Fort's eyes widened at his roommate's words. The last dragon? That was the same phrase the Old One had used in his dreams the last few nights. "What did you just say?" he whispered.

"I'm saying, if there's just one dragon left, maybe it tried to hide," Gabriel said, looking over at him now. "You don't ever wonder if Dr. Oppenheimer knows about one that's still around? You know that guy has tons of secrets. Someone at this school probably knows."

Fort stared at him, not sure what to make of this. It couldn't just be coincidence that Gabriel was using the exact same phrase that the Old One had. And Gabriel *had* said he had nightmares too. But the same dream? It couldn't be possible. Why would Gabriel be dreaming about Fort's father? Could Gabriel have overheard him saying the phrase in his sleep?

"Why are you so interested in some random last dragon?" Fort asked, not sure if he wanted to know the answer.

Gabriel went silent for a moment, then gave him a long look. "What are you doing in here, Fort?"

"I told you, I came to see the skeletons," he said.

"Actually, you said dragons."

"I was mostly just looking for someplace quiet. But you didn't answer my question."

"I'll answer *your* question if you tell me what that book is, the one you hid in the corner there," Gabriel said, nodding toward the spot where Fort had hidden the book of Summoning.

A cold chill passed through Fort. "I told you earlier," he said, hoping to sound braver than he felt. "I can keep a secret."

Gabriel nodded. "That's important, kid. And I admire that about you. But eventually there comes a point where you have to take a leap of faith, and just trust someone else."

"You should take your own advice, maybe."

Gabriel laughed. "You really do remind me of my little brother, Fort. Listen, I don't know what you're doing, and you don't need to tell me. But if I were you, I'd find a good, solid hiding place for that book, and stop throwing it in corners if you don't want to get caught."

Fort swallowed hard. "That's . . . good advice."

Gabriel nodded and turned to go, then paused and looked back. "Just in case you were here for some other reason, I'm going to help you out. Dr. Oppenheimer doesn't have anything on dragons, not in his office. So don't bother breaking in there, I already checked. Now, I'll see you at dinner, yeah?"

And with that, he walked out, leaving Fort more confused than ever.

- TWENTY-THREE -

FORT AND GABRIEL DIDN'T TALK ABOUT what had happened in the display room at dinner, given how many other students were around. But Gabriel didn't mention it later that night, either, and Fort couldn't figure out a way to just bring up Gabriel's dreams. *Hey, roomie, you're not having nightmares about huge tentacle monsters from beyond all space and time, are you? Weird, me too!*

Instead, he waited until Gabriel was asleep, snuck into the bathroom, and retrieved the book of Summoning from where he'd hidden it after the whole dragon conversation. Then he teleported back to the display room, and practiced the spell until he couldn't keep his eyes open any longer.

Before going to bed, he touched the amulet around his neck, wondering if what Agent Cole had told him had been true. There was no way Sierra had *actually* rigged the thing to knock

And beside him, Gabriel seemed to be having a nightmare too, moaning fitfully and tossing around.

Not sure what else to do, Fort reached over and gently tapped his shoulder, only to have Gabriel grab his wrist and twist it painfully, pulling Fort to the floor.

"Ow, hey!" Fort shouted. "I was just trying to wake you up! You looked like you were having a nightmare!"

Gabriel's eyes seemed to focus on Fort, and he instantly released Fort's wrist. "Oh *wow*, I'm so sorry," he said, and he really did sound sincere. "I was . . . Right. Bad dream."

"About dragons?" Fort asked, and Gabriel looked at him sharply. "You know, like in the display room. The skeletons."

Gabriel just stared for a moment, then fell back into his bed and turned toward the wall. "Gonna try to get a few more hours of sleep. Sorry again."

That was enough to keep Fort awake for the rest of the night wondering if Gabriel really was having the same dream somehow, and what that meant. Was there really some last dragon somewhere on Earth? And if so, what did the Old Ones want with it?

More importantly, would Fort be willing to give those monsters something they wanted, something that might make them even more dangerous, in exchange for his father back?

Eventually he gave up and tried to sleep again. As he turned over, he almost knocked his amulet off the bed, and something occurred to him: If these dreams were real, that meant the Old One was projecting them from another dimension. Gabriel had an amulet of his own. If he'd been wearing it while he slept, there was no way he could have seen the same dream.

Except as he turned over, he found Gabriel's amulet sitting on the nightstand.

Uh-oh.

The next few days settled into a kind of rhythm, not that Fort was particularly happy about it. Each morning Sebastian would try to get any information he could out of Fort about how he'd made up new spells without the spell book. Fort always refused, which just made Sebastian punish him in some way or another. Thanks to Gabriel, Sebastian ended up with two sore arms and one sore leg that week.

The two actually seemed to be enjoying themselves after a while, with Sebastian trying to secretly give Fort some disease when he knew Gabriel wasn't watching, then waiting to see how long it took until Gabriel discovered Fort convulsing on the floor.

Good times all around, really.

Weapons practice wasn't exactly fun either. Fort didn't seem to be making much progress working with the staff, but at least Sergeant Tower stayed supportive and positive the entire time. That was more than enough to make him Fort's favorite teacher at the school, even with all the bruises he gained in the class.

"Soreness is just a sign that you're getting stronger," Tower said in their third class, slapping Fort's aching shoulders. "You're hulking out already, look at you! You're doing great, Forsythe. Keep it up!"

Of course, Justine immediately knocked Fort to the floor as soon as the sergeant's back was turned, but she liked to say that was to keep Fort humble.

Cyrus seemed to have disappeared, just like he'd promised, and for all Fort could tell, so had Jia and Rachel. They were either steadily avoiding him, which was fair, or whatever special projects Dr. Opps had them doing were keeping them both so busy that they were never around. Fort wasn't sure which he preferred, but he did feel thankful for Gabriel, secrets and all, especially at meal times. At least he didn't have to sit alone, and in spite of it being a little demeaning, he found he sort of liked being seen as a little brother.

"You want to see some *real* magic?" Gabriel asked at lunch one day, looking around to make sure no one was listening.

Fort rolled his eyes. "No. No I don't. Especially not if it's just you pulling another coin out of my ear."

Gabriel frowned. "I don't know what you're suggesting, but that sounds like a trick. I'm talking about actual magic."

"You mean like the kind we're studying? *That* actual magic?"

"No, nothing so ordinary," Gabriel said, then scrunched up his face. "Hold on, I have to sneeze." He leaned back, then faked a sneeze, sending a rainbow scarf flying out of his nose and into the middle of Fort's green beans.

Fort just stared at his roommate, who wiped his nose innocently, then gave Fort a curious look. "You going to eat those, or can I have them?" Gabriel asked, pointing to the beans.

Each night after dinner they would take the book of Healing down to the room with the dragon skeletons and practice Heal Minor Wounds. While Fort felt a bit more comfortable there with Gabriel around, since apparently his roommate had permission to do anything he wanted at any time, each hour Fort spent studying Healing was an hour he wasn't practicing teleportation, so by the time they were done, he was practically ready to explode.

Fortunately, Gabriel didn't ask any questions about why Fort stayed behind after their study sessions. Of course he knew that Fort had another book of magic, but Gabriel didn't ask, and Fort wasn't going to share, at least not until he found out more of the other boy's secrets anyway.

As soon as Gabriel left each night, Fort would open a teleportation circle and retrieve the book, then get going. He'd experimented with a lot of different teleportation portals since the first night, from trying to high-five himself with two circles right next to each other, to seeing if he could keep a spoon he'd taken from the cafeteria falling forever by creating one circle on the ceiling, another on the floor right below it, and dropping the spoon in.

It had worked for the first few minutes. Unfortunately, spoons moving that fast hurt if you try to grab them because you think you heard someone coming.

He soon ran out of interest in these and instead decided to visit a new landmark around the world every night, just to clear his head. After that, he'd return to the dragon room and create as many portals as he could from one side of the room to the other until he either was ready to pass out, or he thought of a new place around the world to see, to get a second wind.

So far he'd been to the pyramids in Egypt, the Great Wall of China, the Eiffel Tower, Big Ben in London, and the Statue of Liberty, not to mention a bunch of theme parks after they were closed, which was kind of thrilling. Part of him felt bad that he wasn't finding cooler, lesser known spots, but for the teleportation spell to work, he needed to have seen the place, and there were only so many out-of-the-way local secrets that Fort knew about. Most of those were in his hometown, and that was one place he had no intention of visiting now. Not until his father was back, anyway.

Studying as late as he could each night meant he didn't get much sleep, so when he couldn't keep his eyes open any longer, he'd open a tiny teleportation circle back to his room to check to see if Gabriel was asleep, then widen it and jump through after relearning the spell again. It was taking a chance, for sure, but it was still better then getting seen by a guard or a security camera.

And it's not like he needed the help getting caught, if that's what he'd wanted. If anything, as the days went by Agent Cole had gotten more intent on finding the books Fort had taken. Gabriel reported back one morning that two of the suited agents had shown up at their door the night before, checking to make sure Fort was there.

Unfortunately, he'd been off in China somewhere, but Gabriel had claimed he was in the bathroom and told them to stop waking him up. Somehow, they'd listened to that, which made Fort wonder who Gabriel really was again, even as he grew more anxious about getting caught.

The last thing he'd do every night before passing out was remove his amulet and try to reach Sierra. He'd call her name for what felt like hours, but there was never any reply, and he'd lie awake for longer worrying about her. But eventually sleep would come, and the nightmares with it.

By his sixth night of practice, he could barely concentrate even an hour after Gabriel left, he'd gotten so little sleep all week. He slapped his face a few times to wake up, but that didn't seem to be helping, which usually meant he'd gone on too long.

Fort sighed and closed down a portal to the Hollywood sign, then glanced at the book to relearn the spell and finish up for the night.

Except this time, there *was* no teleportation spell. The pages were blank.

Instantly awake, Fort picked up the book and quickly turned the page, his hands shaking with anticipation.

The next page wasn't blank anymore. That meant he'd mastered Teleport and now could access the second spell! Almost afraid to see, he closed his eyes for a moment, crossed his fingers for luck, and took a look.

Restore Dimensional Portal, it said at the top of the page.

If in such a time that a previously created portal between different dimensions needs to be Restored, the careful magic user may ascertain his transdimensional travel will return to an exact previous location by re-creating, instead of creating anew, a dimensional portal. By doing so . . .

Fort stopped and reread those sentences again, just trying to figure out what they meant through his exhausted haze. When he first saw the name of the spell, his stomach sank, thinking he'd need still *another* week to learn the spell he needed. But after rereading the first paragraph a few times, his tired mind eventually realized that no, this was *exactly* the right magic.

After all, he had no idea what it might take to open a portal to the dimension where his father was taken, one out of potentially millions or billions that existed. But *this* spell would just open an old portal, and he knew exactly where one leading to the right dimension had been: below the old Oppenheimer School, the one Damian had created when possessed. It led to the same monsters as the portal that his father had been taken through, so it had to be the same place.

And if it wasn't, well, he could always break into the dome the military had built over the hole in the National Mall if he had to.

He quickly read over the spell words to Restore Dimensional Portal, because no matter what, he wasn't waiting another minute.

"Dad," Fort whispered to the Gettysburg Address brochure he'd left in the Summoning book. "I'm coming for you. *Tonight.*"

- TWENTY-FOUR -

A S TIRED AS HE WAS, FORT WASN'T foolish enough to just jump into a strange dimension without any provisions. Given that he'd now mastered teleportation, Fort used the spell to gather up all the things he'd need for his trip into the monsters' world.

First, since he'd been training on it anyway and didn't have much other magic to depend on, he went looking for one of the metal staffs Sergeant Tower had mentioned so many times.

Finding where they were kept wasn't hard, as he'd seen his old classmates carrying them through the halls to a room near Dr. Ambrose's classroom. A few glances inside that room while walking by gave him all he needed to open a teleportation circle inside it now.

He checked the room first using a smaller circle, then

jumped through when he saw it was empty. He quickly made sure the outer door was locked, stumbling through the room in the dark just in case. Then he turned on the lights and sucked in his breath in surprise.

He'd only been expecting staffs, but his eyes widened when he saw the awesome assortment of weapons and other magical items laid out before him. There in the corner were the bows that he'd heard Chad and Bryce talking about, the ones that shot fireballs. He grabbed one of those, and it glowed red at his touch. Next he took a nearby metal staff that had to be full of healing spells, considering the momentary blue glow when he took it.

There were shields as well, but they looked heavy, and he didn't want to get bogged down, especially since he already had two fairly large items. If the bow had been strung, he might have tried to sling it over his shoulder, but apparently fireballs didn't need string.

Instead, he found some duct tape off with some supplies in another corner and taped each end of the bow to the staff. Without the string, the staff wouldn't get in the way of him firing the bow, and now he could carry the staff over his shoulder using the bow to hold it in place.

Assuming he didn't shoot himself with a fireball, that was.

His next stop was the cafeteria, since he wasn't sure how long he'd be gone. He gathered together a bunch of protein bars (the only dessert the cafeteria offered) in a bag with some bottles of water and hooked that over the end of the staff, leaving his hands free for magic.

It was a bit awkward, with the bag of food hitting his back every few steps, but he felt better being able to cast Teleport at a moment's notice.

Was that everything? He patted himself down, trying to think of what he'd forgotten. He had food, weapons, his amulet, which hopefully would actually hide him from the Old One . . . was there anything else he needed before going on a long trip?

Oh, right! He'd almost left out the most important thing of all! He quickly teleported to the bathroom, considering there probably weren't great facilities in a monster dimension, and with that, he was finally ready.

He teleported back to the display room, bringing with him a pen and paper he'd found with the tape, so he could leave a note. The Gettysburg Address brochure was already back in his pocket, for luck.

Gabriel, he wrote. *If you're reading this, then I've been gone long enough for you to come looking for me. If that's the case, I'm probably not coming back. I'm leaving you the book of Summoning, which I stole from Colonel Charles to use to find my father after he was taken by one of the creatures that attacked D.C. I know he's alive, and I'm going to find him . . . but I had to go alone. It's the only way to keep everyone else safe, just like we talked about. Give this book to Rachel, in the Destruction class. She'll know what to do with it. Tell her, and Jia, and Cyrus . . .*

He paused, tapping the pen. Hopefully none of this would be necessary, but he wasn't going to jump to a strange dimension with the book of Summoning on him, considering what the Old Ones might do with it. And if he *didn't* come back, he wanted everyone to at least know what had happened. The last thing he wanted was for his friends to think he'd just abandoned them and left.

But it also felt really weird to say good-bye. It felt like he was giving up before he'd even started.

Tell them I'm sorry, he finished, and tucked the note into the book.

If you go by yourself, you might rescue your father, but you won't make it back! Cyrus's voice rang through his head, and he hesitated. Was he really ready to get stuck in the monsters' world forever? Or worse, not survive the trip?

Stay safe, his father would have told him. *I'm the parent, and you're the child who will become the first Fitzgerald to be president. You don't have to do this.*

Fort rubbed some wetness from his eyes and clenched his fists. Maybe Cyrus was right. Maybe he *wouldn't* make it back, or see his friends ever again.

But there was no way he was leaving his father there, no matter what it took. And they'd changed the future before, every time Cyrus had maneuvered them around guards at the old school. Why couldn't Fort change it now, knowing what was coming?

Feeling a bit more confident, he hid the book of Summoning where Gabriel had seen it last time, in the corner under some packing material, with his note sticking out from the front cover. Then he took a deep breath, turned to the nearest wall, opened a teleportation circle, and jumped through to the cavern below the old Oppenheimer School.

He landed on stone, but it was so dark, he could barely see beyond his feet. He considered that for a moment, then closed the portal he'd jumped through, and opened one higher, on the ceiling above him, leading back to the ceiling of the display room. Both portals were small, but the light from the display room now passed through the circle to illuminate the cavern, too, enabling Fort to see it clearly for the first time since the monster attack.

Rubble filled most of the area below the old school. There wasn't too much space in the open cavern around him, and he hoped that wherever it had been, the old portal would be close enough for him to still reach.

As far as he could tell, there weren't any dangerous cracks or holes in the stone below him, which was fortunate, as he didn't want to accidentally trip or fall into one while bringing his father back.

Out of curiosity, he checked above him too, up around the open teleportation circle. It was harder to see from the glare of the light, but he didn't find any holes or tunnels leading up out of it.

That was good. If there wasn't any way up, that meant that no soldiers from the base had explored down this far, not since the school had been destroyed. And if no one had discovered the cavern, then Fort could leave the portal open without worrying about someone finding it. After all, if he closed it, he had no way to reopen it, unless he chanced potentially losing the book of Summoning to the Old Ones.

Fort turned back to the floor and readied himself. The memory of fighting the creature was still crystal clear, as it had only been a few weeks before. Damian had opened the portal to the monsters' dimension, and the creature had emerged, digging its way up to where Fort had waited, deep in the basement of the old school. Its hand had burst through the floor and grabbed him, then dragged him back down here.

Fort had fought the creature off, and it had tried to escape back into the portal, but he'd almost not let it. He'd felt so much rage toward the creature for taking his father from him that he'd almost killed the thing before finally letting it go, realizing that the Old One was the one in control, not the monster.

Time to see how true that was. If the Old One had kept his father alive, like he'd seen in his dreams, then Fort would find him. If not . . .

"Gen urre'otre platrexe phor," Fort said softly, and the rock and rubble glowed from an eerie green light in his hands. He concentrated, closing his eyes, and in his mind's eye a glowing circle appeared on the stone just in front of him. He opened his eyes, confused, and the circle disappeared. But closing them again, he could see it clearly, like he'd stared at the sun and burned its image into his eyes.

Moving his head around, he could see another circle hundreds of feet above him, this one also bright, but much smaller from a distance. That had to be the portal Damian had opened when trying to bring the other Old Ones through.

And there were more, many more, in almost every direction, some so far away they were just tiny specks of light, like stars in the dark. A whole bunch of them were grouped off in one direction, and Fort wondered if that was the NSA, where Damian had originally practiced his Summoning magic.

It didn't matter. The only portal Fort was concerned about was directly in front of him.

He turned back to this one, and slowly unleashed the magic, feeling the itchiness of the Summoning power flow out of his hands and into the ground. The glowing circle in his mind disappeared, and he took a deep breath, then opened his eyes to find the portal now glowing in real life, lighting up the rubble all around him.

At first, it was just a circle of magical fire, but soon he could feel something *opening*, splitting the barriers between dimensions, creating a doorway to another world.

Another world where his father had been waiting for almost eight months now.

No. Don't think about it. He couldn't let the possibilities stop him. He was so close! Fort took a step closer to the edge of the chasm, his heart racing. No matter what he found below, he'd be bringing his father back.

Another step, and he stood directly over the glowing circle. The darkness around the flames was so intense that he couldn't see much in the other dimension, but he *knew* this was where the creature had come from. It had to be. It was also strangely quiet, but that was probably for the best: The last thing he wanted to do was land in a nest of the creatures.

He checked to make sure his staff and bow were secure, and that the bag of food wouldn't bounce around too much. *This is it,* he thought, quickly removing his amulet. *Sierra, if you can hear me, I hope you're okay. I'm going to get my father, and I'll be back soon. Stay safe.*

But no response came, and he put the amulet back on, unwilling to wait another moment. Instead, he closed his eyes and stepped into the portal.

But instead of passing through it, his foot came down on solid rock.

Rock that filled the entire portal, completely closing it off.

- TWENTY-FIVE -

N O," FORT WHISPERED, DROPPING to the stone and running his hands over it frantically. It couldn't be true. There *had* to be a way in. The monster had emerged from this very spot, the portal proved it! How could it be totally blocked now?!

"No!" he shouted this time, banging his fists on the rock. Pain shot through his hands, but he barely noticed it in his anger. "Let me in!" he shouted, hitting the rock again. *"Let. Me. In!"*

But there was no response, and his voice just echoed eerily through the cavern below the former Oppenheimer School. He wouldn't accept this. It couldn't be true. Fort leaped to his feet, barely able to think. How could this be happening? There was no *way* he could get this close, only to lose his father again!

Anger turned to rage, and he began lashing out, stomping on the rock with all of his strength, yelling, screaming at someone, *anyone* to open the passage. He cursed the monsters, Damian, the Oppenheimer School, Colonel Charles, and everyone else he could think of until he ran out of names, then just started screaming gutturally.

After what felt like hours but was probably only minutes, his throat began to itch from his shouting, and his kicks and punches lost some of their energy. He slowly fell to his knees, fighting back tears.

"This can't be happening," he whispered, shaking his head. "I'm *so close*."

For a time, he just knelt there on the rock, not sure what else to do. His anger disappeared as the minutes passed, replaced by a roller coaster of despair and determination.

What was the point? He was never going to find his father. It had been far too long.

But if he gave up now, what would happen to his dad if he *was* still alive down there?

It wasn't giving up if he couldn't get through the rock! He didn't have any other options.

But there had to be some way through. He could teleport

throughout the entire world, but a boulder could stop him in his tracks?

But to teleport, he had to know the destination, and there was no way of knowing what lay beyond the rock, or where his father might be. No, he *had* to get through the rock somehow. There must be magic that would do it, a Destruction spell, or . . . or Ethereal Spirit, the Healing spell!

For a moment, a fragile hope buoyed Fort's spirits, and he stood back up. Ethereal Spirit turned your body insubstantial, letting you swim right through solid objects. He could relearn that, and . . .

Except he hadn't learned it. Sierra had stolen it from Jia's mind without meaning to and planted it in Fort's, back when he was trying to pass his Healing test in the original school. If he tried to learn it now, it could take months or longer to even reach the spell.

Maybe he really *did* need Jia or Rachel, just to get through to the other dimension. But that would mean one of them would be lost, and he wasn't willing to even consider that. Besides, Cyrus had said Fort alone could rescue his father, if he was willing to not make it back himself. How was *that* possible if this obstacle stopped him?

That meant there must be a way through, and all he had to do was think of it. He sat back down on the rock, racking his brain for ideas. Unfortunately, every new possibility that occurred to him would have required one of his friends, and he slammed his palm down on the rock, the frustration and anger coming back quickly. There had to be a way he could do this alone! If he couldn't bring one of the other students, then maybe a magical item. He felt around to the staff and bow on his back, but a fireball wasn't going to damage the stone. The staff's Healing magic would be just as useless, and the only other item Fort remembered in the armory was a shield, which didn't seem like it'd accomplish a whole lot here either.

But maybe there were other items? Didn't he hear someone talking about a hammer? He tried to home in on that memory, but could only bring to mind the bathroom, for some reason. Wait, that was it, the bathroom, and Chad and Bryce talking on either side of his stall.

Trey had wanted to switch to Healing, that was it. But before that, they'd mentioned what he was working on. A hammer.

A hammer infused with an earthquake spell from the Destruction book.

Fort climbed back out of the portal so fast he almost tripped over his staff. He immediately opened a teleportation circle back to the weapons room and leaped through it, emerging into darkness once more. He clicked on the light again and started his search.

Fort glanced around, finding row upon row of staffs, more bows, a lot of bandages and amulets on chains, but no hammers.

There were a few items covered with cloth on the tables in the room, too small for Fort to have bothered with before. But at this point, he was running out of options. None of the covered stuff looked big enough to break a rock, but magic wasn't really about size.

The first item he uncovered was some kind of metal sculpture, almost like a small turtle. That for sure wasn't it, so Fort kept moving, finding a large black key next, then a pin of tiny wings, like pilots would sometimes give out on airplanes, and finally . . .

Finally, a tiny silver hammer lying on top of a pillow. It couldn't have been more than three inches long.

Fort peered in close and found a note attached to it with a small piece of string, almost like a gift tag on a present.

The Earthshatterer, the note said. *Work in progress. Don't touch! EXTREMELY dangerous!*

Really? *This* was the Earthshatterer? He picked it up in his hands, and nothing happened, no glow like when he'd grabbed the staff and bow earlier. Maybe it wasn't done yet, like the note said.

But as of right now, he had no other options. He might as well try it; if he went back to the cavern and the hammer didn't do anything, he wouldn't be any worse off than he was now.

Of course, if the hammer did *too* much, it might collapse the whole cavern, sending a few tons of rock down to bury him beneath the old Oppenheimer School.

But Cyrus said he'd bring his father back alone. If the cavern collapsed, his dad wasn't going to get back through. So it *must* be safe . . . ish.

Either way, better to put himself in danger than his friends. Like Gabriel said, protect the ones you love, no matter the cost.

But that didn't mean he shouldn't be prepared. Fort grabbed the hammer and created another teleportation circle, this time back to the room with the dragon skeletons, where he'd hidden the Summoning book. Now that he'd cast Restore Dimensional Portal, the words had reappeared on the page.

He wouldn't need it again, he hoped. But better safe than

sorry, especially if he did end up taking the entire cavern down with him. If he cut off this portal, there was still the one below the National Mall in Washington, D.C., and he'd need the spell again to try there, if the unthinkable happened.

After the itchy magic filled him once more, he hid the book, then teleported back to the cavern below the old school. There was the glowing portal, just as he'd left it, and he stepped inside, then got down on his knees to confirm there weren't any cracks or fissures in the rock, somewhere he could aim the hammer. Unfortunately, just like before, the stone looked completely solid.

He still had no idea how that was possible. Could the monsters have some sort of magic that restored whatever they tunneled through? Or maybe worse, was there something else down there with them that *could*? Maybe the red-eyed things from his dream?

It didn't matter. His father was in there somewhere, which meant Fort was going in too.

He leaned forward, careful not to accidentally tap Earth-shatterer against his own body at all. He assumed the earthquake spell only worked on, well, *earth*, but it wasn't something he was willing to bet his legs on.

Now just inches away, he pinched the tiny hammer between two of his fingers, then brought it slowly down toward the rock, sweat dripping down his forehead from the tension. Suddenly the weight of the rock above him seemed to be stifling, and he couldn't figure out how it hadn't fallen yet.

No. Don't think about it. Concentrate on how it's going to open the portal for you.

"Please, Earthshatterer," he whispered to the hammer, trying not to roll his eyes at the name. "Just split this rock below me, that's all you have to do. Don't go all crazy on me, okay? If I get buried here, you do too."

With that, Fort closed his eyes, took a deep breath, then gently tapped the hammer against the rock below him.

With a sound like an explosion, the rock vaporized into dust, sending Fort tumbling into the darkness below.

- TWENTY-SIX -

FORT SCREAMED IN SURPRISE AS HE fell into an enormous open cavern from such a height that he could barely see the ground as it rushed up toward him. Right before he hit, he was able to concentrate enough to cast a teleportation spell and opened an entrance and an exit right next to each other, just above the ground.

He dropped through one circle and shot in the opposite direction from the other, his momentum sending him high into the air, up toward the glowing portal leading back home. As he neared it, he began to slow again, until he reached the pinnacle of his flight, and started to fall once more.

Quickly, he canceled the two teleportation circles, then cast the spell again, this time creating one below him, and the other standing vertically on the ground.

He dropped back through the circle, but this time it sent

him skidding out on the cavern floor, which fortunately was relatively smooth. The landing was still rough, but he hadn't dropped far enough for it to be dangerous, and he managed to not bruise himself too badly. After he came to a stop on the ground, he lay there in place, trying to catch his breath while his heart threatened to explode out of his chest.

The light from the portal was just barely enough to see by, illuminating his strangely shiny surroundings. The rock nearby looked so shiny, in fact, that he would have thought it was wet, even though the ground felt dry. Whatever the rock was, it was oddly dark, almost black, even, just like the ground beneath him. Was this some kind of obsidian, or . . .

The ground beneath him rumbled, and Fort's eyes widened.

This wasn't stone he was standing on.

A giant eyelid opened beneath his feet, sending him flying. A blazing red eye watched him go, and a roar shook the cavern.

He'd landed on one of the *monsters*.

His flight crashed him into more of the shiny rock, which he now recognized as the creatures' scales. Which meant he'd just been thrown into another of the monsters.

Fort frantically tried to catch a grip as this next creature also began to rise, but the scales were too smooth, and he fell out into open air. Looking down, he now saw that the *actual* ground was still hundreds of feet below. He quickly opened another circle directly below him and spat himself back out into the air in the middle of the cavern, hoping to get a better look.

But when he emerged from the teleportation circle this time, all he could see were shiny black scales moving *everywhere*. From wall to wall, the entire cavern was full of the monsters, all curled up with each other.

"Oh, this is *bad*," he said as he dropped again, only to quickly open another circle directly below him which led to the actual ground this time.

He emerged right beside the massive feet of the monster he'd initially landed on, who had now stood. Unfortunately, it wasn't done making noise, and its roars shook the room, rousing the others. The enormous foot in front of Fort rose into the air, then reversed, coming straight down on the spot Fort was standing.

As it hit, Fort opened another circle, barely escaping before the creature's foot slammed into the ground. His spell sent him back into the air, falling into the now writhing mass of creatures, all of which were struggling to stand as well.

This ping-ponging up and down wasn't working—he had to get out of here! He quickly sent himself teleporting across the cavern, over toward one of the walls, but things didn't look a whole lot better from that side.

He needed some kind of safe place to stop for a moment, because he couldn't keep teleporting around like this. The ground was out, at least if he didn't want to be trampled. Trying to land as far on the other side of the cavern as he could see, he emerged from a teleportation circle to find a red glow coming from a narrow ledge, still hundreds of feet away.

Whatever was there, it looked like it was at least out of the monsters' reach, which meant he could catch his breath, if nothing else. Fort started to cast another teleportation spell, only to get swept out of the air by a giant hand slamming into him, massive claws curling over his form and yanking him back down toward the ground.

The hit knocked Fort for a loop, but he managed to clear his head just in time to look down into the open jaws and oversized teeth of one of the creatures. Frantically, Fort tried to grab ahold of one of the fingers, but it was too huge, and the monster shook its hand, dislodging Fort instantly.

He tumbled down into its mouth, spinning wildly as he fell.

He tried opening a teleportation circle right above the tongue, but his now-dizzy aim was completely off, and the circle ended up around the creature's nose.

Instead, he landed on its slimy tongue and slid toward the throat, catching wind of a smell weirdly like fireworks bubbling up from its stomach. The creature reared back to swallow, sending Fort flying down its throat.

He screamed and quickly opened a circle below him, emerging back out in the cavern, still falling, but at least not heading for stomach acid. Another creature lunged for him, and Fort disappeared into a circle, then shot up from the ground again, only to slam into a third monster's leg. He frantically tried to catch himself but failed, and fell backward right into the same circle, popping out just as the first creature's hand passed, landing on the back of it.

The creature immediately felt his weight and shook its hand, sending Fort flying off upside down, straight at one of the walls. He winced and created a circle on the wall, leading to a spot directly below the ledge on the other side, hoping his momentum would carry him up. He came rocketing out of the second circle and into the air once more, only to just miss the edge of the ledge before falling back to the ground.

With a grunt, he opened a circle directly below him leading to the ceiling above the ledge, just as a new creature rose up, its open mouth coming straight at him. It closed its jaws around the circle right as Fort hit it, but he emerged safely out of the ceiling above the ledge . . . if still falling much too fast.

With no time to open another circle, Fort hit the ground hard and let out an enormous groan of pain. He lay there for a moment, unable to move, all the air knocked out of his lungs. The last few minutes had been a haze of terror and adrenaline, and now that he was safe, if broken, he let the horror of what he'd just gone through wash over him, and he shivered.

The shivering only made his body hurt worse.

When he could finally breathe and convince his poor body to move once more, he crawled to the edge, where an elaborately worked metal railing had been built to keep someone or some*thing* from falling over it. That was interesting, as there was no way the monsters below could have made anything like that. So who else was down here, then?

He pulled himself up by the fence and glared down at the creatures below, now all roaring in annoyance.

"I hope I woke you *all* up," he said, giving them a death stare. "And I hope you don't get back to sleep any time soon!"

One of the creatures slammed a hand into the wall below him, and Fort had to catch himself on the fence to keep from tumbling back into the cavern. Realizing he was pushing his already terrible luck, Fort quickly backed away and tried to figure out where he was now.

Red circles of light with the intensity and color of exit signs lit the ledge, and Fort realized for the first time that the ledge's opening looked like it'd been purposely dug to be too small for the creatures' arms to reach into. With their massive claws, he figured the monsters could still dig a larger opening, but they hadn't bothered for some reason.

In fact, it was odd that they would all stay put in that cavern. Granted, it was pretty huge, but there were a lot of them crammed in there, and they didn't seem like the most peaceful of monsters, at least not in his experience.

Maybe the Old Ones controlled them here, too, just as they did when sending them against Washington, D.C., and the old Oppenheimer School?

The Old Ones, or something else.

The red lights and fence on the ledge certainly suggested some kind of being watched over the monsters. Fort slowly crept toward the nearest wall, trying to ignore the shooting pains in his legs and torso. The wall looked like it led to a tunnel with more of the red lights, which seemed to be the only way out.

Without any other choice, Fort entered the tunnel, pushing himself up against the wall as much as possible to keep hidden. The red lights barely illuminated the tunnel, so if whoever watched over the creatures had eyesight like his, they'd never see him.

Considering they'd built *only* these lights, eyesight like his probably wasn't a safe guess.

The tunnel ended in another cavern, this one not nearly as big as the monsters' home. Red lights dotted the ceiling, arranged in lines that led off in various directions. Unfortunately, the ceiling was higher now, so the lights didn't work as well, and Fort could barely see enough to keep from tripping.

Behind him, he heard the creatures' roars intensify. Maybe they were annoyed at losing him? The sounds made him nervous, since somebody was bound to come check on the creatures, if that really was someone's job. Not wanting to find out, Fort hurried along one of the red lines of lights toward what he hoped was another tunnel out.

Another roar made him look back for just a moment, but

one moment was too long. Something smacked him in the back of the head so hard it sent him spinning to the ground. He landed hard and quickly tried to grab his staff to defend himself, but it was lodged beneath him, and he couldn't free his shoulder from the bow.

Slowly, all around him, more of the red circles of light turned on, appearing two by two in a circle that quickly surrounded him. Had he just . . . walked into one of the lights? Was that what he'd hit? But if that was the case, why were they turning on now that he'd fallen down?

And then a pair of the red lights blinked, and that's when he knew these weren't the same glowing circles of light on the ceiling. These were *eyes*.

TWENTY-SEVEN

FORT ROLLED OVER AND LEAPED TO his feet, yanking the bow and staff off of his back. He pulled back on the bow where the string would have been, and a ball of fire appeared in the center of the bow, ready to fire.

"Back *off*," he said, the light of the fireball illuminating bits and pieces of the creatures, whatever they were. From what he could tell, the monsters weren't that large, but they seemed to be carrying metal weapons of some sort. One had a wicked looking pickax, while another held a spiked hammer in each hand.

The glossy red eyes, though, were the most familiar, and most eerie part of them. These were the same creatures he'd seen in his dream, the ones that had taken his father away.

Two of the red eyes advanced on him, and he loosed the fireball, shooting it right between them as a warning. It exploded against the floor behind the creatures, and for a moment, the bright light blinded Fort. He stumbled backward to stay out of their reach, only to have one of the red eyed creatures behind him slam a foot into the back of his knees, knocking him back to the ground.

He twisted around as he fell and sent another fireball flying. His angle was way off, though, and it ended up hitting the ceiling. This time he made sure to close his eyes, but the creatures weren't so lucky, as he heard several of them groan in pain.

Unfortunately, when Fort opened his eyes again, he found that his fireball had knocked out most of the globes of light dotting the roof of the cavern, leaving the room even darker than it had been.

He scrambled back to his feet, holding the staff diagonally before him like Sergeant Tower had taught them. As one of the red-eyed creatures stumbled close to him, still blinded, Fort swept out with his staff at its hand, trying to disarm the creature.

Instead, as it hit, the staff glowed blue, and Fort felt a cold energy pass from the weapon into the creature.

The creature paused, then took a step back. "Ah, I think it healed my hand," it growled, low and guttural.

"What is it?" another one rasped.

"Looks like another human," said a third.

"Yes!" Fort shouted, holding his staff in a defensive position, even if it was apparently useless at anything beyond healing. "I *am* human, and I'm not here to hurt you."

Several of the creatures laughed at that, which wasn't exactly comforting.

"You, hurt us?" one said, and a high-pitched whirling noise was the only warning Fort had before a wooden object slammed into his face, knocking him back to the ground.

He shook off the hit and immediately tried to push to his knees, but froze as something cold and sharp pushed into his neck. "I meant to say, I don't mean any harm," Fort said, wincing as the blade bit into his skin. "I came looking for another human, one older than me. Have you seen him?"

This time, one of them sighed, almost sadly.

"We know where he is, yeah," one of them said.

"But you don't want to see him," said another. "It's best you go before *they* find out you're here."

"If it's not already too late," said the first.

Fort gritted his teeth. Of all the people discouraging him from finding his father, the last beings he'd expected to do so were the monsters who'd taken him. "I'm not leaving without him."

"Then you're a fool," said one of the creatures. "We're trying to do right by you. But if they find out you're here, then we won't have a choice."

"They'll make us take you to Dragon's Teeth, just like we did the one you're looking for."

Dragon's Teeth? "Take me there!" Fort said, and tried to stand up, but the blade at his neck just pushed in harder, and he winced. "I have to find him, and I'll do anything. *Please* take me to Dragon's Teeth. See? I'm putting down my weapons and everything."

He laid his staff and bow down on the ground. For the first time he realized he must have lost his bag of protein bars somewhere in all the falling back in the cavern of the monsters, but that didn't matter, not if these things were going to take him to his father right away.

The red-eyed creatures went silent for a moment. "You can't be thinking of taking him," said a new voice, higher-pitched than the rest, if only slightly. "He doesn't know what he's asking. We have to let him go before they—"

"Quiet, boy," another said. "Those who haven't been through

the ritual haven't yet earned a say. I think the masters might be pleased if we take him to Dragon's Teeth. It'd be like our present to them. They might bless us."

"Those *masters* have only cursed you!" shouted the higher-pitched voice. "You're all fools if you don't see what those monsters have done to you."

The others growled in low, ugly tones. "Don't be talking about the Old Ones that way, whelp," one said.

"You haven't been through the ritual yet," another said, more kindly. "That's when your eyes will open fully. You'll understand when you're older."

"I understand more than you think," the young one said. "And I'm *not* going to help you take another human to Dragon's Teeth. Not again."

"Keep talking like this, and you'll be next," one of the older ones said.

This was rapidly getting out of hand, and the last thing Fort wanted was for the one creature sticking up for him to get punished. "It's okay!" he shouted. "There's no need to argue. I *want* to go. Just tell me where it is, and I'll come along quietly, I promise."

Back in the cavern, the monsters were roaring louder than

ever, and the red eyes around him started to notice. "What's got the Dracsi all riled up?" one asked. The blade bit into his neck again, and Fort hissed in pain. "Are there more of you, human? Tell the truth!"

"No, I promise, I'm alone," Fort said.

"Well, not exactly," said a voice that Fort really, *really* didn't want to hear right now.

Another fireball hit the ceiling, blinding him along with the red-eyed creatures this time. The blade disappeared from his neck as something swung over Fort's head, the wind tousling his hair. He ducked to avoid whatever it was, and watched one of the monsters go flying into a cave wall.

"More humans!" another shouted, only to get blasted backward by a bolt of lightning square in the chest. Somehow, the first bolt didn't seem to do much damage, but a second and third hit knocked the creature out.

"No," Fort whispered as another creature collapsed to the ground, vomiting everywhere like it'd just contracted some horrible disease. The rest tried to run, but the rocks on either side of the nearest tunnel pushed together, trapping them within.

"What *are* these things?" one of the red-eyed creatures shouted, only to get knocked backward, its eyes soaring much farther than a body should have. As another fireball lit the room, Fort saw the reason: The red eyes weren't eyes at all, but goggles of some kind, illuminated from within by the red light.

At this point, only one creature remained standing, the one with the spiked hammers. "Come on!" it shouted, whirling its hammers around, judging by the high-pitched whine they were making. "I'll take the lot of you on all by myself!"

Twin missiles of magical energy struck the hammers, disintegrating them.

The red eye . . . no, the goggle-wearing creature paused. "Um, okay, maybe not?" it said. "How do you feel about surrender?"

"Not real good," said the same familiar voice, and a shield shined in the remaining light as it slammed into the creature's face, knocking it out. The shield-bearer turned, lighting up his face for the first time.

"Hey, kid," Gabriel said, giving him a smile. "Nice to see you're making friends."

- TWENTY-EIGHT -

OH, PLEASE NO, FORT THOUGHT AS A fireball lit up the center of the room, floating in another newcomer's hand. He looked up to see Rachel glaring around angrily—fireball in hand—and Jia, leaning on a silver staff exactly like Fort's, looking ready to keep fighting. Gabriel leaned down and offered Fort his non-shield hand.

"Hey, you okay, Fort?" Gabriel asked, his smile fading into concern. "They didn't hurt you, did they?" He helped Fort to his feet and brushed some dirt off of his back.

"What were you thinking?" Rachel shouted. "You came here by yourself, after everything Cyrus told you?"

"He was just trying to keep you two safe," Gabriel said. "We can't fault him for that."

"Oh, I can!" Rachel said. "I can fault him for *days*."

"Do you think there are more of them?" Jia asked, glancing around the room. "Maybe I should go check that tunnel, in case some are hiding."

Rachel rolled her eyes. "You're not supposed to *enjoy* this sort of thing."

"Says the girl who takes guys down in practice and screams, 'That's what I'm talkin' about!' over them," Jia pointed out.

"How . . . how are you here?" Fort asked, finally getting the words out.

"How do you think?" Rachel said, glaring at him. "You're lucky I'm the forgiving type. In that I don't forgive you at *all*, but I'll still come after you and keep your sorry behind alive." She pulled a bag off of her shoulder and dropped it at Fort's feet.

The book of Summoning fell out, with his note on top.

"But . . . I haven't been gone *that* long," he said, still not believing this. "How did you find my note that quickly?"

"Oh, Rachel's been keeping an eye on you," Jia said. "She's been using—"

"Shh!" Rachel shushed, her eyes wide. "That's not important!"

Jia snorted, then pushed past Rachel. "Don't listen to her,

she's all embarrassed about this. She learned the first telepathy magic spell in the book of Mind magic, Detect Mind, when you brought the books to her. Basically she's had it going since that night, watching over you, making sure you didn't do anything crazy without us along."

"You were *watching* me?" Fort asked, both shocked and offended.

"I couldn't see anything!" Rachel said, and Fort could tell she was blushing a bit, even in the light of her fireball. "It just told me where you were. Or it *did*, until you started wearing that amulet. Where'd you even find that? I told Cyrus to make you get rid of it."

That was what Cyrus had been trying to tell him? "One of the TDA agents made me put it on," he said. "But that doesn't matter. I've been wearing it the whole time I was here. You couldn't have known."

"You took it off for a minute or so," Jia pointed out, over Rachel's shushing her. "That was the first time we saw you leave the school since you went to New York, so we knew you'd mastered teleportation. It took a little while to find out how to get to you—"

"Basically they came looking for you in our room, hoping to

find clues, and I told them where you practiced," Gabriel said. Fort gave him a betrayed look, but Gabriel shrugged it off. "Hey, you might be protecting *them*, but I'm watching out for *you*, roomie. You're not going to make *me* feel even an ounce bad about it, so don't bother."

"How annoying is teleportation, by the way?" Rachel said, rolling her eyes. "I knew you were below the old school, where you just left a dimensional portal wide open for anyone to walk right through, but because I'd never been down here, I had to teleport us all up to the base above, then tunnel down here using Destruction magic. That's why we took so long."

"I think we got those monsters all riled up," Jia said. "A few of them tried to grab for us while Rachel floated us down, before we worked out where you'd gone."

"Floated you?" Fort said to Rachel. "I knew you could make tornados, but I didn't know you could *fly*."

"We've had an interesting few days, me and Jia," Rachel said. "I'll tell you about it when you've apologized to me a few thousand times."

"Anyway, that's how we got here," Gabriel said, clapping Fort's shoulder. "And now that we're all together—"

"You can *leave* together," Fort finished for him. "You can't be here! If you stay, then . . . then bad things happen, okay? I know it for a fact. Cyrus—"

"Cyrus told us, too," Jia said. "Both what would happen if we came . . . or if you went alone."

"Yeah, nice try," Rachel said, glaring at him. "You think you're just going to leave us behind and get trapped here forever? We'd just spend the next few weeks trying to get you out, and probably all die trying."

"So, what, then?" Fort said. "You all just planned on showing up and carrying me back home, whether I wanted to go or not?"

"We *should*," Rachel said. "You deserve it. But first, we're going to do this." She leaned down and set her fireballs against the book of Summoning.

Fort started to stop her, but then paused and changed his mind. After everything he'd done, and now putting his friends in danger, this might be the right move. Besides, now there really was no way the Old Ones could get ahold of it.

"We, uh, never said we'd be doing that," Gabriel said, his voice low as he stared at Rachel.

"I don't remember needing to ask your permission," Rachel said, glaring at him.

"Rachel," Jia said, and began whispering to the other girl as Rachel tried waving her off.

"Fort," Gabriel said, turning back to him, though he still seemed annoyed about the book. "We talked about it, and we're with you," he said. "But none of us are going to get 'lost' here, or whatever Cyrus said. Because I have a plan."

"Oh, a *plan*," Fort said. "Those have gone so well for us in the past."

"Yeah, but this one Cyrus told me would work," Gabriel said. "But he also told me if I told any of you, that you'd mess it up, so I have to keep it to myself."

"Yeah, we didn't buy that either," Jia said as Rachel shook her head. "Still, we can't leave your dad here, Fort."

Fort just stared at his roommate in confusion. "What could you do that would get us all home safely that none of the rest of us thought of? Cyrus told me that there was no way, that it didn't matter *what* we did."

Gabriel punched his shoulder, giving Fort another bruise. "Guess I'm just more creative. Now let's get a move on. We're not going to rescue your dad just sitting around here."

Something groaned from the corner, and Gabriel immediately tensed up, running over with his shield. Jia got a crazy look in her eye and followed right behind him as Rachel just stared at her in shock. "She's losing her mind, but I kinda like it," she whispered to Fort.

"All of you are losing your minds," he told her, but moved quickly to see what was going on.

One of the red-goggled creatures was leaning against the wall. As Rachel brought her light closer, Fort saw that it wasn't a monster at all, but instead, looked almost . . . human. A short human, at least. With just the hint of a beard, and—

"They're *dwarves!*" Rachel shouted, bouncing up and down in excitement. "Are you seeing this? Real, actual, dwarves!" She sent her fireball flying around the room, revealing more of the creatures as it circled, then landing back in her hand. "Look at their beards! I wonder why they wear the goggles? This is so cool!" She leaned down and stared at the still-groaning dwarf, just inches from his face.

"Okay, let's not play with them," Jia said, pulling Rachel off of the dwarf.

Gabriel leaned in next, a curious look on his face. "Are they really dwarves? But why would they be here, with those monsters?"

Rachel shrugged. "We're underground, and that's sort of

a traditional dwarf place to live. Look." She pointed at the weapons strewn about the floor. "They've got pickaxes and stuff. Maybe they're miners. Lots of dwarves are."

"How do you know all of this?" Gabriel asked her.

"How do you *not*?" she said. "Isn't it common knowledge?" She leaned over and pulled Jia's hands back as the other girl started healing the dwarf. "Um, what are you doing?"

"Curing the disease I gave this one," Jia said, looking confused. "We can't just leave them here like this. What if they're hurt?"

"They tried to *kill us*," Rachel said.

"Only in self-defense," Jia pointed out. "Fort, were they hurting you before we got here?"

Fort shook his head. "Not really. Threatening a little. But some of them wanted me to escape, before their masters heard I was here." He shivered. "That's what they called the Old Ones."

Jia's hands flew into the air, the healing energy disappearing. "Okay, maybe we do just leave them as is. No one said anything about Old Ones."

Before Fort could respond, something below his shirt began to feel uncomfortably warm. He reached in and pulled out his amulet, which was getting hotter as he held it. "Look at this," he started to say to his friends, only to watch as Jia, Rachel, and Gabriel all gasped in pain and doubled over. "Whoa, what's going on?"

Rachel hissed in agony, looking up at him with terror in her eyes. "You can't . . . hear it?"

"It's . . . it's filling my *mind*!" Jia shouted, holding her head in both hands.

"What is?!" Fort shouted, but his friends all fell to their knees, still moaning in pain.

Not knowing what else to do, he quickly touched his staff to Jia first, then Rachel, and finally Gabriel. Each time, cold, blue magic passed into their heads, and they relaxed, suddenly free of whatever had been attacking them. As they did, his amulet went cold again, like whatever had been pushing against it had ceased.

"That's what those things feel like?" Gabriel said, sweating profusely.

"Now you see why I wanted to burn those books in the first place," Rachel told him.

"Will someone tell me what just happened?" Fort asked, positive he didn't really want to know the answer.

"It was just like the dwarf told you," Jia said, shaking her head. "That was an Old One in our heads, the one that possessed Damian. It knows we're here. And . . ."

"And they're coming for us," Rachel finished. "*All* of them."

- TWENTY-NINE -

YOU STILL HAVE TIME TO ESCAPE," A voice growled, and Fort turned to find the younger dwarf that Jia had just healed pushing himself up to a sitting position.

Gabriel was on him instantly, shield held ready to smash it against the dwarf's face. "What do you know about it?"

"That thing was just in my mind too," the dwarf said, wincing. "Didn't realize you all were so delicate. My kind have to listen to Ketas all the time. Maybe we're just used to the pain."

"Ketas?" Fort said. "Is that what you call the Old One?"

"That's his name," the dwarf said. "Or maybe his title. I don't know."

"What did it tell you?" Jia asked.

The dwarf looked up at them for a moment, then sighed.

"To capture the humans. They want you waiting for them in Dragon's Teeth when they arrive."

Gabriel nodded and pulled back the shield to strike.

"Wait!" Fort shouted, jumping between him and the dwarf. "He wouldn't have just told us that if he planned on doing it." He threw a look over his shoulder at the dwarf. "Um, right?"

"I told you to leave, didn't I?" the dwarf grumbled. "You've got a little time before they get here, so I'd use it. Otherwise, Q'baos will take your will, just like she took the will of my people, and will soon have mine."

Gabriel narrowed his eyes but slowly lowered the shield. "How long do we have?"

"Half a feeding cycle, maybe," the dwarf said. "The elders say they used to travel instantly via flaming circles, but they must have forgotten how, because those haven't been seen for as far back as anyone can remember."

"How long is a feeding cycle?" Rachel asked. "Preferably in minutes or hours?"

Now it was the dwarf's turn to look suspicious. "Those are measurements *they* use, the Old Ones. How do you know of them?"

"We're from the same place they are," Fort told him. "And they want us to take them back."

The dwarf seemed to think about this for a moment. "I'd say you have three, maybe four of those hours then," he said finally. "Why, did you plan on doing some sightseeing?"

"Nope, we're leaving *right now*," Rachel said, pulling on Fort's uniform.

"You said you took the last human to Dragon's Teeth," Fort said, yanking his shirt out of her hand. "Could you take *us* there in that amount of time?"

The dwarf looked at him strangely. "You *want* me to take you where the Old Ones commanded?"

"Yeah, I'm with him!" Rachel shouted. "Are you joking?"

"That's where they took my dad, too," Fort told her. Turning back to the dwarf, he leaned down and extended a hand to him. The dwarf eyed it suspiciously for a moment, then reached up and took it, letting Fort help him to his feet.

"I'll take you, if that's your wish," the dwarf said. "But I promise, you'll wish you'd fled while you had the chance. I only just missed the Ritual when the last human arrived because I was a few cycles too young still. Now I have no choice but to attend, and Q'baos will destroy my will, and yours along with it."

"She's another Old One?" Jia asked. "What's her specialty?"

"All I've seen her do is turn my people into servants, worshipping her with all their spirit," the dwarf said, spitting on the ground. "If she has more power than that, she wouldn't need it."

"That's the magic they used on us back at the old school," Rachel whispered to Fort. "When that Old One with the screaming faces on it took over all the Healing students."

Great. So not only did they have to worry about the Old One who used Mind magic, apparently named Ketas, but also one who knew . . . wait, the dwarf had said she took over his people's spirits. Was that the sixth kind of magic? The power to not just take over a mind, but change them into willing slaves permanently?

"Fort, we can't take the chance," Jia said, coming up alongside Rachel. "Last time, one Old One nearly killed us all. The others never even made it fully through the portal. We won't have a chance against all of them together."

"She's right, we have to go *now*," Rachel said.

"No, we don't," Gabriel said, moving to stand next to Fort. "This dwarf will take us to Fort's father, and then Fort can teleport us back to the portal. We can do this. And we're not leaving without trying."

"What do you keep calling me?" the dwarf asked. "A de-wharf?"

"No!" Rachel shouted, shaking her head. "How do you all not get this? It's not just us in danger. If we leave the portal open, they might find it before we're back! We're not taking that chance, no matter what." She turned to Fort, and her face softened a bit. "Look, I know how hard this is, but you can't put the whole world at risk for . . . you know, for . . ."

"For my father?" Fort asked quietly. "Watch me."

He turned toward the dwarf. "Which way to Dragon's Teeth?"

The dwarf pointed toward one of the tunnels. "There. But what did you call me again? It sounded WHOA!"

Gabriel grabbed the dwarf in midsentence and threw him over his shoulder. "I'm with Fort," he said to Rachel and Jia. "If it makes you feel better, go back to the portal and guard it. If the Old Ones show up before we do, then just collapse the cavern. We'll find another way out."

Rachel growled loudly in frustration, while Jia sighed and walked over to join Fort and Gabriel. "They'll have a better chance if we go with them," she said.

"You've got to be kidding me!" Rachel shouted. She turned to walk away, then stopped, started moving again, then slammed her foot against the ground a few times. Finally, she shot a fireball off toward the ceiling, watched it explode while shouting insults, then finally came back to the others. "Let's get this done *quickly*," she growled. "The moment we get even a hint that the Old Ones are close, we teleport back to the portal, Fort. Do you understand me?"

Fort nodded, unable to hide his smile. "I do. And thank—"

"NO," she said. "Don't you dare. Come, dwarf, lead the way."

"My kind are called Dracsi-kin," the dwarf said. "And *I* have a name."

"What's your name?" Jia asked.

"What's a Dracsi?" Gabriel asked.

"Don't answer either of them!" Rachel said. "Let's *go!*"

"I am Sikurgurd," the dwarf said as Gabriel carried him toward the tunnel he'd pointed out earlier. "And Dracsi are the large beasts you must have seen as you arrived. You know, big teeth, scales, that sort of thing. The Old Ones named us Dracsi-kin because we were made by D'hea to care for them. We haven't been allowed any other life, and the Old Ones ensure we never rebel with the Ritual."

"That's when the *Q* one takes your spirit?" Jia asked.

"Q'baos," the dwarf confirmed. "Dracsi-kin who have mastered their inner control of magic are forced to take the Ritual. I hadn't yet finished my apprenticeship when the last human arrived, and—"

"Tell us about *him*," Fort said. "The human you said was taken to the Dragon's Teeth. Is he okay? What happened to him?"

Sikurgurd seemed to shrug, but it was hard to tell with him hanging upside down behind Gabriel. "I don't know. Only those at the Ritual could have told you."

"Was the human alone?" Gabriel asked.

"Strange that you should ask," the dwarf said. "I've heard different stories. Some say it was just one, but others claim there was a human closer to our size—"

"Fort!" Jia shouted as Gabriel immediately came to a halt. "That could be Michael!"

Michael? He'd been a fourth student, back at the original school at the NSA. Damian, Sierra, Jia, and Michael, Colonel Charles's son who'd been studying Destruction magic, and who was also . . . oh wow.

"Yeah, the monsters took him also," Jia said, confirming what he was thinking. "If there's a chance he's still . . . we have to bring him back too, Fort!"

243

"Does anyone else remember that there are horrible tentacle monsters on their way as we speak?" Rachel asked. "Just me? No one else, then? That's what I thought."

"I agree with the excited human," Sikurgurd said. "You are all doomed."

"*Thank* you!" Rachel said. "Now are we at least getting close to this Teeth place?"

The dwarf nodded in the direction they were going. "We'll pass through the city up ahead, and then hit the mines on the other side. There are carts leading down to Dragon's Teeth. We don't mine there anymore, so if we can get that far, you'll be safe from my people. The city, on the other hand, won't be easy to pass. Every elder Dracsi-kin is hoping to please Q'baos by finding you themselves."

Rachel covered her mouth to scream relatively silently, while Fort just leaned toward the dwarf. "Sikurgurd, you know, if we get out of here, you could come with us," he said. "We can't just leave you here to . . . to have your spirit taken from you."

For the first time, the dwarf's eyes lit up as brightly as his goggles had. "I'd *never* leave my people," Sikurgurd said, looking ready to strike Fort. "I'd sooner cut off an arm, or feed myself to a Dracsi!"

"Can't you fight them?" Gabriel asked, resuming their forward motion.

"We have few Dracsi-kin young enough as it is," Sikurgurd said. "And our elders would defend Q'baos and the other Old Ones to their deaths if need be. We'd be forced to fight our own families, and so are trapped."

"Hey, I think I see lights up ahead," Jia said, pointing past Gabriel.

"That is Dra, my city," Sikurgurd said, sounding a bit proud. "It's not the largest of our settlements, but it *is* the deepest."

"How big are we talking?" Gabriel asked him. "You said it'd be hard to sneak by."

"As I said, we have a smaller population than others," the dwarf said. "Still, I would imagine we wouldn't have to deal with more than ten or twenty million of my kin before we reach the mines."

- THIRTY -

ILLION?!" RACHEL SAID.

"There are another one or two million young ones," Sikurgurd said. "They won't be a problem for us, so that's something."

"Not really!" she responded.

Fort wasn't feeling much better than Rachel about the whole thing, but he pushed Gabriel to continue on. It didn't matter if there were two hundred or twenty million dwarves waiting for them. Somehow, they'd find a way through any obstacle . . .

"Whoops," Gabriel said, coming to a stop as he rounded the corner. "The way's blocked."

Fort looked past him to find a gate made of lightning, the same one he'd seen in his dreams. Ten or fifteen bolts of lightning arced across the exit from the tunnel, any one of which had enough power to stop their hearts dead.

"Oh, don't worry about that," Sikurgurd said. "I told you, I learned how to control magic. I can open it."

Gabriel gently set him down on the tunnel floor, and for a moment, the dwarf looked a bit dizzy. "Head rush," he said, leaning against the wall. "I'll be all right."

Rachel began tapping her foot impatiently.

Sikurgurd quickly recovered, then approached the gate of lightning, his hands held out before him like he was trying to calm a wild animal. As he neared it, he slowed to a stop and closed his eyes, moving his hands in elaborate gestures.

First one, then more of the lightning bolts began to flicker, then die as Sikurgurd moved his hands up and down the gate, until finally the way was clear.

"How did you do that?" Rachel asked him in amazement. "I can create lightning, but I'm nowhere near good enough to be able to control it like that."

"Oh, I can't create it," the dwarf told her, waving them through. "None of my kind can. D'hea created us without the ability, and instead, made us fairly resistant to magic of all kinds." He beat his hand against his chest. "Makes dealing with the Dracsi much easier, after all. But we still needed to control magic, for the lightning if nothing else." He nodded back down the way they came. "It's required to feed the Dracsi, so D'hea made sure we could still manipulate magic, even if we couldn't cast it ourselves."

Fort would have loved to have asked Sikurgurd a thousand follow-up questions, but now wasn't the time. "Shouldn't we be quiet?" he asked instead. "I thought we'd reached the city."

"Oh, we should be safe while we're in the tunnels," Sikurgurd told him. "There's not another group of feeders scheduled for a while."

As they passed the gate, the dwarf released his hold on the lightning, letting it cascade back across the tunnel, closing off their exit. With no real choice, Fort led the others around a corner, then stopped abruptly, throwing out his arms to keep the others from falling as he almost had.

He and his father had once walked on a glass path that over-hung the Grand Canyon, standing over a mile above the canyon floor. Nothing felt like it could possibly go deeper than that, at the time.

But now, Fort stood on the edge of a dimly lit cavern that had to extend for dozens, maybe *hundreds* of miles below him, with masses of Dracsi-kin milling about each and every level down as far as he could see.

Lightning tubes began at their height, and ran up, down, diagonally, and in every other direction, connecting both to the gate behind them, and continuing on from there. Elaborate crystal gondolas ran throughout the cavern along some of the tubes, zooming up or down along with the lightning, only to coast as the electricity passed, waiting for the next bolt to strike.

And everything was covered in gold, silver, and gems of all kinds. The city of Dra had to be one of the richest in existence, if you went by rare minerals. But the dwarves weren't collecting or hoarding the gold and jewels; instead, they'd built with them, using gold for roofs and creating elaborate decorations with gemstones.

The biggest display of wealth lay in the middle of the cavern, rising all the way up to their level from potentially the bottom floor. From what Fort could tell from the random lightning blazing by, it looked like a sculpture. From here, he could make out the very top of a human or dwarf head, so enormous that Fort could barely see down to its forehead. That meant the sculpture could be an entire body or more, depending on how far down it extended.

The strangest, most wonderful part of it all was that the sculpture was made entirely of diamond.

"Welcome to Dra, humans," Sikurgurd declared almost sadly. He gestured across the open cavern before them. "The tunnel to the mines is directly across from us, but there's no way to get there without descending into the city first."

Fort looked where he'd pointed, and slowly filled with despair. The cavern had to be at least a few miles across, and getting there while avoiding an entire city full of dwarves couldn't be done, not in the time they had.

"I'm sure it's not as fancy as human cities," Sikurgurd was saying. "We've heard tales of you using something called 'wod' to build, making your homes out of living things." He sighed. "I would love to see that. No Dracsi-kin has ever seen wod, alive or dead. It must be magnificent."

"Yeah, wood's pretty amazing," Jia said. "What's that statue in the middle?"

"That would be Q'baos," Sikurgurd said, his face contorting in disgust. "The city of Dra was built on the site of the very first mine for the Dracsi, but the substance of the statue can't be digested by them, so instead, the miners created a tribute to Q'baos as they dug, merging all the useless gems into it as they went."

Fort had a similar reaction to Sikurgurd's as he realized that what he thought was a forehead was actually a screaming human face, just like he'd seen on the Old One back at the previous Oppenheimer School. "How can you merge two diamonds?" he asked. That didn't seem possible.

Sikurgurd appeared confused. "Any child can do it. Diamond is as malleable as every other substance left to us by D'vale, who created this place. All you do is—"

"Wait, you're saying an Old One created this place?" Jia asked. "But why?"

"For the Dracsi," Sikurgurd said, sounding even more confused now. "Haven't I mentioned? We were brought here to care for them, once they were changed into their present form. The Dracsi have only ever been able to digest metallic minerals, so we mine the gold and silver to feed them. Whatever we have left, we use to house ourselves." He sighed. "The Dracsi would be perfectly able to feed themselves, if we let them out of their caves. They're better diggers than we are, and prefer the heat of the underrealms anyway. Helps them digest their food."

"Can't they just . . . escape?" Jia asked. "There didn't seem to be much holding them back when we saw them."

"D'vale infused their cave prisons with some kind of magic to keep them confined," Sikurgurd explained. "There are thousands of them down here in the underrealms, and obviously they're very strong. But the magic in the rocks keeps them trapped, so if we didn't care for them, they'd not live very long."

"Okay, *enough*," Rachel said, shaking her head. "There's no way we can cross this whole city, not in a few hours. We have to turn back."

"Can we take one of these lightning carriages?" Gabriel asked, looking down into the city. "They move pretty fast."

"You'd be fighting your way through hordes of my kind," Sikurgurd said. "People are headed to their daily tasks now, so the carriages are always full. Four went by before I could even get on one when I was on my way here.."

"Fort, *think* about this," Rachel said, looking him in the eye. "Do you really want the Old Ones to return because of you? Would . . . would your father—"

"*Don't,*" he growled, cutting her off. "Don't . . . just don't."

She sighed. "You're right, that was too far. But still, we can't just—"

"We won't put anyone in danger," Fort said, turning around so he didn't have to look at her. "But we can't go back now. We *can't.*"

"What about using the Teleport spell?" Jia asked.

Gabriel shook his head. "It doesn't work like that. You can only teleport if you've seen the location you're going to. And even from here, I can't make out that tunnel."

He was right. There was no way they could open a teleportation circle, not without at least some kind of telescope or something. If only Fort could have read Sikurgurd's mind, and seen what the mining tunnel looked like. Or . . .

Or seen it in a dream?

Fort's eyes widened, and he turned back to his friends. "Jia, that actually might work."

Gabriel gave him a questioning look as Fort quickly cast a teleportation circle on the wall next to them. It opened into darkness, but Fort didn't wait for Rachel to light it, and quickly stepped through.

He emerged into a long, dark tunnel, dimly lit on one side by light filtering through some vertical rock formations that more than anything resembled the teeth of a dragon.

"It's okay, you can come through," he whispered back through the teleportation circle. "I got us here."

Gabriel was first through the circle and looked around in amazement. "But how? You've never been here."

"Not physically," Fort said. "But it looks like I've had some pretty realistic dreams of it."

He didn't add what he'd seen at the end of the tunnel in those dreams, the thing that terrified him almost as much as the Old Ones.

But whatever was there, they'd handle it. Because after almost eight months, he had *finally* caught up to his father, and nothing was going to stop Fort from bringing him back home.

"I told you not to come here," Sikurgurd said, watching them from the other side of the teleportation circle.

"You were right," Rachel said as she stepped through after Jia. "What's in here, anyway?"

The dwarf just looked at them sadly. "It's called Dragon's Teeth. What do *you* think?"

A long, low growl echoed through the tunnel, shaking the ground beneath their feet with its power.

A small movement out of the corner of Fort's eye caught his attention, and he saw Jia reach out and squeeze Rachel's hand supportively. He hadn't realized how close they'd gotten since coming to the new school.

"I'm sorry about this," Sikurgurd said as they all stared down the tunnel. "I really am. But if the Old Ones can go back to your home, maybe they'll leave my people in peace."

His words made Fort move, but it was already too late. Sikurgurd had his eyes closed and was slowly closing his hands together. "Hey!" Fort shouted, and leaped for the teleportation circle, but it closed as he reached it, with the dwarf on the other side.

"Betrayed again," Rachel said, glaring at Fort. "Does he not realize we can just open another circle?"

"That's what makes me nervous," Fort said. He attempted to open a circle back to where they'd just come from. The magic filled his hands, but just like when he'd tried to teleport somewhere he hadn't seen, no circle opened.

"Um, why aren't you teleporting?" Jia asked, sounding a bit panicky.

The ground shook with another growl as Fort turned to his friends sadly. "Because I *can't*. I think we're trapped here."

- THIRTY-ONE -

WE'RE *WHAT*?" RACHEL SHOUTED. "*This* is why I said we shouldn't come. Among the other reasons, all of which are still valid!"

Fort winced. "I think we should probably be quiet," he whispered. "If that really *is* a dragon down there, we don't want it to know we're here."

"DO YOU IMAGINE I CANNOT HEAR YOU, HUMAN?" said a voice so powerful it shook dust from the ceiling.

They all stared at one another for a moment before Gabriel nodded and turned to walk toward the voice.

"What are you *doing*?" Rachel hissed at him.

"I'm going to see if that's really what we think it is," Gabriel said. "And if it is, I want to know if it's the last one."

Their conversation back in the skeleton room came flooding

back to Fort, and he wondered again who might have been visiting Gabriel in his dreams. If he'd heard the Old One too, what had the creature offered him?

Fort hurried after him, with Rachel and Jia right behind. "We need to be smart about this," Jia whispered. "Remember how they found the books of magic? Humans were riding dragons. That means we were allies somehow."

"Or we used them as horses," Rachel murmured.

Another growl shook the tunnel, this one the most intense yet. Jia glared at Rachel, who put up her hands in surrender. "Okay, okay, no more snarky comments!"

The tunnel was just like Fort remembered it from his dream. As they continued on, they started to see small golden stones lying on the ground. Picking one up, Jia showed it to them in surprise. "Um. This is *actual* gold."

"And it belongs to someone," Rachel told her, nodding in the direction of the growling. "Maybe leave it there for now?"

"I GROW IMPATIENT, HUMANS." The voice shook the tunnel again, sending gold nuggets rolling back down the tunnel. It was the very same voice he'd heard in his nightmare, speaking to his father. "I WILL WAIT NO LONGER."

Instantly, Fort's body froze in place, no matter how hard

he struggled to move. Everything immediately went dark as Rachel's fireball extinguished, but from the groaning Fort heard nearby, he suspected he wasn't the only one paralyzed. Air rushed around him as he felt his body rise into the air, out of his control, and begin floating along the tunnel at a dangerously fast speed. Without any light, though, there was no way of telling exactly what was happening.

That was, until he and the others emerged from the tunnel into the same cavern Fort had seen his father in.

The mounds of gold here rose several stories high in the air, lit only by a red glow coming from the center of the room. That glow filled Fort with a terror just like he'd felt when he first saw the Old One floating above the floor in the officers' mess at the old school. He wanted to look away as he rose toward the glow, but he still had no control over his own body. He couldn't even close his eyes.

As the gold fell away below him, Fort found himself staring into the gigantic red eyes of a beast as large as an airplane, covered in golden scales and curled lazily up around another pile of nuggets. Its wings flexed, sending mountains of gold flying, and it slowly moved its head closer to get a better look at them.

It was then that Fort noticed a second, less intense light glowing in the dragon's hand, and his shock almost overwhelmed his fear, if just for a moment.

The dragon's claws shone with a rich blue glow, the same light as Healing magic.

"DO YOU KNOW WHO I AM?" it asked them, and Fort felt the paralysis leave his face, letting him speak.

Fort's mouth felt dry as a desert, but he swallowed a few times until he found he could speak. "I think I do," he said, his voice cracking.

"I AM D'HEA," the dragon said, snaking its head up and around them, moving out of Fort's sight. "I AM THE CREATOR OF DRAGONKIND, FATHER TO THOSE BORN OF PURE MAGIC. I AM THE CREATOR OF THE DRACSI AND THEIR KIN, CURSED BY MY BRETHREN TO DO SO. AND I AM THE FORGOTTEN ONE, DOOMED TO REMAIN WITHIN THIS TOMB FOR ALL ETERNITY."

"You're an Old One," Fort whispered. "The Old One of Healing magic."

"Oh *no*," Jia whispered from his side.

"HEALING?" The dragon began to laugh, sending golden nuggets tumbling off their mounds. "YOU HUMANS NEVER UNDERSTOOD MAGIC. THAT IS WHY YOU *STOLE* IT

FROM MY CHILDREN, LEARNING SECRETS THAT WERE NEVER INTENDED FOR YOU!"

"We didn't steal magic!" Rachel shouted, and Fort was thankful that she, at least, wasn't intimidated by the creature. "We're here to find someone, not take anything."

"My father was here," Fort said. "I saw him in a dream. You were speaking to him."

The dragon's head came circling back to stare at Fort. He sniffed loudly, pulling them all forward momentarily, only to fall back into place when he was through. "YOU DO SMELL LIKE ONE OF THE LAST HUMANS I SAW," he said.

"One of?" Gabriel said. "Was there another?"

"His name was Michael—" Jia said, but the dragon snapped his jaws, sending jets of fire exploding into the air to either side of his snout. "DO NOT MAKE DEMANDS UPON ME, HUMAN. IF I WOULD NOT SUFFER FURTHER FOR DOING SO, I WOULD RIP YOU APART FOR MY CHILDREN'S SAKE. YOU DO NOT KNOW WHAT YOUR BETRAYAL OF THEM DID!"

"We didn't betray the dragons," Jia said, sounding as scared as Fort felt. "They were helping humans. We've seen proof. They were allies!"

"LIES!" the dragon screeched, loud enough to set Fort's head pounding. "I CREATED MANY CREATURES, BUT MY GREATEST ACCOMPLISHMENT WAS THE DRAGONKIND. INSTEAD OF EVOLVING THEM FROM ANOTHER BEING, I PULLED THEM FROM MAGIC ITSELF, GIVING LIFE TO SOMETHING THAT HAD NONE BEFORE. IT WAS THE ULTIMATE FORM OF CORPOREAL MAGIC!"

"We didn't do anything to them!" Rachel shouted. "You really think we tiny humans would be able to hurt a dragon? Like you said, we can barely use magic to begin with!"

"AND ALL THAT YOU KNOW WAS SHARED WITH YOU BY THE DRAGONS," the Old One, D'hea, said. "YOU WOULD STILL BE SERVING MY BRETHREN IF NOT FOR MY CHILDREN. YET YOU STILL EXIST. WHERE ARE THEY? WHAT HAPPENED TO MY DRAGONS?" He turned and roared, shooting fire from his mouth hot enough to melt an entire mound of gold. "THEY ARE GONE, BECAUSE THEY SIDED WITH HUMANITY AGAINST MY BROTHERS AND SISTERS!"

In spite of his fear and the heat of the fire, Fort almost couldn't believe what he was hearing. Humans had learned magic from dragons? Could that really be true? The Old One of Mind magic, the one the dwarf called Ketas, had said something about humanity serving the creatures. Had dragons broken that servitude?

And if so, had they paid for it with their lives?

"What if there was *another* dragon?" Gabriel asked, and the creature whipped his head around toward the older boy. "One of the Old Ones came to me in a dream and offered me something if I gave them the last dragon. Are you interested in that information too?"

So they *had* come to Gabriel too? But what had he been offered?

"THERE *ARE* NO MORE DRAGONS!" the dragon roared, sending fire shooting out again around the cavern. "MY BRETHREN MADE SURE OF THAT!"

"You're wrong," Gabriel said. "But if you let us go, and give us back his father and my brother, then I'll tell you the whereabouts of the last dragon. Because I know *exactly* where it is."

THIRTY-TWO

GABRIEL'S WORDS SEEMED TO SHOCK the dragon just as much as they did Fort and the others. His brother had been taken as well? That could only mean—

"*You're* Michael's brother?" Jia whispered as the dragon turned away in silence. "Then you're also Colonel Charles's son? But I thought your last name was Torrance?"

"He's my stepfather," Gabriel said, sneering. "My brother took his name, but I never will. That man sent Mike to learn magic when he wasn't ready, took him from me. I'll never forgive him for that."

Suddenly a lot of Fort's questions about his roommate were answered. That explained why Gabriel was getting special treatment from everyone, since his father was in charge of the school. His tour of the skeleton room now also made sense, as he'd probably been at the school before they'd even arrived.

And he *had* been having the same dreams Fort had. But had Gabriel known what Fort had planned? There was no way he could have . . . except that he knew Fort had stolen one of the books of magic, and if he was Colonel Charles's son, it probably wasn't that hard to figure out which one.

All this time, he'd had so much more in common with Gabriel than he'd ever known. They'd both had loved ones taken by the Dracsi and would do anything to get them back.

Part of him wished he'd known all along, so he could have talked to Gabriel about it. The other boy could have shared at any point but hadn't wanted to for some reason. There had to still be more to it.

And how on earth could Gabriel ever know the location of the last dragon, even if there really was one? They'd talked about it in the skeleton room, but he hadn't said he *knew* of one. Or was he bluffing?

"YOU MUST BE LYING," the dragon said finally, whirling around to glare at them. "IF ANY OF MY CHILDREN YET EXISTED, I WOULD KNOW. THEIR FATE IS WELL KNOWN TO ME, AND NONE ESCAPED!"

"I'm not lying," Gabriel said. "Use your magic to confirm it, I don't care. If you don't want him, then I'll give him to the Old One with the tentacles. He was willing to give me my brother for it."

The dragon sneered. "KETAS. HE WAS THE ONE WHO EXACTED MY FAMILY'S REVENGE UPON ME, FORCING ME TO CHANGE MY CHILDREN INTO THE MONSTERS THEY ARE NOW."

"You did something to the dragons?" Jia asked. "What did you . . . wait, the *Dracsi*?"

"YES, THE CURSED DRACSI WERE ONCE MY DRAGONKIND," the Old One said, whipping his tail about in sadness and rage. "KETAS CONTROLLED MY MIND AND USED MY POWERS TO EVOLVE THEM INTO THOSE MINDLESS BEASTS, A WEAPON HE AND THE OTHERS USED AGAINST HUMANITY.

"BUT YOUR KIND USED THE MAGIC MY CHILDREN TAUGHT YOU AND EXILED US FROM OUR HOME. AND NOW, WHENEVER AN OUTSIDER IS BROUGHT, KETAS USES ME AGAIN TO TURN THE OFFENDER INTO A NEW DRACSI, REPLENISHING THEIR RANKS."

Fort's eyes widened. The dragon created Dracsi out of any outsiders? If that was true, then—

"You turned my brother into one of those . . . those *monsters*?!" Gabriel roared, his muscles bulging as he struggled against the magic holding him in place. "If you hurt him, I'll spend every last day of my life *hunting you down*—"

The dragon turned to him, his hand glowing, and Gabriel's body stretched out until it was flat, then compressed to the size of a mouse, only to grow back to normal height a moment later, leaving the boy stunned and silent.

"I AM MASTER OF CORPOREAL MAGIC, WORM," the dragon said. "YOU THINK I INFLICT PAIN FOR THE PLEASURE OF IT? I CAN MANIPULATE A LIVING BODY IN ANY WAY I WISH, AND CAUSE AS MUCH OR AS LITTLE DISTRESS AS I REQUIRE. IF YOU SPEAK TO ME IN SUCH WAYS, I WILL ILLUSTRATE IT AGAIN, THIS TIME CAUSING EVERY NERVE IN YOUR BODY TO FLARE IN PAIN."

". . . I'm sorry," Gabriel said, catching his breath. "I shouldn't have said that. But our deal still stands. I know where there's a dragon on Earth. My friend has Summoning magic, and he can use it to take you there."

"Um, Gabriel, maybe don't give everything away?" Rachel hissed.

"I HAVE SAID THAT NO DRAGONS LIVE ON IN THEIR TRUE FORM," the Old One said. "IF YOU DON'T LIE, THEN MY BRETHREN DID."

"Why would they?" Fort asked, not sure if Gabriel was telling the truth or not, but it seemed like their best shot now. "They could have asked us for the book of Summoning, or for us to just open a portal, and that would have gotten them back to Earth. But they didn't, they wanted the last dragon. Why lie?"

The dragon whipped his tail again in frustration. "THERE CANNOT BE ANY MORE DRAGONS! IF ONE OF MY CHILDREN WERE LEFT BEHIND, ALONE, IN DANGER . . . I CANNOT EVEN CONSIDER THE POSSIBILITY!"

"Don't think about the dangers it was in," Fort said, his father's image in his head. "Just imagine what it'd be like to have your child back! And we can give that to you, if you give us back our humans."

"And let us go!" Rachel said.

The dragon sneered. "YOUR KIND ALWAYS DID

BELIEVE THEY WERE SUPERIOR TO THEIR WORTH.
YOU ARE AS TRAPPED HERE AS I AM! NO MAGIC
CAN PENETRATE THESE WALLS. EVEN IF YOU HAVE
THE POWER OF SPACE MAGIC, IT WILL DO YOU NO
GOOD, NOT WHILE MY PRISON STANDS. D'VALE
HERSELF BUILT THIS CAVERN, AND ONLY HER
POWER CAN OPEN ITS GATES."

D'vale? The dwarf had mentioned that name. She was the
Old One who made the lightning. Which meant she was—

"Destruction magic!" Rachel shouted. "I can do that! I can
get us out of here!"

"DESTRUCTION? HER POWER IS THAT OF THE
ELEMENTS, HUMAN! YOU WARP ITS MEANING TO
YOUR SIMPLE ENDS."

"Yes, I warp its meaning, sure, but I can crack us through
these walls, if that's what it takes!" Rachel said. "Just let us go,
and I'll get us right out of here! And then you'll be free to go
looking for this dragon yourself, maybe."

"I'll take you there," Gabriel said. "Just as soon as I have my
brother back safe and sound."

"And my father," Fort added.

The dragon pondered this for a moment. Out of nowhere,

control of his body returned to Fort, and he gently floated down to the floor, near one of the walls. "SHOW ME YOUR POWER, LITTLE HUMAN," the dragon said to Rachel, climbing over the nearby mound of gold. "TEAR DOWN THE WALL THAT D'VALE CREATED, AND I SHALL CONSIDER YOUR BARGAIN."

"Okay, give me a second," Rachel shouted up at him, then turned to Fort and moved in close. "Is Gabriel telling the truth?" she whispered. "I don't care *what* this thing looks like, it's still an Old One. If we bring it back to Earth, there'll be no stopping it. You saw what it did to Gabriel."

"We'll figure something out," he whispered back.

"Oh, perfect," she said, looking sick. "Improvising has gone so well for us in the past."

She walked over to the wall and began to concentrate, as Gabriel took her place. "We're going to make this work, no matter what it takes," he said to Fort. "I need to know you're with me."

Fort looked at his roommate, now someone completely different than he'd thought. "I want my father back, and you know what I'm willing to do." He leaned in close. "Do you really know where the last dragon is?"

Gabriel nodded. "I'm not going to say where, in case the Old One is listening. But my father has it trapped. He captured it a few days ago and won't shut up about it."

"He captured a dragon?" Fort said incredulously.

"Like I told you before, it's the last dragon: What makes you think it isn't hiding as something else?"

"So it's human?"

"Dr. Opps is the one who told my father what it really is," Gabriel said. "Dad doesn't believe him, because he's a fool. But once we get my brother and your dad back, we'll bring the Old One over to the good colonel, and let those two discuss what it is. And then they can work it out between themselves who gets to *keep* it."

THIRTY-THREE

WHAT IS TAKING SO LONG, HUMAN?" the dragon asked Rachel. She had both of her hands pushing against the cavern wall, the red glow emanating from her fingers lighting up the nearby gold. "ARE YOU UNABLE TO ACCOMPLISH THIS SIMPLE TASK?"

"I've . . . *got it*," she groaned, then flashed Fort a look. He quickly ran over to her and leaned in close.

"So listen," she whispered, sweat running down her face. "This might . . . be harder than . . . I thought. There's . . . something in the rock . . . that eats any magic . . . that you send at it."

Fort nodded, even though he had no idea what she was talking about. "But you just said you can handle it."

She glared at him. "That was . . . so that thing didn't . . . *eat* us. But I might . . . have an idea."

She let go of the wall and turned back to the dragon. "Don't worry!" she yelled, wiping the sweat from her forehead. "Should only be another minute at most!"

"IF IT IS MUCH LONGER, MY BRETHREN SHALL ARRIVE, AND I WILL BE FORCED TO TURN YOU ALL INTO DRACSI," the dragon said, not sounding particularly bothered by that.

"She's got it!" Fort shouted up, then leaned back in. "So, um, what's the idea?"

She made a face. "Dr. Opps and Dr. Ambrose have had us . . . experimenting. You know, like you did against that Ketas Old One thing, made up that Cause Great Harm spell or whatever it was using the spell words you knew, and trying to say something else with them?"

"Yeah, Sebastian mentioned that," Fort said.

In spite of the situation, she smiled. "He's so bitter, he's not working with us now. But forget him. One of the spells I found, it uses my magic missile spell . . . in a different way. It fills something with magic, instead of shooting it."

"I get it!" Fort said, a bit too loudly. She shushed him, and he leaned back in. "So you're going to feed whatever's in the wall so much magic it can't handle it all!"

"That's what I'm going to try," she said. "Unfortunately, last time I did this, I exploded the whole lab." She took in another deep breath. "If Jia hadn't been nearby, Dr. Opps and I wouldn't be around anymore."

Fort shook his head. "Then we come up with another way. I have a little tiny hammer that might break the rock, and—"

This made Rachel snort and begin to laugh. "Okay, thank you for that," she said. "But seriously, you know how Cyrus . . . he said one of us would be lost?" She winced. "I think this is what I'm here to do."

"What?!" Fort said. "No way. We'll think of something else. I can't let you—"

"I just wanted to tell you that I know why you did all of this," she said, ignoring him. "And while you're completely wrong and made terrible choices, I forgive you. Because I get it. If it'd been my mom or dad . . . well. I'd be right here too."

"You're *not* doing this!" Fort said, and grabbed for her arm to pull her away from the wall, but she just raised a hand and a gust of wind knocked him off his feet, sending him careening across the cavern floor. "No!" he shouted as he hit a pile of gold and came to a stop.

"Everyone stay back!" Rachel shouted, and turned back

273

to the wall, her hands glowing much brighter now. "Jia, be ready!"

The red glow began flowing into the wall, only to disappear as fast as it arrived. Rachel groaned in pain, and the flow intensified, becoming too bright to look at.

"Rachel, stop this!" Fort shouted, pushing to his feet, but Gabriel grabbed him before he could go to her.

"She's going to be okay!" Gabriel told him. "Just let her do it."

"You don't know that!" Fort shouted, trying to get free, but Gabriel just tightened his hold.

"I *do* know that," his roommate said quietly. "I told you, I have a plan, and Cyrus confirmed it. She's not going to be hurt!"

Rachel started to scream, and her whole body glowed with the same red light of Destruction magic. But now the light was slowly filling the wall as well, which bulged and pulsated grotesquely, like it might explode at any minute.

"Everyone get down!" she yelled, and Gabriel pushed Fort to the ground, covering them both with his shield. A blue glow lit up the side of the cavern suddenly, but it was quickly overwhelmed by another burst of red, and then the wall exploded.

Rock went flying everywhere, and Fort shouted Rachel's name over and over, but no one responded. A stone larger than Gabriel struck his shield, only to bounce off, its protective magic saving them from being crushed. Dust cascaded into the cavern, dropping a cloud over everything that made it even harder to see.

"Rachel?!" Fort yelled, pushing out from under Gabriel as soon as things settled down. "Rachel!"

Through the dust, a blue light flickered, then solidified, and Jia walked Rachel out of the cloud in a bubble of Healing magic. Fort quickly ran to them, only to bounce right off the bubble, falling back to the ground.

Inside, he saw Rachel soundlessly laugh at this, even as she wiped tears from her eyes. Her mouth moved like she was saying something, but her words didn't make it through the protective bubble. Jia waved a hand and the bubble popped, and Rachel's laughter filled the cavern.

"*Thank* you for that," she said to Fort. "Totally worth almost dying."

"Um, you're welcome," Jia told her. "You're lucky we didn't all experiment with blowing things up."

"A CORPOREAL SPHERE," the dragon said, peering

down through the cloud of dust at them. "I WOULD NOT HAVE THOUGHT A HUMAN COULD CAST SUCH A POWERFUL SPELL. NOTHING CAN PENETRATE SUCH A THING AS LONG AS THE SPELLCASTER LIVES."

Jia's eyes widened. "Seriously? I kinda just cast it randomly and thought it was a fun protective bubble."

The dragon narrowed his eyes, and fire began to escape his mouth.

"I'm kidding!" Jia said quickly, putting her hands up to ward off any fire. "I mean, *of course* I take Corporeal magic too seriously to ever just experiment with it." She flashed Fort a terrified look.

"THERE IS NO TIME TO WAIT," the dragon said. "WHICHEVER OF YOU HUMANS HAVE STUDIED SPACE MAGIC, REMOVE US FROM THIS PLACE NOW, BEFORE MY BRETHREN ARRIVE."

Fort nodded and stepped forward, peering into the cloud of dust. Beyond it, a hole as large as the dragon now opened in the middle of the cavern wall, and he stepped around some enormous rocks to better see what was on the other side.

They were on the shores of what looked like a lake, only

it looked more like liquid silver than water. And the heat was so intense, he could feel it all the way from inside the cavern.

Tubes ran from the lake of molten metal in various directions, most likely as food for the Dracsi. Well, he could look when they arrived back in the den he'd first landed in.

"Everyone ready?" he asked, and opened a teleportation circle.

"Um, no, I almost just died," Rachel said from behind him. "And *great*, you're not even going to give me a minute. Ugh. Fine!" She strode past him and leaped through the portal, with Fort just a few steps behind.

- THIRTY-FOUR -

THEY DROPPED INTO THE CAVERN OF the Dracsi, the same one where Fort originally landed, the only light coming from two fireballs that Rachel created, holding one in each hand. Now that Fort could actually see the nest of Dracsi properly, he wondered how he had ever lived through his first trip here, as the entire cavern was *full* of the creatures.

"MY CHILDREN!" the dragon said as he passed through Fort's circle, sounding stricken at the sight of the Dracsi.

The sight of the Old One sent the Dracsi into a frenzy, each struggling to get closer to the much smaller dragon. The abrupt movement quickly became dangerous, with the huge creatures threatening to stomp them at every turn.

Fortunately, Jia was able to get her Corporeal Sphere up to protect them before anyone was hurt.

"Is it him?" Gabriel shouted, making his way over as Fort slowly turned the creature over.

"No," Fort said, looking up at his roommate. "It's . . . I think it's an elf."

"Watch out!" Jia shouted, and Fort turned in her direction, only to be yanked to the ground as the elf's eyes flew open, and it wrapped its hands around Fort's throat, an animalistic rage filling his eyes.

"Let him go!" Gabriel shouted, bashing the elf in the face with his shield. The creature immediately released Fort, snarling at this new threat, but Gabriel just slammed it again, and it fell unconscious.

"What's wrong with that thing?" Rachel shouted.

The Old One let out an ear-splitting shriek. "MY CHILDREN!" he yelled, his voice filled with desperate grief as, one by one, the dragons' bodies slowly began to fade away, leaving behind the same blue glow that had filled the room a moment ago. It was almost like they were returning to the magic from which they'd come. "I WILL MAKE MY BRETHREN PAY FOR WHAT THEY'VE DONE TO YOU!"

"He killed them," Rachel said as now even the blue glow disappeared, leaving no sign of the Dracsi.

"No, he *released* them," Jia said. "Turning them into those monsters did something to their minds, like with the elf. I'm not sure they were ever going to come back from that, not after living as Dracsi for that long."

"RETURN TO THE MAGIC," the Old One shouted. "BUT REMEMBER WHAT THEY DID TO YOU. REMEMBER, AND AWAIT YOUR REVENGE, AS IT WILL COME SURELY AND SWIFTLY TO MY FAMILY!"

Fort stared down at the elf on the ground before him, a new fear gripping his chest. If this elf had lost his mind . . . what had happened to his father?

"Fort!" Gabriel shouted from behind a particularly large dragon that had just started to dissolve. "I think I found him!"

Fort felt all the heat drain out of his body as he raced over to where Gabriel was standing. As he rounded the dragon, he saw the body on the ground, and he almost collapsed, tears streaming down his face.

It *was* his father. And he was alive!

"Dad?" he whispered, touching his father's face. "It's me. It's Fort!"

His father's eyelids fluttered, and he opened them to look up into his son's face. For a moment, madness filled his eyes, and his face twisted into something unrecognizable, but then he seemed to focus, and his expression turned instead to wonder.

"Fort?" he said.

Then his eyes rolled back into his head, and he fell unconscious.

"Jia!" Fort shouted as Gabriel ran off in a new direction. "JIA! It's my dad! He needs healing!"

She and Rachel both ran over as Gabriel continued searching the floor for his brother. "I've got him," Jia told Fort, but he wouldn't move, he wouldn't let his father go, not now, not after he'd just found him. "Please, Fort, you have to give me room."

Rachel gently pulled Fort away, and somehow he resisted fighting her, instead watching intently as Jia concentrated, then put her glowing blue hands down onto his father's chest.

"Fort, as soon as Gabriel finds his brother, we need to get out of here," Rachel hissed at him. "If we can get to the portal, we can close it and leave the Old One trapped here. We can't let him get back to Earth, no matter how much he hates the others."

"Jia, is he *okay*?" Fort asked, barely hearing Rachel's words.

"Shh," Jia said, crinkling her forehead. "Give me a minute. I'm trying to see what's wrong."

"Fort," Rachel said. "Did you hear me? We have to get out of here before the Old One, or—"

"Hey!" Gabriel shouted from the far side of the room. "Where *is* he?" He ran over to the Old One, who was ignoring him, tears turning to steam as they rolled down his scaled face. "I don't see him. Where is my brother?!"

"Uh-oh," Rachel said.

"LEAVE ME TO MOURN," the Old One said.

Gabriel angrily slammed his shield against the dragon's leg, more to get its attention than from any possibility of hurting it. "We had a *deal*. Tell me where my brother is *now!*"

"IF HE IS NOT HERE, THEN MY FAMILY MUST HAVE TAKEN HIM," the Old One said, snaking his dragon head down to within inches of Gabriel. "BUT THAT IS NOT MY CONCERN. AS OF NOW, OUR BARGAIN IS COMPLETE. I HAVE RETURNED TO YOU THE ELDER HUMAN." He lifted his head and sniffed toward the tunnel leading to the portal. "AND I CAN SENSE SOMETHING OF MY CHILDREN IN YOUR REALM! PERHAPS YOU WERE NOT LYING ABOUT THE LAST DRAGON AFTER ALL."

- THIRTY-FIVE -

GABRIEL SCREAMED IN RAGE AND pulled back his shield to strike again, only to freeze in place.

A moment later, so did the rest of them.

"ATTEMPT TO INTERFERE, AND I WILL DESTROY YOU," the Old One said, slowly beating its wings. Dust kicked up all over the room as the remaining dragons disappeared, and the Old One rose into the air.

"No!" Rachel shouted, struggling against her paralysis. "We can't let him get away, Fort! Use your magic!"

Fort concentrated, and his hands glowed green at his side as a massive teleportation circle opened right above the dragon, covering the tunnel to the portal and leading right back to Dragon's Teeth. There was nowhere for the Old One to go, as Fort extended the circle to just inches away from the walls on each side. At his size, there was just no way the dragon could get past it.

The Old One paused in midair, then shrank to the size of a house fly and flew through the gap between the wall and portal.

"NO!" Rachel shouted, but it was already too late. Their paralysis once again faded, and there could only be one reason why: The Old One had made it to Earth.

"We need to get after it!" Rachel shouted. "There's no time to waste!"

"We're not going anywhere until my father's okay!" Fort shouted at her.

"What?" Rachel said. "Think about what that dragon can do! And there's a teleportation circle still opened to the school, from where we came in!"

"He's okay to move," Jia told Fort. "I don't know what's keeping him unconscious, but he seems fine physically. We won't hurt him if we take him with us."

Fort gritted his teeth. He didn't like it, but he also didn't want to stay in this dimension another second, especially with the Old Ones on their way. He leaned down to pick up his father, and Jia helped from the other side. Together, they lifted him up and held him between them.

As soon as they had him, Fort opened a teleportation circle vertically in front of them, one that emerged just inches below the portal, set diagonally to shoot them out to the stone floor beyond.

"Because the portal is in midair, you're going to need to run through the circle here," he told the others. "Your momentum will take you through the portal, but be careful how you—"

Rachel didn't bother listening to the rest, and instead leaped through the circle. Gabriel's eyes flickered in multiple directions, but when he saw Fort waiting for him, he nodded and leaped through next.

A moment later, his upside-down hands extended back through the teleportation circle at the top. "Hand him to me!" Gabriel shouted, and Fort and Jia passed his father into Gabriel's arms. The older boy lifted Fort's father through the portal, leaving it clear for them to follow.

Once they were all back in the cavern below the old Oppenheimer School, Fort immediately closed the teleportation circle beneath them. He started to do the same to the dimensional portal, then stopped.

If they were somehow going to force the Old One to return to its dimension, they'd have to get it back here and through the portal, which presented a big problem. Obviously he couldn't close the portal now, or they'd be trapped with the dragon on Earth. But if he left it open, there was no telling what might come through. The Old Ones had to be almost to Dragon's Teeth, and it wouldn't take them long from there to find out what had happened to the Dracsi.

"We're going to have to guard the portal until I bring the Old One back," he told the others.

"*What?*" Rachel shouted. "Did you lose your mind like that elf? The Old Ones are coming! You think we'll be able to stop them from walking through this thing?"

"That's why I need to get the dragon back in it before they arrive," he said. "There's no time to argue. I'm the only one who can teleport it back here, so I'm going after it. Rachel, you and Gabriel should stay here—"

"No *way*," she said. "You won't be able to fight that thing without me."

"If it comes to fighting it, we've already lost," he told her. "It can freeze us in place. No, you need to stay, because you're the only one who can collapse this place and bring a ton of rock down on top of anyone who tries to come through."

She growled, but nodded. "This is all on you, Fort, from start to finish. You need to fix this!"

Fort turned to Gabriel, thinking he was going to object to being left behind, but he just nodded and put a hand on Fort's shoulder. "I'll make sure she's okay," he said. "Good luck with that dragon."

Happy to not have to argue, Fort nodded. "Jia, I'm going to teleport you and my dad to the school's hospital, then see if I can find the dragon. If it *did* go through the teleportation circle, it shouldn't be hard to find. If not, I'll just turn on the news."

"Of course," Jia said, moving to pick up his father from Gabriel, with Fort helping. "I'll call Dr. Ambrose in too."

"Thank you," he said, knowing the words weren't enough, but they were all he had. "Be back soon," he told Rachel and Gabriel, then opened a circle in front of him, and together with Jia, carried his father through.

They found two doctors in white coats staring at them as they emerged, one already on the phone for the guards. When they saw Fort's unconscious father, both immediately moved to take him, gently carrying him to one of the free beds.

"What's his situation?" one of them asked Jia.

"Unknown," she said. "Physically he's okay, but . . . he's sort of been trapped as a giant monster for the last six months or so."

The woman just stared at her for a moment, then began checking his vital signs. Jia turned to Fort, who couldn't look away, and gently pushed him toward the teleportation circle. "Go," she said.

He nodded in acknowledgment but stood still, unable to leave his father. After all this time, his dad was just feet from him, back where he belonged. But why hadn't he woken up? He'd said Fort's name, so at least he hadn't gone feral like the elf had after who knew how long being a Dracsi.

"Fort," Jia said. "He'll be fine."

As much as it killed Fort to be anywhere other than at his dad's side, he knew that Jia was the one who could really help heal him. And right now Fort had to make sure no one else got hurt because of the risks he'd taken to save him.

With one last look at his dad, Fort forced himself to turn and run out of the room. He stopped just outside, unsure where to go next. If the Old One had come here, there should be some signs of him, like screaming students and the guards defending the school. But the facility was also big enough that he might not be able to hear it from where he was.

He needed to get somewhere more central first, and then see what was happening. He teleported himself to the armory, the place he'd most feared the Old One would go, but thankfully, the room was empty.

Unfortunately, the screams coming from beyond the armory's door told him that the hallway outside wasn't.

Fort unlocked the door, then ran down the hallway as alarms began to blare. The screams were coming from a few hallways away, so he raced as fast as he could only to stop dead, shocked into paralysis by the trail the Old One had left.

Two guards had been merged with the wall, somehow still alive and otherwise unharmed as they tried to free themselves. Another was tied up in her own arms, which were now long enough to wrap around her body over and over. Two more had been connected at the back, and both were trying to pull away in opposite directions, just trying to escape.

"Help us!" one of the guards shouted.

But there was nothing Fort could do, not without Healing . . . or rather, Corporeal magic. Instead, he sprinted through the hall, knowing that he had to get the Old One out of here above all else. Jia and the other healing students could help the Old One's victims.

As he continued following the trail of guards, gradually Fort began to recognize where he was going. He came to a halt, realizing that of *course* that was the dragon's destination. Instead of running any farther, he opened a teleportation portal straight to the display room, hoping he wasn't making a mistake.

He wasn't. The dragon stood before the ancient bones of his children at the other side of the room, the rage-filled power pulsating off of him so strong that Fort could feel it on his skin.

Just in front of him, Sergeant Tower lay unconscious, a silver staff lying a short distance away. Considering that his body hadn't been magically changed, the dragon must have fought him physically. Still, it looked like he was breathing, so that was something.

With the Old One distracted by the skeletons, Fort held his breath, then opened a teleportation circle directly below the dragon, one that spit out right above the portal back to its dimension.

But instead of falling through his circle, the dragon instead just hung in midair, neither falling nor even moving in the slightest.

"I WARNED YOU NOT TO INTERFERE!" the dragon

said, his head turning to face Fort, eyes glowing with rage. "ARE THESE THE LAST DRAGONS YOU BARGAINED WITH, THE EARTHLY REMAINS OF MY CHILDREN?! YOU WOULD TAUNT ME WITH THEIR BONES?!"

An invisible force grabbed Fort by his throat and yanked him into the air, flying straight at the dragon. He struggled to breathe or free himself, but the magic was far too strong. "Didn't taunt . . . ," he gasped. "These aren't . . . the last . . ."

Darkness pushed in on his vision as his lungs cried out for oxygen, but the dragon didn't release him. Instead, it just sneered. "THEN WHERE IS MY CHILD? WHERE IS THIS FABLED LAST DRAGON?!"

Fort's mind scrambled as he slowly lost consciousness. Gabriel seemed sure he knew that the last dragon existed, but Fort had no idea where it could be. "I . . . can take . . . you," he bluffed, but whatever the dragon replied, it was lost to Fort as he passed out.

A moment later, he awoke on the floor, blue magic fading around him as the dragon healed him. "ENOUGH LIES," the dragon said, his face just inches from Fort's. "AND ENOUGH BARGAINS. BRING ME TO MY CHILD, OR I WILL RAZE THIS EARTH TO ITS MOLTEN CORE."

Fort started to respond, trying to think his way out of this, but one of the dragon's claws pushed into his chest, and he gasped in pain. He nodded. "I'll . . . bring you."

"NOW," the dragon said, and slid the claw beneath Fort's back, picking him up in his hand. "TAKE ME *NOW*."

- THIRTY-SIX -

THE DRAGON HELD FORT LIKE A RAG doll in his hand, claws digging into him painfully as he waited for Fort to open a teleportation circle. Just thankful to be breathing, Fort had no idea where to start on a search for the last dragon, or even if taking the Old One to it was the safest choice. For all Fort knew, any new dragon they found could be just as much of a threat as its Old One creator.

And anything that happened would be Fort's fault, just for going after his father.

He shook his head, unwilling to think about that until the Old One was taken care of. For now, he had to stall until he figured out what to do. Fort reached out and opened a tele-portation circle to the first place that occurred to him, and the dragon leaped through without pause.

They emerged from the circle at the Great Wall of China,

with the dragon's momentum crashing them right through the wall. He quickly recovered and beat his wings hard, sending them soaring into the air to hover over the wall as visitors below looked up and screamed.

That's when Fort realized his first mistake: It was broad daylight here. Of *course* there would be a ton of tourists around. And far too many of them were recording the dragon with their phones, which meant this was going to hit the news in a matter of moments.

"I SENSE NOTHING HERE," the dragon roared, and the tourists below all ran at the power of its voice. Fort didn't blame them: He'd have loved to run away right now too.

"They must have moved the dragon, then!" Fort shouted, bluffing for all he was worth. "I'll take us somewhere else!" Preferably somewhere the sun wasn't shining.

A shot rang out from below, and Fort glanced down to find local police aiming their weapons at the dragon. It roared in rage and started to dive toward them, so Fort immediately opened another teleportation circle right in front of the creature, more for the police's sake than his or the dragon's.

They emerged over the Eiffel Tower, diving straight for it. Paris sparkled before them as the sun began to rise, so at least he'd picked somewhere with less light out, but the dragon hadn't stopped its dive, and they were quickly closing in on the streets.

Even at this early hour, people were up and about, and any that saw the creature coming for them screamed. This time Fort joined in as the dragon pulled up at the last possible moment, skimming just above the various cars and pedestrians. His tail swung out for balance right into a café's awning as the dragon took a tight turn down a narrow street, and Fort looked back to find the awning still attached to its tail.

"I CAN SENSE SOMETHING!" the dragon shouted, sounding almost excited as they careened toward the Arc de Triomphe in the middle of a traffic circle. "SOMEWHERE CLOSE, ON AN ISLAND!"

"Okay but *look out!*" Fort shouted, and teleported them away just before the dragon's wings hit the Arc. They emerged in the sky above London, just in front of an enormous Ferris wheel. The dragon braked, then swung out to the right to avoid hitting the wheel, its massive wings passing within inches. He circled around Big Ben and Parliament as his head snaked in every direction.

"IT IS *CLOSE*," the dragon declared, then took off away

from the direction of the rising sun, which unfortunately seemed to be heading them straight for an airport. A massive passenger jet was coming down right above them, but the Old One barely seemed to notice it, all its attention on the dragon it sensed. At the last possible moment, it swooped right over a plane so close that Fort could see the pilots' horrified faces.

Fort just about threw up as the plane's airstream hit, almost knocking the dragon from the air. "WHAT EVIL IS THIS?!" he shouted, barely righting himself as he turned to face the offending airplane. "RETURN TO ME, METAL BEAST, AND I SHALL DESTROY YOU!"

"I think that was an accident!" Fort shouted, not wanting to point out who'd really been at fault. "Don't you want to find your child?"

The dragon sent a jet of fire after the plane in a huff, then turned and continued west.

As they flew, Fort wondered where they were heading, and if the dragon had actually managed to locate the last of its kind. Was this where Colonel Charles would keep a dragon imprisoned, in the United Kingdom? That seemed unlikely. But what else . . .

Wait. The UK had its own school for magic, the one that

Cyrus had attended briefly. What if they also had a dragon skeleton, found with the book of Clairvoyance?

If that was the case, Fort was going to be left with one *extremely* angry Old One on his hands.

"Actually, I think this is a false alarm," Fort said, screaming over the wind. Behind him, he heard the sounds of jet engines, and looked back to find two military planes coming up fast. "I'm taking us somewhere else!"

"NO!" the dragon shouted. "I SENSE IT HERE!"

The planes behind them launched a missile, and Fort screamed as one passed right over them. "We can't stay here!" he yelled, and opened another circle just in front of them. He had no time to think, so he dumped them out in the first place that came to mind as the planes sent more missiles in their direction.

Unfortunately, the first place he could think of was New York City.

They shot out of a teleportation circle on the side of the Empire State Building with the missiles just behind them. Fort shut the circle as quickly as he could, but it was too late; the missiles emerged just before it closed, gaining quickly on them.

"Dive!" Fort shouted, right as the missiles were about to hit, and for once the dragon listened to him, plummeting to the streets below. The missiles passed harmlessly above them, but that wouldn't be the case for long. What if they hit a building in the city, or kept flying across the river and hit something in New Jersey? Anyone hurt because of the missiles would be his fault, and he wasn't going to let that happen.

Fort quickly opened another teleportation circle as they plummeted, this one just in front of the missiles, leading the only place he knew they wouldn't cause any damage. He desperately hoped he'd aimed accurately, because it wasn't easy casting a spell while falling through skyscrapers in New York, but the missiles flew right through the circle, and he sighed in relief.

Hopefully two explosions on the moon wouldn't make the news, not with a dragon attack in multiple cities.

Just as he began to think they might be okay, the dragon tightened its grip on him, crushing the air from his lungs as the Old One pulled out of his dive, barely above street level. The dragon's feet plowed into a row of parked cars, sending them crashing into each other as a row of traffic honked at it, and Fort waved his apologies at the New Yorkers, too breathless to do anything else.

Fortunately, it was still night here, so not as many people were around to see them as they soared back into the air. But they were still far too noticeable for Fort's taste, and it was only a matter of time until another round of jets came after them, or *worse*. Missiles were one thing, but Colonel Charles's soldiers with magical bows and lightning bullets would be a lot more dangerous.

"I SENSE ANOTHER," the dragon said, to Fort's surprise. He slowed to hover over the skyscrapers, then chose one to land on. They landed with a crunch, and part of the building gave way beneath the dragon's weight, but at least they were stopped. Fort had never been so happy to not be flying in his life. "AWAY FROM THE SUN."

So, west? Okay. At least that kept them moving, and harder to track. "We'll keep looking until we find it," Fort promised, inwardly still trying to think of a plan as he opened a teleportation circle a few feet away.

The dragon leaped off of the building, sending Fort's stomach dropping, and they emerged in the middle of Chicago, where it was even darker than in New York. The lights below were almost peaceful in the silence of the night sky, though Fort wished he were seeing it from anywhere but a dragon's hand, especially one that was going to wipe out humanity if it didn't find its last remaining offspring.

"FARTHER," the dragon said, and Fort opened another portal.

They emerged below the St. Louis Gateway Arch this time, and Fort hoped that wherever this last dragon was, it'd be near a landmark that he'd seen at least once. "FARTHER," the dragon repeated, and Fort jumped them again, this time into the Rocky Mountains in Colorado.

Wait, why hadn't he thought of this *before*? He'd seen pictures of national parks, mountains, lakes, all kinds of things that wouldn't have many humans nearby. If the dragon was around one of these spots, Fort could surprise it, have it fly straight for another teleportation circle, and send it back into the cavern before it could realize what he'd done. It'd be *hugely* dangerous, but might be the only way to—

"NO," the dragon said. "I SENSE IT NEAR MORE HUMANS. A LARGE AMOUNT OF YOUR KIND. BRING ME FARTHER AWAY FROM THE SUN, TO A LARGE GATHERING OF HUMANS."

Fort sighed. A large gathering of humans meant a big city,

which only put more people in danger. But what else could he do? He hadn't figured out a way to get the dragon back to the portal, and there was no way he was going to stop until he did. None of these innocent people deserved whatever the Old One might put them through when he didn't find his offspring. Not when he wouldn't even be here if Fort hadn't gone looking for his father.

But for now, all he could do was take the dragon where it wanted to go and hope he came up with an idea in the meantime.

"Let's try another city, then," Fort said, and opened a teleportation circle to the first place he could think of that matched the dragon's description.

The lights from the Hollywood sign illuminated the landmark enough to see it, even through the portal, and before Fort could take a breath they soared through it, emerging into the sky above Los Angeles.

- THIRTY-SEVEN -

THE LIGHTS OF L.A. SPREAD OUT below him, extending in every direction except for the hill directly below with the Hollywood sign. Fort let the dragon fly for a moment, concentrating on where to position his teleportation circle back in the cavern.

He had to put it directly above the portal to the Dracsi dimension. If it was anywhere else, the dragon might hit Gabriel or Rachel. But if it was that close, there was no way he'd be able to get free before they passed through.

But maybe this is what he deserved? The Old One coming to Earth was his fault, and he'd known from the start that one of them was going to be lost to the other dimension. If this was what it took to make up for his actions while still rescuing his father, then that was what Fort had to—

"THERE!" the Old One shouted, and they began to dive in

the direction of the Pacific Ocean. "I SENSE IT, DIFFERENT THAN THE ONE ACROSS THE SEA. THIS MUST BE THE TRUE CHILD I SEEK! I AM COMING FOR YOU, LITTLE ONE!"

What?! The last dragon might actually be here? Fort hadn't even considered that!

He had to get a teleportation circle open while they were still flying. That was the only way to get the dragon through it, to use its speed against it. Closing his eyes and mentally saying good-bye to his father and friends, Fort opened a circle . . .

Only for the dragon to dive beneath it. "DO NOT INTER-FERE," the Old One said, squeezing Fort tighter. Once again, Fort found it almost impossible to breathe, and the world began to get even darker than it was under the starry sky.

And then the dragon released the pressure as it did a barrel roll in the sky, avoiding something loud before them. Fort gasped for air as they passed directly under a police helicopter, then went blind as the helicopter's lights focused right on him.

"MORE OF YOU TRY TO STOP ME!" the dragon shouted. "YOU BEG ME TO DOOM YOUR SPECIES!"

As the first helicopter turned to follow them, a second came up from another side. *That* wasn't good. So far they just had their lights trained on the dragon, but if they started shooting, or even tried to head it off, there would be no way of stopping the creature.

"Hey!" he shouted, waving his hands toward the helicopters. "It's okay! I've got this under control!" Yes, it was a complete lie, but he still had a better shot at fixing things than they did.

"Set the boy down safely on the ground," said a voice over a loudspeaker from the helicopter. "We do not want to hurt you."

"HURT ME?" the dragon said, sneering as it turned its head toward the helicopter.

"No!" Fort shouted, now waving at the dragon to get its attention. "Remember the last dragon? Don't let them distract you!"

The dragon seemed dismissive of this, but turned away from the helicopters, and Fort silently let loose the breath he'd been holding . . . only to scream as the dragon dropped again, rocketing toward what looked like a black, bubbling lake of awfulness right in the middle of Los Angeles.

Tar pits. The La Brea Tar Pits. And the dragon was diving straight for them.

"Wait, I can't breathe in there!" Fort shouted, just seconds before they hit.

Almost as an afterthought, the dragon absently tossed Fort into the air the moment before it plowed into the tar like a missile. Fort's momentum sent him up and flying over the tar pits before gravity regained its hold on him, pulling him back toward the lake of blackness. He quickly opened a circle and fell through it to crash on the ground just in front of the pits, landing hard enough to send pain shooting through every part of his body.

"Get away from the pit!" shouted someone over the helicopter loudspeaker, and Fort knew they were talking to him. The dragon had given up its hostage, which meant they could attack now.

But if he let the police try to fight the Old One, they'd be the ones to suffer for it. So instead, Fort pushed to his feet, waving up at the bright spotlight they'd turned onto him.

"Don't shoot!" he shouted. "Let me handle this! I really do have it under control!"

If only that were true.

More helicopters hovered overhead now, and police cars came racing up to the tar pit with sirens blaring. The more that arrived, the more Fort was convinced they'd try to just grab him and forcibly remove him from the scene, dooming them all. If only the dragon would finish whatever he was doing, so Fort could figure out another way to get it back to the Dracsi dimension. What could possibly be taking so long—

His thoughts were interrupted by the dragon flying out of the black lake to land just behind Fort, hot tar dripping from its scales. And in its hands was an egg at least three feet tall.

Only, the egg was *broken*. Whatever had been inside it was gone, or hadn't lived through the heat of the tar.

The Old One gently lay the egg down on the ground, then turned to the police assembling before them, his eyes blazing with fury.

"FOR THIS TRAVESTY," he shrieked, *"I SHALL WIPE YOUR KIND OFF THE FACE OF YOUR EARTH!"*

THIRTY-EIGHT

NO!" FORT SHOUTED, LEAPING BETWEEN the Old One and the police. "You don't know what happened to that dragon!"

"YOU LED ME TO NOTHING BUT DEATH," the Old One roared, shooting fire straight at Fort and the police behind him.

Fort dove to the ground, and the heat almost singed his uniform as it passed just a foot or two above him. He threw a look over his shoulder to find that, thankfully, the cops had escaped unscathed by hiding behind their vehicles.

"I didn't know what we'd find!" Fort shouted, pushing to his feet and holding his hands up in surrender. "But these humans did nothing to that dragon. No human did! *You* were the one who told us that dragons were on our side. We were partners, just like you saw with the skeletons!"

"AND FOR THAT CRIME, MY BROTHER AND SIS-TERS DESTROYED MY CHILDREN!" the Old One roared again, this time lunging forward, swiping directly at him. Fort quickly threw up a teleportation circle, and instead of cutting him in two, the Old One's claws passed through empty air above the Grand Canyon.

"Then blame *them*!" Fort shouted, closing his circle as the dragon pulled his hand back. "By taking it out on humanity, you're doing the exact same thing your family did. Would your dragons want you to hurt the ones they were protecting? Especially for *their* sake?"

The Old One reared back, screaming incoherently, his face still contorted with rage. "YOU HAVE NO *IDEA* WHAT IT IS LIKE TO LOSE YOUR CHILDREN!"

"Kid, get out of the way!" one of the cops shouted. "You're in the line of fire!"

"I've got this!" Fort shouted, and summoned a huge tele-portation circle behind him, just in case they decided to ignore him and fire anyway. Now if they did, their bullets would fly out harmlessly over the Atlantic Ocean, a spot Fort remem-bered from a flight to Florida once.

He quickly turned back to the Old One, his hands still held

up. "It's true, I don't know what it's like to lose a child. But I do know what it feels like to lose my parents! I've never known my mother, and my father only got turned into a Dracsi because I was too slow, too weak to stop it. And yes, I'd have done anything to bring him back . . . but maybe I didn't have that right. Maybe it's not worth putting all these people in danger because I was so sad and angry!"

The Old One sneered. "YOU CANNOT POSSIBLY UNDERSTAND THE DEPTHS OF WHO I AM, AND WHAT MY DRAGONS MEANT TO ME, *HUMAN*. THEY WERE THE EMBODIMENT OF ALL MAGIC, MY GREATEST CREATION. NOW I HAVE NOTHING LEFT, *NOTHING*!"

"Maybe *not*, but . . . ," Fort said, then trailed off as an idea occurred to him. It wasn't perfect, and even suggesting it might get him killed, but if it did work, it could save all the police behind him, let alone the rest of humanity. "But that didn't have to be the last dragon."

"YOU CAN SEE FOR YOURSELF THAT IT IS GONE!" the Old One shouted. "THERE *ARE* NO MORE DRAGONS."

"Your children are gone," Fort said quietly, hoping this wasn't a huge mistake. "But that doesn't have to be the end of their species. You brought the others out of magic, created them out of nothing, right? Why can't you then—"

The Old One reared back in surprise. "CREATE ONE ANEW?"

Fort nodded and braced himself for anything, readying a teleportation spell back to his bedroom in his aunt's apartment.

But instead of incinerating him with fire or ripping him apart with his claws, the Old One seemed to be . . . thinking. "IT COULD NEVER HEAL THE LOSS," he said finally. "BUT PERHAPS IT WOULD IN SOME WAY PUT RIGHT THAT WHICH HAS BEEN MADE WRONG."

"A new dragon could be created in honor of the ones that came before it," Fort said, still waiting for the creature to change his mind.

The dragon picked up the egg on the ground and wrapped his massive hands around it. Even next to the Old One, the egg looked gigantic, but Fort supposed any animal the size of a dragon would have to come out of a pretty big egg.

The dragon closed his eyes, his hands glowing bright blue as the egg slowly knitted itself closed, its cracks filling over until it looked whole and unbroken. The light in the egg now grew even more intense than the dragon's hands, and Fort covered his eyes to keep from going blind. Behind him, he could hear the police shouting and footsteps heading around the sides of his teleportation circle, only to stop as they were blinded just as he was.

"It's okay!" Fort shouted, hoping they'd listen. "He's not going to hurt anyone!"

"What is it doing?" one of the cops yelled.

"Righting a wrong!" Fort shouted back.

The blue light was now so strong that Fort could feel its chill even from several yards away. The cold light of Healing—no, Corporeal magic—passed through his body, and all the aches and pains he'd gotten in the last week disappeared, from training with Sergeant Tower to falling in the Dracsi cavern to even a bit of a runny nose, healed like they'd never existed to begin with.

"I . . . I AM NOT AS STRONG AS I ONCE WAS," he heard the Old One say, his voice sounding less powerful than it had. "I HAVE BEEN IMPRISONED SO LONG. I AM NOT SURE I CAN—"

"You *can* do this!" Fort shouted, feeling energized from the Healing magic. "Remember what they mean to you, and don't let anything stop you from bringing them back!"

The Old One went silent, but the light intensified, painful even through Fort's closed eyes. He brought his arm up over his face and turned around, hoping this magic wasn't going to kill them all, now that he'd finally talked the dragon down. Only, as he turned, someone grabbed his shoulder and yanked him to the ground.

"I've got the kid!" one of the cops shouted. "He's out of danger!"

"Take that thing out!" another shouted.

"NO!" Fort screamed, but the police officer who'd grabbed him held him in place. "He won't hurt you if you don't attack him first!"

"We're doing this to keep the city safe, kid," the cop on the ground growled at him. "I don't know what that thing is, but if we let it go, who knows what it'll do."

"Don't shoot unless positive you have a confirmed target!" one of the cops shouted. "On my mark. Three! Two!"

"Please, no!" Fort shouted, but as he did, the light abruptly disappeared, dropping the whole world into darkness.

The policeman holding Fort loosened his grip in surprise, and Fort didn't wait. He leaped to his feet and ran in the direction where he hoped the Old One was.

"Kid, no!" the cop who'd grabbed him yelled. "Hold your fire!"

Not waiting to see if they did, Fort threw a teleportation circle beneath the spot he'd last seen the dragon, then dove through it blindly, hoping the Old One wouldn't pick now of all times to float above it.

He flew through the circle and into the display room back at the new Oppenheimer School, crashing hard to the concrete floor, only to feel the whole room shake as the dragon landed next to him, not moving.

Cradled protectively in the Old One's arms was a bright blue egg, glowing with an inner light. And from that light, Fort could just make out the fact that something inside was moving.

- THIRTY-NINE -

I T WAS TAKING FAR MORE HEALING BANdages to wake the Old One up than Fort was comfortable using. That, and having an unconscious dragon meant he could have teleported the creature back to Dragon's Teeth without any worry.

But for some reason he didn't feel right, leaving it at the mercy of the other Old Ones. If Fort sent the egg back with him, they'd surely make him turn the new dragon into another Dracsi. And if he kept the egg safe on Earth, he'd be taking the Old One's child from it, which also felt horribly wrong.

Still, what was he doing, *healing* a creature that had threatened all of humanity?

After the seventeenth bandage, the Old One's eyes cracked open, and he groaned, then glanced up at Fort strangely. "YOU . . . RESTORED MY BODY? WHY?"

"Because that egg needs his father," Fort said, backing away and hoping he hadn't just made a very bad mistake. But the last thing he was going to do was take this new dragon's dad from it, not with his own father lying on a hospital bed not far from him right now.

The Old One's eyes widened, and he scrambled to his feet, relaxing after he saw the glowing blue dragon egg. Fort had carried it from the Old One's arms when he wasn't sure if the creature would wake up or not.

The dragon reached out a trembling hand and gently lay it on the egg, an odd expression on his face. "IT WORKED," he said, sounding almost surprised. "IT TOOK ALMOST ALL OF MY POWER, BUT THE LITTLE ONE IS ALIVE AND WELL." His eyes unfocused, and he put his other hand on the egg as well. "THOUGH THIS DRAGON . . . IT WILL BE DIFFERENT FROM MY LAST CHILDREN. MAGIC HAS CHANGED, HERE ON EARTH. IT . . . WANTS SOME-THING."

Magic wanted something? *That* was terrifying. "Okay, great, but we still need to get you back to your dimension," Fort told him. "You're going to have to find some place to hide from your family—"

The Old One's eyes refocused, and it sneered. "RUN? I WOULD SOONER DIE. I WILL FACE THEM AND MAKE THEM *PAY* FOR WHAT THEY'VE—"

"And put your egg in danger?" Fort said incredulously. "You've got to be kidding!"

The dragon moved his head in closer until his teeth were just inches from Fort's fate. "DO NOT SPEAK TO ME AS IF—"

"Then don't put your new child's life in danger!" Fort shouted back, so angry that he didn't even care if the Old One attacked. "You need to think about them, not just yourself and your need for revenge!"

"I WOULD SOONER PERISH THAN THREATEN THIS NEW LIFE," the Old One said, backing off a bit and standing up, still holding the egg carefully in his arms. "YOU . . . YOU MAY BE CORRECT, HUMAN. AND I DO NOT SAY THAT LIGHTLY. BUT WE SHOULD GO. WE MUST HURRY BACK IF WE ARE TO HAVE ANY HOPE OF HIDING FROM MY BRETHREN."

Really? The dragon was pulling an "I'm ready, we're waiting on you now" on him? In spite of wanting to run back to the medical ward and check in on his father, Fort knew he couldn't just teleport the Old One back and hope for the best.

He needed to see this through, if just so he could look his dad in the eyes when the man woke up. With a long sigh, Fort opened a circle back to the portal beneath the old Oppenheimer School. "Let me go first," he told the Old One. "I don't want to scare Gabriel and Rachel."

The dragon barely seemed to hear him, busy staring at its egg, so Fort stepped through the teleportation circle, ready to tell Rachel how right she'd been all along.

Except Rachel wasn't there. Neither was Gabriel. The portal still burned in the floor of the cavern, but otherwise, there was no sign of anyone.

"Uh-oh," Fort said, only to be knocked out of the way by the dragon pushing through the portal behind him.

"WHAT TRANSPIRES?" the Old One said, turning his body to protect the egg. "WHY DO YOU PANIC?"

"Because my friends were here, guarding the portal," Fort said. "And now they're gone. Do you . . . *sense* any humans nearby?"

The Old One shook his head. "YOU ALONE, FOR MANY MILES AROUND."

Oh *no.* "Come on," Fort said, and moved to the portal.

But the Old One held back. "IF THERE IS DANGER, WE

MUST SHIELD THE EGG. I CANNOT BRING IT INTO PERIL. *YOU* JUST SAID—"

"I know what I said!" Fort shouted. "But my friends could be in trouble! We have to go *now!*"

The dragon sighed, then slowly held out the egg, his hands shaking. "HIDE IT," the Old One commanded. "USE YOUR SPACE MAGIC AND HIDE THE EGG SOMEWHERE SAFE UNTIL WE FIND YOUR FRIENDS. I . . . I OWE YOU THIS MUCH."

Fort just stared at the creature for a moment, then nodded and took the egg, forgetting how heavy it was. He thought for a moment, then opened a circle and deposited the egg in the safest place he could think of, right on the bed in his old room at his aunt's house. "Okay," he said, closing the teleportation circle. "No one will get to it there." Unless his aunt decided to use her rowing machine. But still, it was much safer than the school, for sure.

The dragon nodded, his face now downcast. But instead of waiting, he grabbed Fort around the waist and dove into the portal, spreading his wings at the last possible moment before they hit the Dracsi cavern floor.

As soon as Fort could breathe again, he looked around in the dimly lit room, expecting to see, well, something. Not Dracsi, not anymore. But the elf should have been here, at least.

The cavern was completely empty, though. "Where are they all?" Fort asked the dragon as the Old One set him down on the ground.

The creature hissed as it landed, and Fort backed away nervously, his hands in the air again. "*THEY* HAVE ARRIVED," he said, sending a cold chill down Fort's back.

"The Old Ones? They're here now?"

"THOSE STILL ALIVE," the dragon said. "KETAS, MY BROTHER IN MIND; Q'BAOS, MY SISTER IN SPIRIT; AND D'VALE, MY SISTER IN THE ELEMENTS."

So the Old Ones of Mind, Spirit, and Elemental magic, which was Destruction, if Fort remembered right. That only left Time and whatever the seventh form of magic was. That at least was fortunate: The last thing they needed was an Old One who could see the future.

Still, the three here could read and take over your mind, take over your spirit and force you into servitude, or . . . Destruction. So, blow everything up. That wasn't much better.

But where had his friends gone? Had the Old Ones attacked the portal and taken them prisoner? If they had, why hadn't they just passed through it? That was their goal all along, and without Gabriel and Rachel guarding it, the portal had been standing open for however long Fort had been gone.

No, if they'd known about it, they'd be on Earth now, and the dragon seemed convinced they were still in the Dracsi dimension. So what had happened to Gabriel and Rachel?

"THEY WILL SENSE MY PRESENCE," the Old One hissed. "WE DO NOT HAVE MUCH TIME!"

"Do you sense any humans now?"

The dragon slowly nodded. "Two. They are with my brethren."

And there it was. However it had happened, the Old Ones had his friends. And all because of him. Somehow, Cyrus had been wrong: In trying to save his father, he'd lost two friends, not just one.

"Then there's nothing for it," Fort said, feeling numb inside. "We have to face your family. We need to get them back."

"THERE IS *NO* FACING THEM," the Old One said, sneering at Fort. "PERHAPS ONE, MAYBE TWO OF THEM, BUT NOT THE THREE. THEY WILL DESTROY ME AND TAKE YOUR SPIRIT. YOU WILL BE THEIRS, BODY AND SOUL. WE HAVE NO HOPE AGAINST THEM ALL AT ONCE."

"Can't you paralyze them before they cast any magic?" Fort asked. "That's your whole thing, you control bodies! You should be able to stop them before they're even able to move!"

"THEY WILL TURN MY MIND OR SPIRIT AS SOON AS I APPEAR, AND I WILL HAVE NO CHOICE BUT TO OBEY THEM," the Old One said. "THEN YOU WOULD FACE FOUR, NOT THREE." He lifted a claw, and Fort felt the dragon's invisible magic squeeze all around him. "AND *YOU* ARE NOT A MATCH FOR EVEN ME. THERE IS NO HOPE, HUMAN. YOUR FRIENDS ARE LOST."

No! It couldn't end like this, not with him losing both Rachel *and* Gabriel! Cyrus had said he'd only lose *one* friend, and even that was too many. "There's got to be a way!" he shouted. "If we can't outmagic them, then we'll have to out-think them. If they're going to attack you first, since you're the greatest threat . . . maybe we can use that?"

The dragon snorted. "HOW, BY HAVING *YOU* ATTACK THEM?"

Fort's eyes widened. "No. By having me be a *distraction*."

- FORTY -

DWARVES FILLED THE CITY OF DRA, LINing the edges of the cavern on every level, from the very top to as far down as the eye could see. The huge roaring cheers were so loud that they were almost painful, and powerful enough to send tremors through the rock.

The dragon floated down slowly and carefully in circles around the enormous statue of the Spirit Old One that rose from the center of the city. On his back, a human boy wearing a silver amulet around his neck watched the dragon's flight carefully, offering suggestions every few seconds that sounded vaguely like orders.

The packed crowds of dwarves weren't cheering for the dragon or the boy, though. The object of their worship instead lay at the very bottom of the city, where three Old Ones posed regally in diamond chairs, sculpted individually to fit their forms. Before the Old Ones, lines of younger dwarves stood in silence, having yet to go through the Ritual that would take their spirits and replace them with absolute loyalty to Q'baos.

That would change in a matter of minutes.

As the dragon neared the ground, the dwarves' cheers cut off at once, like someone had abruptly muted them all. The three Old Ones all rose from their thrones and turned to face the descending dragon.

A purple light glowed from the hands of Q'baos, the Old One immortalized in the statue that the dragon was currently circling. A matching glow appeared around the dragon's head, and the dwarves began to cheer once more. The dragon's heart now belonged to the Old Ones, they knew, and that alone was reason to celebrate, even if they hadn't been controlled by Ketas, the Old One of Mind magic.

The dragon's speed increased since it no longer felt apprehension about the Old Ones below, and the boy on his back was forced to hold on tightly to avoid falling off.

As they neared, dozens of elder dwarves cleared a path between the assembled younger ones, opening a place for the dragon to land. He did, though it was a bit of a rough landing, almost knocking the boy off of his back.

After landing, the dragon immediately bowed to the three Old Ones, who sat back down on their thrones.

To the side of the three thrones, two humans stood, one a girl, the other a large boy. Both stepped forward. The girl's eyes were filled with hatred, controlled as she was by Ketas.

The boy, however, just looked worried when he caught the eye of the boy on the dragon.

"WE WELCOME OUR FORMERLY IMPRISONED BROTHER," said D'vale, the Old One made entirely out of flames. "WE REGRET THAT HIS DISLOYATY NECESSITATES THE USE OF OUR SISTER'S POWER"— she nodded at Q'baos, the Old One of Spirit magic—"BUT WE WILL DO AS WE MUST, AS WE HAVE ALWAYS DONE."

IT SEEMS THAT HE HAS BROUGHT US A GIFT, the master of Mind magic said, his words beating inside the skulls of everyone present. ONE THAT BELIEVES A TRINKET AROUND HIS NECK MIGHT PROTECT HIM. BROTHER, PRESENT THIS HUMAN TO US TO PROVE YOUR DEVOTION. IT IS THE YOUNG ONE WHO HURT US, WHEN WE LAST ATTEMPTED TO RETURN TO OUR HOME.

The dragon nodded and lay down to let the boy climb off of his back, which he did. The boy then moved slowly toward the three thrones, his eyes on the Old Ones.

The young dwarves behind the boy began to shout in protest, but the Old One of Mind magic glowed yellow, and they all fell silent, still rebellious, but now unable to speak.

"You wished to find the last dragon?" the boy said as he stopped within a few feet of the thrones. "I regret to inform you that there are no more. The one you see before you is the last of his kind."

The three Old Ones looked past him to the dragon. "THAT IS NOT THE LAST," Q'baos said. "THERE IS ANOTHER."

Ketas gestured at Gabriel, who stared at the boy sadly. THIS ONE HAS GIVEN US THE LOCATION OF THE LAST DRAGON IN EXCHANGE FOR HIS KIN. NOW WE WILL RETURN TO EARTH AND RETRIEVE THE DRAGON.

Gabriel stepped forward. "I told them where it is, Fort, in exchange for them returning my brother to me."

The boy standing before the Old Ones raised an eyebrow at this, then shook his head. "I am afraid I cannot let that happen."

"YOU?" Q'baos said. "YOU BELIEVE THAT YOU HAVE THE POWER TO STOP US?"

The boy nodded, and the Old Ones began to laugh.

"OUR BROTHER," Q'baos continued, gesturing toward the dragon. "SHOW ME YOUR DEVOTION. USE YOUR MAGIC TO TURN THIS ONE'S BODY INSIDE OUT. BUT KEEP THE HUMAN *ALIVE*. WE WANT TO SHOW THE YOUNG DWARVES THE PRICE OF DEFYING US."

The dragon nodded and scrunched up his face, like he was trying hard to do as ordered. A minute passed, then another, until finally, he let out a deep sigh, shaking his head. "I WANT TO DO AS YOU SAY, WITH ALL OF MY SOUL, BUT I DON'T KNOW *HOW*. I DON'T KNOW THAT KIND OF MAGIC."

WHAT? Ketas leaped up from his seat, followed immediately by the others. He leaned in to the boy, to get a closer look, only for his tentacles to flail about as he hissed, retreating quickly. NO! he shouted. WE HAVE BEEN DECEIVED—

His words cut off as blue light surrounded the three Old Ones, freezing them all instantly.

"Unfortunately, all he knows is a bit of space magic," the boy said, nodding at the dragon. "Perhaps if you had not been so arrogant, you would have checked his mind before stealing his spirit?"

The boy reached out his still-glowing hand, and blue light now flooded over the dragon. The creature's wings shrank into his back, and his front legs pulled up, shortening into arms as his tail disappeared into his back.

As the dragon morphed into a human, the opposite happened to the boy, his body enlarging as it grew wings and a tail. A moment later, the Old One had resumed his dragon shape, while Fort stood behind him, staring down at his now-human hands in wonder.

"ONE MORE THING," the dragon said, and Fort's whole body began to glow blue, as did those of every dwarf assembled except for the young ones, and Rachel, too. A moment later, and all traces of Q'baos's Spirit magic had been expunged from the assembled crowds. The effort seemed to have exhausted the dragon, but he still looked up at the Old Ones in triumph. "*NOW*, MY BRETHREN, WE SHALL SEE WHO IS PUNISHED FOR THEIR CRIMES."

- FORTY-ONE -

THE ASSEMBLED DWARVES ROARED IN anger and began to rush the thrones, but the dragon snarled, stopping them all in their tracks. "THEY ARE *MINE* TO JUDGE," the Old One told them.

"They've held us under their spell for generations!" one of the dwarves yelled.

"We're owed *justice*!" shouted another.

"I CARE NOT," the Old One said. "COME ANY CLOSER, AND I WILL DEAL WITH YOU AS HARSHLY AS I DO THEM."

That did the trick, and the dwarves quickly backed off, only to turn their attention to the massive diamond statue in the middle of their city. "Tear it down!" one shouted, setting off a huge swell of shouts as they all ran for the base of the statue.

Up and down the city of Dra, Fort could hear the dwarves

shouting and stamping their feet, sending massive quakes through the entire cavern, just as they had when cheering for the Old Ones. Yet this time their shouts were full of righteous anger, and their stamping threatened to knock down the whole city, not just the statue.

"YOU DESTROYED MY CHILDREN," the Old One said, turning back to his brethren. "YOU IMPRISONED ME FOR MILLENNIA. YOU HAVE GIVEN ME NO CHOICE BUT TO—"

"WE NEVER HARMED YOUR DRAGONS," D'vale, Old One of Elemental magic said, sounding almost amused. "*YOU* DID THAT. AND THERE IS STILL ONE DRAGON LEFT ON EARTH. KETAS HAS SEEN IT FOR HIMSELF, HAS BEEN IN THE DRAGON'S MIND."

"LIES!" the dragon snarled. "I SAW THE EGG FOR MYSELF, THE ONE THAT MY ALLY TOOK AND HID. THE DRAGON WAS GONE!"

Ketas had been in the mind of the last dragon? Wait, but that meant—

"BELIEVE AS YOU WILL," D'vale said. "BUT BLAME US *NOT* FOR YOUR OWN CRIMES."

"Give me back my brother!" Gabriel shouted at the three.

"You promised you'd return him if I gave you the location of the last dragon, and I did!"

Now that Fort wasn't under the control of Q'baos, the extent of Gabriel's betrayal hit him hard. Part of him couldn't believe what Gabriel had done, but a smaller, darker part of Fort wondered if he himself would have done the same, if it had been the only way to get his father back. Would he have betrayed the entire world too? He couldn't imagine it, but the idea of leaving his father behind absolutely ripped him apart inside.

But that was a question for another time. For now, he moved toward Gabriel, hoping to get some answers. But a fireball beat him there, flying straight at his roommate before Fort could move to stop it.

Gabriel saw it coming, though, and his hands glowed green as he opened a teleportation circle in front of himself, sending the fireball somewhere unknown.

Gabriel could cast Teleport? Since *when*?

"Traitor!" Rachel shouted, another fireball already on its way toward Fort's roommate. As he dodged, she lowered her hands to the ground, and the earth beneath his feet jumped, sending Gabriel flying. He opened another circle in midair and emerged right behind Rachel, moving to bash her with his shield, only for Fort to teleport him away before his blow could land.

"What did you *do*, Gabriel?" he shouted, moving between the two.

"He tried to knock me out and go looking for the Old Ones!" Rachel shouted, lightning playing between her hands. "I got here after he told them where the last dragon was, but that one took over my mind before I could stop him." She pointed at Ketas, the Old One with tentacles coming out of his skull helmet.

Fort turned to Gabriel, his mouth hanging open, but his old roommate just stared at Fort sadly. "It's like I said, kid. You do whatever you have to do to save the ones you love. They have my brother. I hate them with every inch of my body, but I can't beat them. So this was my only option."

D'vale began to laugh again. "WAIT UNTIL YOU SEE WHAT HAS BECOME OF YOUR KIN. THE TWO HUMANS WE TOOK WERE MEANT TO TEACH US WHAT YOUR KIND HAD BECOME WHILE WE WERE EXILED. WHAT WE DISCOVERED, HOWEVER, IS THAT THE OLDER HUMAN NO LONGER HAD THE

ABILITY TO CREATE MAGIC. BUT THE *YOUNGER* ONE WAS FULL OF POWER. AND WE UNLOCKED IT."

Gabriel clenched his fists as he stared at the creature, then turned to the dragon. "You're in control of them, right? Make them give me back my brother!"

"I CANNOT CONTROL THEIR ACTIONS," the dragon rumbled. "AND I CARE NOT FOR YOUR KIN. I TIRE OF THIS, AND WILL HAVE MY VENGEANCE NOW!"

"Me too," Rachel shouted, and sent lightning sizzling toward Gabriel. He dropped to the ground, then threw his shield right at her, but she slammed it with rock from the ground, sending it flying.

With Rachel distracted, Gabriel ran for the three Old Ones. Fort ran after him, not sure what the other boy intended, but it couldn't be anything good. "Gabriel, what are you doing?" he shouted, but his roommate didn't turn around.

"Stop him!" Rachel shouted. "Fort, he's going to—"

Before she could finish, the dragon landed on the ground between Gabriel and the other Old Ones, roaring fire at the boy. Gabriel threw up a teleportation circle, but instead of using it to block the magic, he instead leaped through, emerging just past the dragon.

And that's when Fort understood what Rachel had been warning him about.

"Gabriel, NO!" Fort shouted, and opened his own circle. He leaped through it to emerge at Gabriel's side just as Gabriel opened another teleportation circle right below the three Old Ones, dropping them, himself, and Fort all through it.

They emerged in the now-empty cavern of the Dracsi, Fort's momentum sending him crashing to the ground. He landed hard on his shoulder but quickly scrambled to his feet, a growing horror filling him as he turned toward the Old Ones.

All three were now moving, free from the dragon's spell, thanks to Gabriel.

"There, you're not paralyzed anymore!" Gabriel shouted at them. "Now return my brother. We had a deal!"

The Old Ones looked at him and laughed, the sound still so horrifying that Fort could barely comprehend it. "WE DID INDEED HAVE A BARGAIN," D'vale said.

"WE WILL SHOW YOU WHERE YOUR BROTHER IS, AND ALLOW YOU TO USE YOUR SPACE MAGIC TO BRING HIM HERE," said Q'baos.

Ketas raised his tentacles, and Gabriel shouted in pain as yellow light glowed around his head.

I HAVE GIVEN YOU AN IMAGE OF WHERE YOUR KIN IS, Ketas said in both their minds. BRING HIM HERE, AND LET *HIM* DECIDE WHAT HIS FUTURE SHALL BE. IF HE CHOOSES TO RETURN HOME WITH YOU, THEN HE SHALL. IF NOT, WE WILL DESTROY YOU *AND* THIS ONE. He pointed his tentacles at Fort.

"Deal," Gabriel said, and opened a teleportation circle.

- FORTY-TWO -

FORT WATCHED HELPLESSLY, KNOW-ing he couldn't attack the Old Ones, as they could take over his mind, steal his spirit, or even destroy him. And he couldn't just pull Gabriel away, not when Gabriel was so close to getting his brother back.

But the other boy had betrayed them all and freed the Old Ones, not to mention revealing to them wherever the last dragon was. And if dragons really did come from magic, then the whole world truly could be doomed.

But why did the Old Ones seem so confident that Gabriel's brother, Michael, wouldn't choose to return home? All Fort knew about Michael was what he'd seen in Sierra's memories, back when she and Damian were still asleep beneath the Oppenheimer School. He'd seemed like a goofy kid, and Sierra had liked him. Michael had studied

Destruction magic, and if Fort remembered right, had set his room on fire.

So, pretty normal all around. But then why would they take the chance? Had they used Spirit magic on him? That seemed pretty likely, but didn't really fit with giving him the option to make a choice.

Maybe whatever had happened to Michael had been done to Fort's father, too, and that explained why his dad hadn't woken up? But Michael hadn't been turned into a Dracsi, so that didn't seem too probable.

Either way, they'd have to be ready to run at a moment's notice, so Fort inched closer to Gabriel. From this distance he could see into the circle, but whatever lay beyond—Fort assumed it was the home of the Old Ones—was almost incomprehensible to his mind.

There was nothing solid there, just . . . madness. Shapes dissolved into sounds, and colors became ideas. Everything felt . . . *sharp*, like it could cut your mind the way a fever dream feels. Fort took a step toward the circle, drawn either by some sort of insane gravity, or through the horrible appeal of madness. He forced himself to look away.

Fortunately a figure appeared on the other side, blocking out the insanity. "Michael?" Gabriel said, his voice cracking as the boy from Sierra's memories stepped through the teleportation circle, which quickly closed behind him.

This Michael had the same red hair, the same face, but somehow his body seemed to be constantly changing, at times almost fluid like a liquid, only to quickly shift to nearly diamondlike density. His whole body faded away until it was close to transparent, like a cloud, then caught fire like D'vale, and then back again. And his eyes . . .

Fort turned away, unable to even look at them further. Michael's eyes looked just like what had lain beyond the teleportation circle—lunacy personified.

"HELLO, GABRIEL," Michael said, waving his hand and leaving a trail of mist behind it. "IT'S BEEN A LONG TIME. HOW ARE YOU?"

"*Mike,*" Gabriel said, tears streaming down his face. "What . . . what did they *do* to you?"

"THEY OPENED MY EYES, GABRIEL," Michael said, and Fort flinched at their mention. "OUR BODIES ARE MADE OF STAR MATTER. WE ARE ONE WITH THE UNIVERSE, AND MORE! EVERYTHING IS CONNECTED, AND I CONTROL IT *ALL.*"

"Mike, they're going to let you come home with me," Gabriel said, stepping closer to his brother and slowly holding out a hand. "Do you understand what I'm saying? You can come back to Earth, with me and mom, even with the colonel. We're your family. That's where you *belong*."

"EARTH?" Michael tilted his head, as if he was confused. "NO, I DON'T BELIEVE I WILL. NOT YET. I HAVE TOO MUCH TO LEARN HERE. THE OLD ONES ARE GOOD TEACHERS, GABRIEL. IF YOU LET THEM, THEY CAN OPEN *YOUR* MIND TOO, AND YOU CAN SEE THE TRUTH OF WHO WE ARE, AND WHAT THIS REALITY TRULY IS. THEN YOU AND I WILL BRING THEM BACK HOME AND HELP ALL OF HUMANITY TO SEE, JUST LIKE WE DO."

Fort swallowed hard, readying a teleportation circle. That was it. The Old Ones had given Michael the choice, and he'd chosen to stay with them. And that meant—

"Mike, *no*," Gabriel said, stumbling toward his brother. "*Please*, you have to come back. They're letting you decide! Are they making you say these things? If the real you, the Michael I remember, is in there somewhere . . . just say the word, and I'll help you. I'll fight them and bring you back no matter what! I don't care if I have to burn down the universe to do it."

"OH, GABRIEL," Michael said, putting a hand on his brother's cheek. "THEY ARE NOT MAKING ME SAY ANYTHING. I'VE LEFT YOU AND DAD BEHIND NOW. BUT IT'S NOT TOO LATE. COME WITH ME, AND YOU'LL SEE WHAT I HAVE. LET ME PROTECT *YOU* FOR ONCE, GABRIEL."

Gabriel looked up at his brother and raised a hand toward him. Was he going to leave with Michael, go back with the Old Ones? He couldn't . . . could he?

"Mike, I—"

THE CHOICE HAS BEEN MADE, Ketas declared, and Fort felt the Old One's presence push into his mind, infecting him with its incomprehensible horror. Gabriel also stiffened as a yellow glow appeared over his head, the same thing likely happening to him. HOWEVER, OUR APPRENTICE HAS MADE YOU AN OFFER, AND YOU MAY ACCEPT. BEFORE YOU DO, LET US MAKE SURE THAT YOUR INFORMATION WAS TRUE.

The cavern around them disappeared, replaced by a mental image of a human woman standing before two children, both tied up and looking completely out of it. Lost in his own mind, Fort screamed noiselessly as he recognized first Sierra, then Damian, with Agent Cole standing over them.

"This will all go much easier on you if you reveal where the stolen books went," Agent Cole said, leaning in toward Sierra, whose head lolled to one side.

WE HAVE INDEED FOUND THE LAST DRAGON, Ketas said in their heads. PERHAPS WE WILL SHOW YOU HIS TRUE POWER NOW?

Even through the dimensional distance, the Old One lifted a hand, and Damian straightened in his seat, whatever sedative they'd given him overwhelmed by the presence of Ketas. His eyes went wide, and he began to struggle against his bonds, an inhuman growl coming from his throat.

"What . . . what is this?" Agent Cole said, stepping backward, holding up her weapon, and lifting a phone to her mouth. "This is Cole, get in here! We've got a—"

Damian's bindings ripped in half, and he leaped for her as his body began to morph, wings growing out of his back and his mouth filling with rows of razor-sharp teeth. He lifted Agent Cole with a now-massive hand and flung her against the wall, then roared so loudly the room shook.

THE LAST OF ITS KIND, Ketas told them. MADE FROM MAGIC AND ABLE TO ACCESS ITS EVERY POWER. AND HE IS *OURS* ONCE AGAIN!

Damian was the last dragon?! With everything happening at once, Fort almost couldn't believe what he was seeing. But Ketas couldn't have used Corporeal magic to change him . . . it was something inside himself. And that would explain why he wouldn't talk about where he'd come from before the school, and why he could learn magic so quickly.

Damian in dragon form turned toward Sierra with a low growl and opened his mouth to unleash a fiery death sentence. *NO!* Fort tried to shout, but Ketas had him under his control, and there was nothing he could do but watch—

"MY CHILD!" came a roar from above, and a second dragon dove directly through Damian and Sierra to slam into Ketas. The image of the interrogation room faded instantly, and Fort felt his mind clear as the cavern returned, revealing the father of the dragons raking at his brother's crystalline armor with his claws.

"Fort!" someone yelled, and he glanced up to find Rachel floating down on a platform of rocks, while a sea of dwarves rappelled the wall behind her, using lightning as ropes, controlling it with just their bare hands. "Go, get out of here while they're distracted!"

SAVE ME! Ketas shrieked at his siblings, but it was Michael that moved first. He raised a hand toward the dragon, and the Old One roared as the elements making up his body all pulled apart at once, only to smash back together, crashing to the ground.

"CHILD, LOOK TO OUR FORMER BROTHER TO SEE WHAT HAPPENS TO THOSE WHO DISOBEY," Q'baos said to Michael. She raised her hand, and the dragon went still, then stood up, bowing toward its family.

"Heads up!" Rachel yelled, and Fort looked up just in time to catch a heavy silver staff that she threw. She nodded at the dragon. "Do it!"

Without a second thought, Fort leaped forward and slammed the staff against the dragon's scales.

Blue Healing light filled the creature, and he shrieked again, then turned back to Ketas. "YOU WILL PAY FOR WHAT YOU'VE DONE!" he roared, his hands glowing bright blue. Ketas put up his tentacles to stop him, but it was too late.

The Old One's tentacles pulled up into his body while he screamed in pain and anger. His crystalline armor cracked and fell away as the Old One rapidly increased in size, rising high into the air, his skin growing black, shiny scales. The skull helmet he wore exploded off of a head that now began to resemble something even more monstrous than the tentacles he'd previously had.

"STOP HIM!" D'vale shouted, but both Q'baos and Michael were transfixed, watching Ketas's evolution into a Dracsi. "THEN I WILL DO IT MYSELF," D'vale finished, and turned on the dragon.

The blue light disappeared as the Old One of Corporeal magic abruptly dissolved, each mineral and element in his body releasing from each other at the same time.

"Fort!" Rachel shouted. "We have to get out of here *now*!"

"Go!" he shouted to her. "I'm right behind you!"

She growled in frustration but took off toward the ceiling and the portal home.

The dwarves reached the ground and came running, all wielding axes and other weapons, but now that Ketas's transformation had stopped, Q'baos raised a hand, and the dwarves all skidded to a stop, falling to their knees in worship. They began to chant words of praise toward the Old One, and from off in the distance, Fort could hear more dwarves doing the same, the noise shaking the rock all around him.

"PLEASE, GABRIEL," Michael told him, extending his hand to Gabriel . . . and also Fort. "COME. I DO NOT WISH TO SEE YOU PERISH LIKE MY MASTERS' FORMER BROTHER."

Gabriel looked down at the spot where the dragon had been destroyed, then slowly took a step toward Michael . . .

Only to step through a teleportation circle, with Fort just behind him.

- FORTY-THREE -

IRST GABRIEL, THEN FORT CRASHED through the teleportation circle and the portal back to Earth, slamming into the ground. The moment Fort saw Rachel waiting, he immediately shut down the portal, finally cutting off all access to the Dracsi dimension.

Gabriel rolled to his feet and just stared down at Fort in shock. "What did you *do*?" he whispered.

"I saved your life," Fort said, rising to his feet too.

"You should have left him there," Rachel said, fireballs forming in her hands.

Gabriel shot her a look, then bashed her away with his shield before turning on Fort. Even at his size, Gabriel was too fast, and the hit knocked Fort back into the rock wall hard enough to make the world spin. Fort struggled just to breathe as the air exploded from his lungs.

"*What did you do?!*" Gabriel shouted again, then smashed him with the shield. "You left Mike behind! *Open that portal again. Now!*"

"Get away from him!" Rachel shouted, and a piece of the wall slammed into Gabriel, knocking the boy to the ground. Before Gabriel could move, the rocks beneath him rose up to ensnare his hands and feet.

"Let me *go!*" Gabriel shouted, frantically pulling against the rock, but even his strength wasn't enough to break through stone. "He's my brother! I need to bring him *back!*"

Fort pushed off the wall, still sucking in air. "Michael's . . . gone," he said to Gabriel, shaking his head sadly. "You saw him. He had the choice, and he wanted to stay with them."

"He was under their spell!" Gabriel shouted.

"He said he wasn't," Fort said as Rachel put her shoulder under his arm to support him. "And from how he was talking, I believe him. Besides, you gave the Old Ones *Damian*. If the dragon hadn't stopped them, they could have used him to return to Earth and killed us all!"

"He's my *brother!*" Gabriel snarled. "I'd do whatever it takes to bring him home. Do you really think this wasn't the plan all along? I always intended to do this! I even told Cyrus my plan, and he said it'd work, as long as I stayed behind. But you ruined it. You stopped me from saving him!"

Fort's eyes widened. Cyrus *knew* what Gabriel had planned? Why hadn't he said anything to Fort? Or tried to stop him? What had Cyrus been *thinking*?

"We need to hand him over to his father," Rachel said, sneering at the captured boy. "It makes me sick just to look at him."

"This is *Fort's* fault, all of it!" Gabriel screamed. His trapped hands began to glow green, and a portal appeared below him, then *rose up* through the spot he'd been trapped in. He appeared just above them and crashed down straight into Fort, the rocks tumbling off of them both harmlessly.

"Watch out!" Rachel shouted, and leaped for him, but another teleportation circle opened, and she disappeared.

"Take me back there now," Gabriel said, his eyes wild as he held Fort against the ground.

"I can't!" Fort shouted, hoping his bluff would work. "I never mastered the spell. Bring Rachel back!"

"You wouldn't have gone in without rereading the spell!" Gabriel shouted, and grabbed Fort's hands. "You wouldn't have taken that chance, not with your father over there. I *know* you can cast it!"

Instead of struggling, Fort opened a teleportation circle

below them, and the two dropped into the sky above New York City, Gabriel's hands still locked around Fort's.

"Even if I did still know the spell, I'd never cast it again!" Fort shouted as they plummeted toward the ground. "I won't lose you to the Old Ones too!"

Gabriel released one of Fort's hands and punched him in the gut, then opened a teleportation circle underneath them, which they dropped through and into incredibly warm air. Fort glanced down to find an active volcano below them, lava rising out of the cone in all directions.

And they were falling straight for it.

"You *have* to cast it!" Gabriel shouted, punching him again. "Open a portal, or I let you fall!"

Fort tried to concentrate to open a circle, but a blow sent the world spinning, and everything began to go dark. The lava below him now was so hot he could feel the heat through his clothing, but Gabriel didn't seem to be bluffing.

"Okay!" Fort said. "I'll do it! I promise!"

But the heat was overwhelming now, and he wondered if Gabriel would have the time to—

They passed through another circle, emerging from a vertical circle onto a tiled floor, their momentum sending them skidding down a familiar-looking hallway. Gabriel twisted around until he was behind Fort and put him in a headlock.

"Now," Gabriel said, as Fort heard yelling and footsteps coming toward them. "Open the portal, right back where it was. If you do anything else, I'll drop you into that volcano inches from the lava. You won't have time to save yourself."

"You'd kill me to get your brother back?" Fort gasped, struggling to breathe against Gabriel's grip.

"I'd burn the whole world down," Gabriel sneered. "I was supposed to protect him! When my father heard about the books of magic, I told him Mike was too young, that he should send me instead, but *no*, Mike had the right birthday and had to go. It's his fault that my brother got taken, but *yours* that I lost him again!"

"It was . . . the *Old Ones*," Fort grunted.

"Gabriel!" shouted Colonel Charles from behind them. "Let him go. What is going *on* here?"

"I found Michael, Colonel," Gabriel said, not turning around. "And I'm going to fix your mistake. I'm going to bring him *back*."

"What are you talking about?" Colonel Charles shouted. "Your brother is gone!"

"NO!" Gabriel shrieked. "No, he's not! I never believed that.

You let him go, but I always knew he was still alive! That's why I asked you for the book of Summoning two weeks ago. I studied Space magic so I could go look for him! But then you took the book away before I could master the portal spell, and I thought I'd have to steal it back . . . but fortunately, my new *roomie* had the same plan. So I waited for what felt like years. And *finally* Fort learned the right spell, and we found him!"

"I've got a shot," one of the guards yelled.

"No one fire!" Colonel Charles said. "Son, let the boy go, and we'll talk."

"Don't you call me that!" Gabriel shouted, throwing a look behind him. "You're no father of mine, not since you brought Mike to this school and then left him in the hands of those *things*. But Mike's alive, and I know where he is! Fort has the power to send me back, and I can rescue Mike!"

Gabriel's arm tightened around Fort's throat, cutting off his air. "I'll . . . do it," Fort gasped, and his hands began to glow with magic as his mind raced. If he reopened the portal again, the Old Ones would be waiting, and that was it. But if he didn't, Gabriel would throw him into the volcano instantly.

"I'm not letting go until it's done," Gabriel said quietly to him. "And you're coming with me, to that dimension. If we find Mike again and bring him back, then you'll come home too. If not, then we *all* stay."

Fort nodded, and Gabriel released his grip slightly, just enough to let Fort breathe again.

"Gabriel, *please*, don't do this!" Colonel Charles said, his voice cracking. "I can't . . . I can't lose you, too!"

"Then you shouldn't have let Mike come in the first place," Gabriel said, turning back to look at his father. "This is *YOUR FAULT—*"

That was his chance. Fort opened a tiny teleportation circle into his pocket, and the silver hammer, Earthshatterer, dropped from it directly into his hand. "I'm sorry, Gabriel," he whispered, then slammed the hammer onto the floor next to him.

The tile instantly exploded into dust, and suddenly they were falling. As they dropped, Fort could see a glow coming from Gabriel's hands as the other boy tried to open a teleportation circle.

But he was too slow, and the next floor down was too close.

They crashed into the concrete with a horrifying crunch, and then everything mercifully went dark.

- FORTY-FOUR -

FORT FLOATED IN A SEA OF CONFU-
sion for the next few days, waking to find different
people standing over him, only to fall unconscious
again. Any amount of time could have passed, and he'd have
had no way of knowing. He was vaguely aware of Dr. Ambrose
being present, and Jia at times, but other than that, everything
was a blur.

And then he awoke to find himself in a blank, unformed
place with only the bed beneath him as proof that he wasn't
still asleep.

"Hey, sleepyhead," a voice said, and Sierra faded into view
above him, leaning over his bed. "You had me worried! Are you
feeling any better?"

Fort pushed himself to a sitting position, strangely free of all
the tubes and wires that he'd felt when he'd woken up the past

times. "What happened? Where am I? Is Rachel okay? Are *you*? What about my father? Did he wake up yet?"

"Okay, settle down," Sierra said. "You're still asleep, because you need to heal. If you get too excited, you might wake up. But as far as I've seen in Jia's head, you're going to be fine. And they found Rachel in Colonel Charles's house, of all places, so she's already back."

Fort frowned. "I need to heal? How badly was I injured?"

Sierra winced. "It wasn't pretty. You're lucky Jia was around. She took care of your biggest problems right away, but she had to restore everyone that the Old One morphed, and she's been working with Dr. Ambrose on your father." She patted him on the shoulder. "You always get up to such interesting things when I leave you alone, don't you?"

"My father isn't awake yet?" Fort tried to push himself out of bed, but somehow found himself right back in it. "Is he okay? What's going on?!"

"Oh, he'll be fine," Sierra said, but she looked away, which made Fort nervous. "Hey, don't get all anxious on me, you know I can feel what you're feeling. He just hasn't come to yet. And Dr. Ambrose doesn't know why. Though she did see something odd—"

"Odd? What's odd? Sierra . . . ?"

Sierra sighed. "She wasn't going to tell you, because she's not sure what it is. Part of her thinks it's just that your dad has some odd EEG readings. Don't ask me what that means, I saw the answer in her head and still can't remember it, but it's something they read your electric brain waves with. And before you start panicking again, she just saw something unusual, and she's figuring it out, okay?"

Fort nodded, then noticed something in her mind. "That's not all she saw, is it? You're hiding something."

"It's not important. I'd tell you if it was." He glared at her, and she threw up her hands. "*Fine*. The weird thing in his brain . . . it sort of, *kind of*, only remotely looks a bit like something they saw in *my* mind, okay? And I'm fine, aren't I?"

Fort frowned. Something they'd seen in Sierra's mind? "But you were in a coma. Maybe that's the similarity?"

"See, that's smart thinking!" Sierra said, then cringed. "Except she doesn't think that's it. But again, let's remind ourselves that not only am *I* fine, but I'm actually doing great. And in an effort to change the subject, can we talk about how Damian is actually a *dragon*, of all things? No wonder he was all mopey. I would be too if I were the last of my species."

Fort's eyes widened. "What happened with him?" he asked. "Last I saw, he was about to attack you!"

"I don't know, I was kind of sedated, but from what he said, the Old One stopped controlling him just before he could," she said, looking away again. "Here's the weird thing: I'm not sure we'd have escaped if he *hadn't* dragoned out. That Agent Cole lady? I'm *not* a fan."

"Me either," Fort said. "How did she catch you? I thought you were hiding in the airport."

She made a face. "Remember how she told you that they'd completed their search in terminals four and five of Heathrow Airport? That was a lie. We came out, thinking we were safe, and BAM, they grabbed us."

Fort's eyes widened. "She *used* me to capture you?"

"She's a tricky one," Sierra said, sighing as she sat down on the bed next to him. "The only good thing that came of it all was that they brought us to the UK school for interrogation, since it was closer, and they didn't want to chance bringing us back to the U.S. So at least they saved us some time, having to find it for ourselves!"

"That's where you are now, the UK school?" Fort asked. "Did you see Cyrus? He and Dr. Opps were heading there . . ."

She nodded. "Both of them. Dr. Opps came through, trying to convince Agent Cole to release us, but she of course refused. I think she was about to throw *him* in jail for a while there. But after Damian dragoned out, we freed ourselves, and I decided to remind her of her dream to go to art school instead of staying on as a federal agent." She grinned widely. "I think she quit and is applying to one as we speak."

"I'm so glad you're okay," Fort said. "I tried reaching you so many times. If I'd known you were captured—"

"You would have tried to come find us, but wouldn't have known where. That's one reason they took us to the UK school. No one here other than Dr. Opps or Cyrus knew where it was, so your little teleportation stunt wouldn't get you there."

"So do you have the book of Clairvoyance?" Fort asked, trying not to let his concern for his father overwhelm him.

"I told you, don't worry about him!" Sierra said. "He'll be fine. And no, we don't have the book yet. Apparently it went missing when the kids here went a little bit insane after studying it. Maybe one of them stole the book and hid it, because none of the administrators know where it is. And since the students aren't really thinking clearly, I can't read their minds to figure out where it is."

"Wow," Fort said. "And Cyrus wasn't any help?"

"Not really," she said. "He spends most of his time talking to himself at lakes nearby. I'm not really sure what he's doing." She shrugged. "Anyway, I'm going to try to heal all these kids' minds, both because it'd be cruel not to, but also so we can figure out where the book is. They got all riled up when Damian turned into a dragon, so we figure we'll go somewhere a *lot* less public when we get the book, so Damian can learn Time magic in peace. It's not easy hiding ourselves here in the middle of the school as it is. Dr. Opps is helping, but still. He's been pretty anxious too, but he won't say why. He and Cyrus have been talking a lot, so who knows what prophecies Cyrus has been telling him."

"You should listen, if Cyrus gives you one," Fort said, looking away. "He warned me I'd lose someone if I went after my father, but I thought that meant a friend would be left behind, not that Gabriel would turn on everyone."

"He needs to learn to be more specific," she told him, scrunching up her nose. "And if it makes you feel better, Gabriel probably would have taken the book if you hadn't. And this way, you got your father back. Besides, at least you got to visit a different dimension. Look at how boring this school is." She waved a hand, and the dark area around Fort lit up, showing a pleasant hallway lined with windows that opened on a green countryside. "Almost makes me jealous of that puke-green color there."

"Stop trying to cheer me up," Fort said, and she grinned at him.

"Just wanted to keep you from wallowing a bit," she said, patting his leg. "Anyway, I have to go save all these kids, because I'm amazing. You keep healing, okay?"

Fort nodded. "Say hi to Cyrus for me, will you? And, um, don't go disappearing on me this time. I *might* have missed having you around."

She beamed, then leaped at him for a hug. He yelped when she slammed into him, then realized he wasn't injured in his mind, and hugged her back. "I missed you too, Fitzgerald," she said. "But don't worry. I won't be gone long this time. If all goes well, we should have the book and be heading to London in an hour or two to get off this island. And then we're heading for . . ." She trailed off, then shrugged. "Actually, I have no idea where the sixth book might be. But that's why we're getting the Clairvoyant book now, so we can use it to see where we go next!"

Fort laughed. "That doesn't make sense, you know?"

Sierra winked. "That's why they call it magic, New Kid."

And with that, she disappeared, as did the scene in Fort's head, and everything went dark again.

At some unknown time later, something almost woke him up, a voice that could have been Sierra screaming his name, sounding terrified. But it cut off too quickly, and he fell back into a dreamless sleep, filled with a strange sort of dread that something had gone very, *very* wrong.

- FORTY-FIVE -

ORSYTHE," A VOICE SAID, AND something tapped his face. "*Forsythe.* Wake up already, I don't have all day."

Fort opened his eyes, then immediately closed them again. He wasn't in pain, at least, but his mind still felt fuzzy from whatever they'd been giving him. Another slap on his cheek, and he looked up to find Dr. Ambrose leaning over him. "Okay, I'm up," he murmured, and she thankfully stopped.

"Good," Dr. Ambrose said, leaning back. Fort could hear people running outside the door, and muffled shouting. "We've got a lot to talk about, and not much time. First, you should be totally healed now. Jia fixed your ribs, leg, and ankle." She gave him some side eye. "You only fell, like, ten feet, Forsythe. Next time try not to land on everything breakable all at the same time."

"I broke all of those things?" Fort said, sitting up slowly and feeling around his ribs. Everything felt totally normal, which made sense, since Jia's magic would have restored his bones back to their nonbroken state. "Did Gabriel . . ."

"Not as bad," she said, frowning. "We kept him sedated, though, until his father decided what to do with him. He's expelled now, if that helps."

Fort sat up straight, his eyes widening. "Wait, you let him *go*? You know he can teleport, right? You can't just—"

"Who are you talking to, Forsythe?" she said, glaring at him. "Of course I know that. And *I* said we needed to wipe his memories. But Colonel Charles outranks me, and he said he'd be taking his son home. What was I supposed to do, arrest them both?"

"*Yes!*" Fort shouted. "He almost let the Old Ones come back!"

"Let's not get into who's releasing what Old Ones here," Dr. Ambrose said, narrowing her eyes. "I'm told you pulled a stunt just like that yourself. You're lucky no one was permanently injured from that dragon you took on a joyride around the world."

Fort's face turned bright red, and he coughed to hide his embarrassment. "Yeah, okay, it wasn't the smartest thing to do."

"That's the first intelligent thing I've heard you say," Dr. Ambrose told him, sitting down on the bed next to him. "And don't forget, I did warn you about Gabriel. He didn't handle losing his brother well. Not that anyone would, but Colonel Charles thought you might be able to help Gabriel with his grief, because of your father. I'm pretty sure he didn't think that you'd inspire his son to almost destroy humanity instead, but we all have our blind spots."

Fort sighed. "I didn't know he was Colonel Charles's son, or stepson. He never told me. I saw all the special treatment, but I didn't make the connection."

"Next time I'll put up a blinking neon sign or something," Dr. Ambrose said, patting his shin. "How else do you think he would have gotten permission to use the book of Healing after classes? Not to mention that he and his mother have been staying here for months, over in the government-family section of the facility." She shook her head. "They brought a bunch of VIPs down here to keep them safe once the first attack happened, just in case. Probably didn't help Gabriel to get over things, being surrounded by soldiers and having those skeletons on display."

"He was studying the Summoning book," Fort told her. "He almost learned how to make a portal himself. If he had—"

"In some ways, we're all lucky you stole it," Dr. Ambrose said as the noises outside increased. Something was definitely happening. "Plus, even if you took him along with you, another fine choice you made, at least you were around to pull him back. Otherwise we'd all be knee-deep in Old Ones right now."

This was all too much to process, and Fort had much bigger questions on his mind anyway. "How's my father doing?" he asked. "Has he woken up yet?"

Dr. Ambrose shook her head and nodded at the curtain around Fort's bed. "No, and I'm not sure when he will. His body is in great shape for a man his age, so he should be awake. I took an EEG, but it didn't explain anything."

Fort's dream of Sierra came back to him. "But you saw something odd in the EKJ, didn't you?"

"EEG. Electroencephalogram. Measures electrical activity in the brain. And yes, I did see something *unusual* in his readings, but nothing to concern yourself with." She raised an eyebrow. "But how did *you* know that?"

"Just a guess, since he didn't wake up," Fort lied. "But you think he will? He's going to be okay?"

Dr. Ambrose started to speak, then paused. "Yes, I do, Forsythe," she said. "I think he'll be fine. But I can't say when he'll wake up, or why he hasn't yet."

"Can I see him?" he asked, barely able to stop himself from leaping out of the bed and pushing aside the curtain.

Dr. Ambrose looked like she wanted to say no, but instead just sighed. "Okay, but just for a few minutes. We're not done here. There are some pretty big developments happening out in the world right now, and they're not going to wait."

She helped him off the bed, which he was thankful for, as standing turned out to be a bit more wobbly than he expected. But his father's bed was only steps away, anyway, just on the other side of the curtain, and by the time he reached it, he was feeling more steady.

That was good, because the sight of his father hooked up to various machines and IV drips almost sent him reeling.

"I can only give you five minutes," Dr. Ambrose said, and walked over to the door. As she opened it, Fort saw soldiers waiting expectantly for her. "Say whatever you need to quickly, okay?"

He nodded, but she'd already turned and left, closing the door behind her. And finally, it was just him and his father.

His dad looked exactly the same as he had back in the Dracsi cave, which shouldn't have been surprising, as that was just a short time ago. Still, it felt like years, and even now, the fact that his father was lying there in front of him brought tears to his eyes.

He just looked so vulnerable, so small, when he'd always seemed so big in so many ways.

Fort pulled a chair over and sat down, taking his father's hand. There was so much to say, so much to apologize for, but now that he actually had his dad back, he had no idea where to begin.

"We never did see the Einstein statue, huh?" Fort said, and his voice cracked. The only response was the beeping of the machines, though, and for a moment, Fort just looked at his father, not sure if he could go on.

"I just want you to know," he said finally, "that I am so deeply, *truly* sorry that . . . that everything happened. You'd never have been taken if I'd just . . ."

He wiped his eyes, his hand coming away almost soaking. Fort let the tears fall as he softly sobbed, laying his head against his father's hand. "But I fixed it. I came to find you. I didn't stop . . . I would never have stopped . . ."

As he said it, an image of Gabriel freeing the Old Ones appeared in his mind, and he squeezed his eyes closed, willing himself not to think about it. Would he have done the same thing, putting the entire world in danger to bring his father back? The thought made Fort sick to his stomach.

"I . . . I lost a friend," he said quietly, picking his head back up. "His brother was taken. I didn't know that, but my friend tried to rescue his brother, too, and I . . . I stopped him. To save him, but I still stopped him. And now I lost him, just like Cyrus said I would. And I have no idea what he'll do next."

Silence, except for the beeping from the machines.

"If I'd just waited another few seconds," Fort whispered. "Maybe Michael would have changed his mind. Maybe I should have teleported him back too. But the Old Ones were going to attack, and I didn't . . . I couldn't know. But whatever happens next, it's my fault. Just like you being taken."

No response.

"Did I do the right thing? Gabriel could have let them loose on our entire world! But he was just trying to save his brother. I don't know what I should have done! Tell me, *please*." He squeezed his father's hand harder now, not even bothering to stop the tears. "Please, please, please, just tell me what I should do. I don't know, and I keep messing up!"

Someone knocked on the door, and Fort realized he didn't have much time left. He cleared his throat and looked up at his father. "You're going to be okay now," he said, hoping he wasn't lying. "Dr. Ambrose and Jia will make sure of that. You're going to be okay, and we'll go home, probably with no memories of any of this, and everything will be back to normal. It has to be. And I'll . . . I'll make this up to you, for the rest of my life if that's what it takes. I'll—"

The door opened, and Dr. Ambrose entered, closing it softly. "Forsythe," she said, not unkindly. "I gave you as long as I could. But I need to speak to you about something."

"*What?*" he asked, rubbing his eyes again as he let his irritation show. "What is so important? This is my *father!*"

She sighed. "I know. But something's happened in the UK, and it won't wait."

She reached and flipped on a television above his father's head, and the news appeared, showing what looked like a strange black dome surrounded by blue.

"Those were satellite pictures," Dr. Ambrose said as a news anchor appeared on-screen. "Whatever that dome is, it's covering half the United Kingdom."

- FORTY-SIX -

FORT'S EYES WIDENED. THE UK? THAT meant . . .

Sierra? he thought as loudly as he could.

There was no response.

"We lost contact with the Clairvoyance school a few hours ago," Dr. Ambrose said as the television showed closer footage of the black dome from a helicopter. On the water, military ships anchored just past the point where the dome hit the ocean. "Right around the time *this* appeared. It's closing off almost all of England and Wales. We have reason to believe it originated at the Clairvoyance school."

"What?!" Fort shouted. "Sierra and Cyrus are there! We need to get them out!"

"Sierra's there?" Dr. Ambrose said, but Fort stopped listening. Instead, he retreated back into his mind, yelling Sierra's name over and over, but again, there was no response.

"Oppenheimer is at the school too," Dr. Ambrose said as a huge sinking feeling in his stomach made Fort want to throw up. "But that's not why I'm here."

"I can go," Fort said, standing up taller. "I can teleport in there, and get them out. I can save them—"

"That's the absolute *last* thing that's happening," Dr. Ambrose said. "You're not going anywhere. None of you three are. But Colonel Charles wants to speak to all of you, and . . ."

She continued on, but Fort's attention was caught by something she'd glossed over. "What do you mean, 'you three'?"

Dr. Ambrose looked away. "We know the dome originated from the Clairvoyance school because we received a message from them. And not from the headmaster or a teacher."

Fort frowned. "Cyrus said the students all lost their minds somehow, when they first learned Time magic." Of course, Sierra had said something about fixing that, but he wasn't going to let Dr. Ambrose know she'd been talking to him.

"From their message, it doesn't sound like things have gotten much better," she said. "Something about saving the world and bringing back the one true king. They claimed they created the dome to keep us from interfering, but if we did what they said, they'd release Oppenheimer and everyone else they've got. We just have to meet their demands."

Fort felt a chill go down his spine. "And what were their demands?" he whispered.

She turned back to stare him dead in the eye. "Why do you think I'm here, Fitzgerald? They want *you*. You, Jia, and that Rachel girl. Now get some clothes on. You've got your first military briefing in five minutes."

ACKNOWLEDGMENTS

Huh. So a bunch of students who can see the future have decided to hold a country hostage, demanding Fort, Jia, and Rachel. That sounds ominous. But hey, at least Fort found his father, right?

Though if his dad is okay, why hasn't he woken up yet . . . ?

Ah well, I'm sure it'll all end happily.

Hahahah, it totally won't. I feel so bad for Fort, knowing what's coming!

But you know what I feel good about? How many people have given their all to get this book into your hands. I run everything by my wife, Corinne, first, but from there, Michael Bourret, my agent, helped shepherd every one of these books from start to finish. Of course, none of these would even exist if not for Liesa Mignogna, my editor at Aladdin; every book I've written has been made immeasurably better by her. If the books are batarangs, she's sharpened each one to a fine point.

I can't thank my publisher at Aladdin, Mara Anastas,

enough, for always supporting me and my little stories. Aladdin's marketing team including Caitlin Sweeny, Alissa Nigro, and Anna Jarzab have been just killing it with these, as has Cassie Malmo, my publicist; Elizabeth Mims and Sara Berko; Laura DiSiena, who designed the book; Michelle Leo and the education/library team; Stephanie Voros and the sub-rights group; Gary Urda, Christina Pecorale, Jerry Jensen, Christine Foye, Victor Iannone, and everyone else in sales; and the ever fantastic Vivienne To, who I wish could draw dragons on every cover of mine.

And one last thank you to *you*, the reader. I'm so, so sorry for what you're going to go through in the next book. I hope you're not too attached to anyone!

"I SHALL FREE YOU FROM THIS HORRIBLE NIGHTMARE," they heard the dragon shout, though he was now lost in a sea of Dracsi, each one growling its love for their creator. "YOU SHALL BECOME DRAGONS AGAIN, EVEN IF IT MEANS . . ."

Whatever else he said was lost when blue light as bright as the sun exploded in the cavern.

All around them the Dracsi began to roar in surprise, twisting and turning—though they didn't necessarily seem to be in pain. Their bodies glowed with the same blue light, and as Fort watched, entranced, Gabriel grabbed his arm, a huge smile on his face.

"We're actually going to do this, Fort," he whispered, tears in his eyes. "We're going to bring them *back*."

The nearest Dracsi to them began to shrink abruptly, wings emerging from its back as its arms extended down in front of it, matching the length of its legs. The shrinking grew more rapid now, and as Fort watched in awe, the black-scaled Dracsi morphed into a bright blue dragon, which collapsed to the ground with a heavy sigh.

"MY CHILDREN!" the Old One shouted, and his voice rang out clearly in spite of the roaring Dracsi. "RETURN TO YOUR TRUE FORMS!"

All around them, the giants collapsed in on themselves, most growing wings and becoming dragons once more. But off in the distance, Fort saw something strange. One Dracsi had continued to shrink, and this one had no wings. In fact, it lost its scales too, becoming more and more . . . human.

"There!" Gabriel shouted, but Fort was already banging his fists on Jia's bubble until she shut it down. The moment it disappeared, he was off, not caring about the Dracsi still changing shape in front of him. His eyes were locked on where the person had fallen, and nothing was going to stop him now . . .

"Fort!" Jia shouted. *"Above you!"*

He looked up just in time to find a Dracsi collapsing right over him. Without a second thought, Fort created a teleportation circle in front of him, sliding through it a moment before the newly formed dragon slammed into the spot where he'd been standing. He emerged right next to the human, who had landed on his stomach. Fort dropped to his knees, his momentum sending him skidding to a halt at the person's side.

"Dad?" he shouted, turning the human over. *"Dad!"*

But it *wasn't* his father. This creature had longer ears, light blue hair, and looked like he'd been sculpted from marble.